THE RESTORATION TRILOGY: BOOK THREE

Witch

DENISE WEIMER

Witch

THE RESTORATION TRILOGY: BOOK THREE

DENISE WEIMER

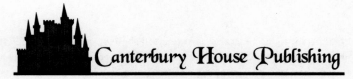

Canterbury House Publishing

www. canterburyhousepublishing. com
Sarasota, Florida

Canterbury House Publishing

www. canterburyhousepublishing. com

Copyright 2017 – Denise Weimer

Book design by Tracy Arendt
Model and Costumer, Kat Nagar
Photographer, Dr. Vincent T. Peng

Library of Congress Cataloging-in-Publication Data

Names: Weimer, Denise, author.
Title: Witch / Denise Weimer.
Description: First edition. | Sarasota, Florida : Canterbury House
    Publishing, [2017] | Series: The restoration trilogy ; Book 3
Identifiers: LCCN 2016055816 (print) | LCCN 2017001967 (ebook) | ISBN
    9780997011975 (softcover) | ISBN 9780997011982
Subjects: LCSH: Historic buildings--Conservation and restoration--Fiction. |

    Man-woman relationships--Fiction. | GSAFD: Love stories.
Classification: LCC PS3623.E4323 W58 2017 (print) | LCC PS3623.E4323 (ebook)

    | DDC 813/.6--dc23
LC record available at https://lccn.loc.gov/2016055816

First Edition: April 2017

Author's Note:
This is a work of fiction. Names, characters, places and incidents are either the product of
the author's imagination or are used fictitiously, and any resemblance to actual persons living or dead, business establishments, events, or locales is entirely coincidental.

For information about permission to reproduce selections from this book:
Email: publisher@canterburyhousepublishing.com
Please put Permissions in the subject line.

To ignore the frantic clanging of the fort's brass bell could mean death. I knew the story well of the young mother who bet wrong on what she believed to be a false alarm at Ft. Knox. Creek warriors scalped her, beat her baby's head against a tree and took her two sons captive. Yet I stood frozen in the garden by Jared and Phoebe's cabin, a basket of snap peas hanging from my numb hands. Mrs. Williams had yelled a few minutes before from her lot, closer to the Augusta Trail. I assumed something happened with one of her children. And now reality set into my fogged brain, defying the bright cheer of the late summer morning. *Indian attack!*

Phoebe and I were alone at her cabin. My widowed father prepared to defend a man accused of thievery before Honorable Judge Jacob Samuels at Greensborough's new courthouse, up the street and across the Augusta Trail, also known as the Upper Creek Trading Path. Phoebe's husband, my brother Jared, blinked off a night of drinking with fellow sentry volunteers inside the fort. I knew what Father would want us to do. Anyone remaining in the town when it came under attack would be left to the mercy of the murdering savages. We had to get to Jared in the fort.

"Phoebe!"

I bolted up the steps of the cabin. My sister-in-law stood behind the rough work table, swollen with pregnancy, a shallow earthenware bowl holding yesterday's milk and a skimmer before her. For a crazy moment I wished I could stop time, churn the butter while she prepared the peas, and share the secrets and giggles of two newlywed young women like we had planned this morning. But the horrified knowledge in Phoebe's brown eyes, wild and wide beneath tendrils of auburn hair escaping her mop cap, confirmed our lives were about to change forever. I grabbed Phoebe's paring knife, slid it into the large pocket tied around the waist of my shift, under my dress, and held out my hand. "We have to run to the fort before they close the gate!"

I pulled as Phoebe ran behind me, a hand under her belly. When I spied the trees bordering the spring and creek beyond the fort, my heart thudded in rebellion. It felt foolish to run toward the enemy. This area provided the likeliest cover for Creek warriors, who would attack from the west, across the Oconee River, but the sheltering walls of the stockade and the soldiers with flintlock rifles would protect us once inside. I forced myself forward, along with the stream of settlers pouring from cabins on the west street, and, paralleling it to the east, the main street. The open maw of the eastern wall slowly narrowed. Men waved sobbing women and screaming children inside. I paused just outside the stockade, looking back. My father, where was he?

The sudden thump of Indian drums and a cry from Phoebe—"the gate closes!"—spurred me inside the fort. My last glimpse outside revealed a family—I knew them all—weeping in panic, arms outstretched, running, but not fast enough.

I whirled toward the clearing, expecting militia powdering and patching their rifles at the loopholes. While civilians rushed around, men shooed women and children into the two rows of cabins and lean-tos, and horses picketed on the outside rows reared and whinnied, Only a handful of men answered the savage war cries. They fired a volley of gunfire from the western side of the fort. My stomach sank. I had forgotten the militia was away.

"We have to find Jared," Phoebe yelled. She grabbed a passing man in dirty linsey-woolsey, elderly, toting a Brown Bessie. "Do you know where Jared Miller is?"

Mr. Smith shook his head. "Jared's busy, Mrs. Miller. We've got under twenty guns to hold this fort. You should go with the others into the officer's cabin. You will be safe there."

As he dashed off, I heard a sentry yell to him, "They are spreading out in the woods, movin' toward the east gate!"

Another man called, "Move around, make 'em think we got a full contingent of soldiers!"

In her desperation Phoebe looked like she might yet dart off in search of her husband, so I pulled her toward one of the larger cabins people crowded into. There, hearing the whistle of incoming arrows and an explosion of gunfire as Indians lunged into the clearing near the east gate, we huddled on the floor with our arms around each other. And I thought of Levi. Why had I not gone with him this spring to Long Creek?

I saw him in my mind's eye, tall, lanky, dark silky locks tied back in a queue, stitching up the ax-inflicted wound of settler, or making the local men roar in approval when the shot from his Pennsylvania rifle extinguished a candle flame at seventy paces. As a doctor and as a former Revolutionary War soldier, he earned the admiration of the fledgling town of Greensborough when he arrived last fall from Augusta, having made his way south from his

8

father's Virginia plantation to claim his land grant north of Greensborough in Wilkes County. And he won my heart.

We begged him to stay in town. Plenty of patients in the area needed tending. He could just set up practice, we said. But no, Levi's botany classes under the famous naturalist, William Bartram, had convinced him to tame his own two hundred acres. Bartram painted the Georgia natives as welcoming, the flora and fauna awaiting a doctor's collection as bounteous. Levi's appetite for independence whetted, he possessed no patience to practice the three years in Virginia required before writing and defending the M.D. thesis his father wished for him. True, even the amount of education Levi already possessed proved rare in the Colonies, so he embarked on his grand adventure. We married at Christmas, and I snuggled in his arms all winter. But when the thaw came, everyone thought me safer here with my family until Levi got his cabin built on Long Creek. Now, I wished more than anything to be there with him.

"Fire!" gasped an older woman, peering out the shutters. "They shot flaming pitch arrows into the shed roofs and barrack walls. We must do something."

"Stay here," I told Phoebe as I got to my feet. "I will come back for you."

I followed a group of goodwives in search of burlap, which we soaked in buckets of water and ran to flap on any burning portions of the fort we could reach. I tried to ignore the running men, and worse, the fallen men, and concentrate on extinguishing the blazes. A young girl who got too close to a loophole fell over right in front of me, an arrow protruding from her chest. I saw the life go out of her eyes before she hit the ground. I raised my horrified gaze just as a figure in knee breeches and a loose blouse soaked with sweat and gunpowder jumped around her falling body.

"Jared!" I dropped my burlap sack and threw myself into his arms.

"Verity." He hugged me. "Did Phoebe make it inside?"

I pushed a long strand of my unbound dark hair out of my face. "In the officers' cabin. She wanted to come find you, but I told her to stay there."

"Good. Get down." He knelt, leaning his flintlock against his side, and dug in his possible for a patch. His other hand grasped his powder horn. "They saw the one block house stood empty. The diversion at the east gate allowed some of them to scale the wall. They be in the fort, Verity. You should go back to the cabin, too."

I felt the color drain out of my face. "But the fires—"

"Do not come out unless you must."

I placed a hand on his shoulder as he prepared his rifle. "God be with you, brother."

The briefest glance speared me as he replied, "And also with you," before he approached the loophole.

I ran back to the cabin. I saw no braves yet. I never had. I had seen Indians in Mixon's General Store trading for striped blankets, powder and liquor, but never braves on the war path. We should have been prepared. We knew Creek Supreme Chief Alexander McGillivary, son of a Scottish trader and a Creek woman, rejected all recent treaties as bogus, and in the last year, Indian arson and scalpings occurred up and down the river. Just two months ago, not far from the fort, Mrs. Fielder and her Negro woman held off marauders by pretending several men protected their cabin.

"I saw Jared," I exclaimed to Phoebe, finding her in the dim interior. "He is fine."

"Oh, thank God. Verity, what is happening?"

"The fires have spread, and the Indians breeched the fort."

Phoebe's brown eyes fixed on me, and her small hand plucked at her skirt. "Oh, no. What shall we do?"

"We pray the men hold off the invaders." Seeing a neighbor of mine listening as she clutched her three-year-old daughter to her bosom, I held out my hand to both women. Then we did just that. Pray. Above the shots, the yells, the weeping, and the war cries, as the acrid smell of smoke became overpowering and sweat ran in rivers beneath my stays.

Then a whoosh sounded from the roof, and the wooden shakes above us ignited. Those of us with burlap jumped to our feet and beat at the flames.

"Dear God, help us! We shall die in here!" someone cried.

From nearby cabins I could hear shrieks like those from hades, where I assumed other settlers burned to death.

Phoebe doubled over, gasping and coughing. I turned to her. "We must attempt to escape. The Indians will also be in the town by now, so that makes the west gate our best bet." I thought of the two boys taken by Indians from Ft. Knox, pursued by settlers to a swamp and rescued. The dark-haired boy was unharmed, while the light-haired boy had been scalped, and to this day lived with those heinous wounds. I attempted to tuck Phoebe's ginger tresses beneath her cap. "If we can make it to the woods, we stand a chance."

She nodded, eyeing the knife I pulled from my pocket. I cracked open the door just enough to see out and caught my first glimpse of several half-naked warriors as they rushed past. Heart pounding so hard I felt faint, I waited until the limited area I could see cleared, then I pulled open the door enough for us to ease out. The bright light, orange flames and intense heat blinded us, and cinders and bits of burning wood drifted down from above. Fire danced like devils across all portions of the fort, but I took Phoebe's hand and edged west. Several women and children followed us.

Past the cabin I saw braves firing into the store room at the fort's center, where I assumed the defenders had retreated. Was Jared there? Would the battle there occupy the enemy enough for us to dash past the walls of flame toward the western end of the stockade?

I never found out. With a whoop, two warriors set upon our little group from behind. Those just exiting the cabin fell by their shots before I turned around. Then Phoebe lunged toward me, a look of intense shock frozen on her face. As she stumbled into me, I saw the tomahawk protruding from her back. Before my eyes, a brave with a single roach of hair woven with feathers and leather seized my sister-in-law's auburn locks from behind, pulled her head back, and with the sun glinting on his blade, cut a bright red path on her forehead. Time stopped. I never remember seeing her scalped. I just remember her disembodied hair in his hand and him retrieving the tomahawk and swinging it again, aiming for her rounded middle. I see the bloodied weapon's path through the air, but I block the memory of that contact, too.

But I do always remember the warrior who came for me, head shaved, face half black and half red, and how I swung my knife in an upward thrust that glanced off his chest. He grabbed my arm and twisted, knocking my weapon to the ground beside Phoebe's crimson-stained cap. When he turned me to face away from him, I thought, *I shall be scalped, too.* Indeed I felt his fingers entangle in my thick, dark locks.

The warrior who killed Phoebe appeared beside me, screaming something in an unintelligible tongue. The one who held me shook his head and said one word, the hot breath of it fanning my neck, "*Yekce.*"

The roached brave spat in the dust and attached Phoebe's scalp to a thong at his waist.

Wheezing, I waited for the knife, but the Indian holding me started dragging me forward. When I struggled, he placed his blade under my chin. He never stopped walking. His companion ran to catch a loose stallion, mounted and whooped out the gate. The shaved Indian found a soldier's steed, crazed and still tethered to its post, and shoved me up onto its unsaddled back.

"No! I will not go with you!" I yelled, and lunged to jump off, but before I could, my captor mounted behind me. He reached around me and, faster than I could see the knot forming, he tied my hands with the rope that had held the horse. Then he kicked the mount's sides, and we galloped out of the burning fort, not to the west, to the east.

We rode through the town, where warriors looted the settler cabins and cut down anyone still moving in the street. Flames rose from all the main buildings, the store, blacksmith shop and new school. In front of the courthouse, I sobbed aloud and screamed for my father when I saw him face-down in the dust, his black coat wet with blood. The man behind me tightened his hold on my waist and called to his compatriots. Whooping, screeching, they rounded up stolen mounts and ponies tethered in the woods, and we thundered past the searing heat of the flame-engulfed fort.

As the Augusta Trail proved wide enough for several horses abreast, I became aware other Indians also bore captives, several other women and a couple of slaves. Hope flared. We would be followed. Our abductors seemed aware of this, too, fleeing so fast the thick forest became a green blur.

I had been to Rock Landing, the crossing at the shoals of the Oconee River. As we approached it, I sat erect. The dry season caused the water level to flow lower than normal, but if I could throw myself into the current at the deepest point, perchance the waters would wash me away. Better my tied hands cause my death by drowning than life at the mercy of savages. I waited until the Indian who held me shifted his weight as our mount stepped onto a large rock just before a swirling eddy, swung my leg over the horse's neck and flung myself into the river. My shoulder hit a rock, and the edge scraped my face, but I went under and kicked in an attempt to let the current have me. A moment later, I raised my joined hands to pull my weight above the surface for a breath. I fully expected arrows to whiz by my head.

The water ahead squeezed through a narrow shoot formed by rocks and branches, taking me with it. Hearing shouts and splashing behind me, I scrambled to pass through the deepest portion. *Please, God, please.* It was stupid, but I had to try.

I dove into the pool ahead arms first, pulled down, and repeated, but the weight of my skirts and the diffusion of the current decreased my momentum. I started to sink. A splash sounded behind me, and a dark head and torso surfaced to my left. I gasped, blinking water from my eyes before I went under again. Not my captor, but Phoebe's killer, who had ridden at the tail of the party, seized me and jerked my chin above water. He screamed what I guessed to be Creek obscenities in my ear. When I tried to escape, he threw me before him into shallow water. And when he dragged me onto the bank and my bound hands brushed the still-bloody scalp of my sister-in-law, I screamed like the bobcats I sometimes heard at night in the forest. He lifted a hand to strike me when the bald brave rode up on his horse and jumped down, coming between us. The men exchanged tense words, then my captor lifted me onto his horse again.

As his arms came around me, I struggled and sobbed. I heard him growl a word in my ear, and I knew any further attempt to escape would prove useless. I slumped against the neck of the stallion as we splashed into the waters dividing any hint of civilization from wilderness.

We rode all day and into the night, hardly slowing. Any whites coming from the other direction dared not interfere, clearing the path at our approach. I did not blame them, for the red and black warriors looked straight from hell. Even the related Muskogee people of Northeast and Piedmont Georgia feared The Upper Creek of extreme Northwest Georgia and Alabama, part of the Chickamauga Alliance. We must be returning to one of their villages. By the time Levi even knew I was gone, I would be dozens, if not hundreds, of miles away.

As night closed around us, exhaustion set in. My thighs refused to grip the flanks of the animal beneath me, forcing the warrior's arms to tighten. We stopped once to answer the call of nature. The captives did so under the gazes of several braves, but we clasped hands and assured each other the men from our village would catch up. If any remained, that was. My Indian pushed a water flask toward me, and I drank deeply.

We rode on, into a dark nightmare of looming shapes where the riders seemed as keen-eyed as the owls hooting from overhanging branches, into a dreamscape where I slumped defeated into my captor and he and I moved as one. As I again and again visualized Phoebe, her unborn child and Father—and most likely Jared, too—all dead, my heart burned in my chest with the hottest pain I had ever experienced.

Then I heard my abductor's voice again in my memory, the word spoken at the river differing from the clipped Indian dialect. *Arrêtez.* French. French for "stop." How did he know French? French traders and soldiers populated the lands to the west. Maybe it was only a word, but maybe it offered a priceless chance to communicate. I did have something to live for. Levi.

When we finally dismounted in a sun-baked field of mid-morning, where pea vines grew waist high and black-eyed Susans opened yellow and brown faces to a cloudless sky, I determined to speak to him, but the first thing I did was collapse. He carried me to the foot of a massive black walnut and leaned my back against the trunk. My trembling limbs must have convinced him of my incapability of fleeing, for he did not bother to secure me. He offered me the water flask again.

After I drank, I wiped my mouth, then placed my hands on my chest and tried to look at him as I said, "Verity."

Crouching before me, he paused before drinking, a silver crescent gorget like chiefs and military men wore shining in the sun around his neck. The silence forced me to raise my gaze all the way. He placed a hand on his own chest and said, "Tenetke." But his eyes, not the name, caused my breath to stop. Flecks of hazel shone around the pupils in the bright sunlight.

"Egads, you are part white," I gasped out. "And you spoke French to me yesterday, did you not? *Arrêtez?*" Seeing his straight brows lower, I hastened to switch to that language. I knew of two reasons the Creek took whites captive, and only one would be acceptable. "Please. My husband Levi is a doctor. Medicine man. He lives on Long Creek, just north of Greensborough. He will give ransom—money—to get me back." I held out my joined hands, entreating.

Tenetke ignored me, reaching instead inside the leather pouch hanging at his waist. He pulled out a walnut shell, opened it, and dipped his finger into some sort of balm inside. He jerked his chin up and looked at the gash on my forehead where I had felt the blood dry some time during the night. I sat still while he dabbed some of the ointment onto the wound. Watching him, I realized he had saved me twice now when his friend would have killed me. I felt certain he possessed some European blood, which made me fear him a tiny bit less. I tried picturing him without the war paint, with dark hair worn like Levi's. I could not. His chiseled physique loomed too powerful and close, smelling of sweat and bear grease. There was nothing tame about him. The eyes were surely a trick of the light.

My lips trembled. "Please," I whispered.

His gaze met mine. "No money," he said in French. "You will be wife now. You *yekce*, strong."

"I am already married. I cannot marry you."

"You marry me in Creek lands, become Creek." As Tenetke spoke, he slipped the gorget from his own neck and fastened it around mine. Like the iron collar I had seen slaves wear as they, too, came into their new land. A tear slipped from my eye and fell down my cheek onto his bronzed hand.

CHAPTER ONE

Normally Jennifer Rushmore's public speaking anxiety guaranteed she'd never address a group, but at the Historic Oglethorpe Summer Gala a couple of months ago, she told the mayors of Lexington and Hermon about her work. That conversation about her restoration of Michael Johnson's ancestors' doctor's house and apothecary had gotten her here - giving a Powerpoint for the whole club.

But now, the hum of the projector, the familiar library setting, and the respectful and interested response of her audience, which included people who had become dear to her over the past six months, lulled Jennifer into a sense of security. And then that magic thing happened any time she shared what she was passionate about, and the words just flowed out. With her guard lowered, she didn't even see the attack coming.

Grace Stevenson, the library genealogist who nagged Jennifer into coming tonight, had told her that many of the Historic Oglethorpe members owned historic homes themselves. Jennifer prepared her presentation with that fact in mind. Posing her job to them as an architectural sleuth, she used photos from her initial visit to Dunham House back in March, revealing what appeared to be a dilapidated, 1870s home hunkered beneath massive magnolias. The fancy millwork and steep roof lines on the one-story cottage suggested Gothic Revival style, while the wide band board and door introduced Greek Revival, and the cornices hinted at Italianate.

Inside, the mystery deepened. Jennifer provided examples of how the different styles of doors, windows and fireplaces competed for dating. Finally, her discovery of an enclosed roofline in the attic and stone and brick piers upholding portions of the house in the crawl space verified an original 1840s structure, expanded during the early Victorian era. Her attentive audience nodded. Some took notes.

Jennifer cleared her throat. The slides provided her security. A year ago, she would have trundled on through them like an aged professor, her introverted, list-checking nature focused on facts and details. Facts and details couldn't hurt you like people could. But now, after learning so many life lessons in the tiny community of Hermon, she recognized her presentation lacked the life that only people could bring.

"And now, I'd like to credit the wonderful local folks who helped transform the Dunham house and apothecary from what you've just seen to what it is today," she announced, advancing the slide to a picture of the fireplace crew, then the roofing crew, at work. "Most of you know these people."

She flicked to a photo of a group of men painting the outside of the house, Earl James in front, grinning with upraised paint brush. Her gaze slid over the audience to the African American man and his wife, Stella. "Earl's expression says it all, folks. Every day, Earl arrived early and cheerful, ready to sand or paint. We couldn't have done this restoration without him and his wife, Stella. Stella painted all the inside trim, stenciling, and most important, the parlor mural you now see of the original Dunham plantation up the road from the house and apothecary."

Jennifer paused as the Hudson River Valley-style painting flashed onto the big screen, eliciting murmurs of admiration from those who had not yet visited the house. "Stella's painting is featured in the article on the Dunham restoration in this month's issue of *Old Houses*," Jennifer said. "Her artistic touch makes Dunham House a very special country house now, just as it was a century ago."

Adorned in her usual bright, flowing clothing, the middle-aged woman met her eyes and smiled. Petite beside her with each silvery curl in place, Stella's mother Dorace nodded. "And her friendship has been one of the biggest blessings of my time here," Jennifer added in an unsteady voice.

"Aw, honey, it's mutual," Stella called out with a wave of her hand.

While Jennifer blinked a sudden mist away, several people gave murmurs of appreciation. What Jennifer couldn't say was that Stella's persistent and loving witness had led to the best gift, in fact, of Jennifer's life: faith in and a relationship with Christ. Neither was now the appropriate time to go into the fact that Stella and her mother, Dorace, had provided the key to explaining why Michael Johnson's great-grandmother had fallen off the family tree in the 1920s. The daughter of Dr. Hampton Dunham and his black housekeeper Luella, Georgia

Pearl found sanctuary in passing as a fully white nurse in Atlanta after an attack by KKK members maimed her black beau. She married a white doctor and gave birth to Michael's beloved grandmother, Gloria. That made Michael and Stella cousins of sorts. Lucky Michael.

Jennifer realized the painting still glowed on the projector screen and focused her attention. "Most of you here know this scene depicts the plantation and sanatorium built up by Dr. Silas Dunham, son of Levi Dunham, the first of the family in this area. Levi's cabin is also shown. Levi's original two hundred acres on Long Creek increased and flourished under the practice of his son, who became renowned for incorporating African and Native American healing arts alongside herbal and traditional medical training. Despite the fact that folks describe him as the richest man in Georgia during his time, we still haven't found the gold he's supposed to have buried."

Laughter rippled through the room. Lubricated by Jennifer's previous show of emotion and attempt at humor, someone called out, "Aren't you supposed to be moving Levi's cabin to Hermon?"

Jennifer smiled, and her gaze sought out, not the speaker, but Michael Johnson, sitting with hands resting on sprawled long legs, beside his father, James. Her heart turned over as the dark-haired man smiled back. "Yes, in fact, Michael and I have a meeting with a cabin reconstruction expert from Arnoldsville this week."

"Maybe you'll find that gold under his cabin, huh?"

More laughter. "Maybe so," Jennifer agreed. "Or maybe he buried it under the outhouse after his sons established their practice here in Hermon, in which case we might find it when my former professor brings an archeology class from UGA later this month."

Carried along in the spirit of camaraderie, she couldn't resist a wink in the direction of fifty-something Horace Greene. Horace oversaw the Dunham property in Hermon when his company, Athens Area Property Management, rented it out after the death of Dunham spinster Ettie Mae, last family member to occupy the house during the mid-1900s. Horace now specialized in historic real estate and allowed his son to helm the company. But his obsessive interest in Jennifer's and Michael's plans for the buildings on the estate remained. At first his inquiries and suggestions raised Jennifer's ire. Now, after his former homecoming queen wife Amy's surprisingly discerning eye selected period-appropriate paint and curtains for Dunham House through her Lexington shop, Drapes and Drips, Horace and Amy topped Jennifer's list of helpful supporters.

But to Jennifer's surprise, Horace did not wink back, or smile. Amy dug a silk-clad elbow into her husband's well-padded side. And that was when things started to go south.

"I admit, finding some gold would help finance all this restoration," Michael put in.

As everyone chuckled, James added in agreement, "Yeah, we didn't know what we were getting into when we decided to follow the terms of Michael's grandmother's will." Contrasting his teasing words, the slender man's warm smile made clear his approval of Jennifer and her work.

A figure in the back Jennifer hadn't seen past the light of the projector stirred. "Exactly what I fear we'll get into with the Gillen's department store," offered a voice no less firm for its rheumy quality.

Jennifer's heart thudded. Maybe if she just moved on, Bryce Stevenson's reluctance to interrupt a professional meeting would override his objections to the proposal she'd put before "his" town council over a month ago. She advanced the PowerPoint, passing several pictures of the refinished interiors of Dunham House with no comment, hoping to pick up the momentum when she reached the apothecary slides.

Michael's smooth, deep voice filled in her gap. "As you can see, the money was well spent. Although Gothic and Victorian furnishing best suited the date of the house, Jennifer cut a stubborn bachelor some slack and went with American Empire. It's a cleaner look. We mixed in my modern furnishings. I had to make it clear I didn't want to live in a doll house."

When the group laughed, Jennifer held up a finger. "But he did agree to a touch of Gothic," she told them with a smile.

Michael's arrival in Hermon had created lots of speculation as to why a young bachelor would move to the boondocks. Even restoring family property at his grandmother's dying wish didn't explain leaving behind a social life and thriving construction company. What most people in the room didn't know, but Jennifer now did, was that Michael was not a bachelor, but a widower. Learning her employer had lost his wife to cancer, as he had his mother, went a long way toward explaining his reclusive tendencies.

Prepared to move forward, Jennifer froze as the aging town councilman spoke again.

"Well, the money might have been well spent, but I believe your grandmother left it for that exact purpose." Bryce rested the weight of his upper body on his cane. "Let's just cut to the chase. Many of us are on the Hermon town council. As wonderful as it's been to watch the transformation of the Dunham doctors' property, we're all aware this enterprisin' young woman is askin' our town to purchase the old Gillen's department store and pay to have it renovated for meeting space and an art studio and gallery for Mrs. James. What's more, Michael Johnson and his father, general construction contractors from Atlanta, presented a bid for that project at our last meetin'. Now, I still don't know what's in it for Miss Rushmore, besides the fact that she's identified Mrs. James as her personal friend and obviously has some loyalty to the Johnsons, but the truth is, she's an outsider. She may know our history, but she hasn't lived it. She hasn't scraped and sweated to put that money in the bank that she's askin' us to spend on what could be another ill-advised whim. I think we can see from this presentation that restorin' a historic structure opens a bottomless financial pit."

Jennifer stood frozen in place. She saw tall, elegant Grace Stevenson's pale face as she turned to her father-in-law and said, "Please, Daddy Stevenson, this isn't a council meeting. You can say what you want there, but I asked Miss Rushmore to speak to Historic Oglethorpe tonight about her restoration of the Dunham property. And you're interruptin' that." She turned back around and, without a glance at her banker husband's carefully composed face, offered Jennifer a faltering smile. "Please continue, Miss Rushmore. I know everyone is anxious to hear about the apothecary."

Somehow Jennifer got through the presentation. She heard her own voice discussing their refurbishment of the horseshoe-shaped shelving built into the curved, plastered walls of the front room of the 1870s doctor's office. She described how the doctors mixed medicines on the compounding desk and examined patients in the middle room, as denoted by the reclining chair still in residence and the extra soot from kerosene lanterns cleaned from the ceiling.

Jennifer even mentioned the letters they found behind a cabinet in the back room. Charlotte, the wife of Dr. Stuart Dunham, had written those letters to Dr. William Dunham, her brother-in-law, while Stuart was an invalid after being wounded in the head while performing operations in a Civil War field hospital. The missives hinted at an attachment between Charlotte and William well before William became a widowed Charlotte's second husband. But Jennifer knew she'd lost her spark. She'd fallen back on reciting facts.

The smug assurance behind Bryce's observations punctured her protective layer, swilling memories of childhood condescension to the surface like dregs from a torn tea bag. Those voices told her she was second-hand, like the trailer park she'd come from, like the clothes she'd worn, and worse, like the child her own sorry parents had rejected. Stella and the pastor of her church Jennifer now attended told her to replace those voices with the truth from God's Word about who she'd become in Christ, but obviously her ability to do so remained shaky.

Finally, with little of the confidence she'd exuded when she read the *Old Houses* article just over a week ago at the coffee bar debut in Mary Ellen McWhorter's antique shop—Jennifer's idea, too—she announced the Halloween opening of Hermon Apothecary Herbals under the management of local herbalist Allison Winters, then thanked her audience. She sat down, skewing the question and answer session she'd promised Grace. A warm round of applause followed her abrupt wrap-up.

Somehow "old man Stevenson," as Stella and Mary Ellen called him, stumped his way to the front of the meeting room with a rapidity that beat out well-wishers and a frowning Michael. He loomed over her in the sudden brightness of the fluorescent lights.

"No hard feelings, young lady," he said, the scruff of bushy white eyebrows contrasting with a long-sleeve Polo shirt and shiny gold watch. "It's not personal, you know. I just don't want to see the town take a windfall. You don't understand all the hard times we've been through since the boll weevil. The owner has a much more sensible plan in mind for that building."

Jennifer stood up. "The owner?" The identity of that individual had long been cloaked in mystery, even to the long-standing residents of the county. "You know who owns the Gillen store?"

Bryce winked. "Sure I do. I know everything about Hermon."

"Well, who is it?" Jennifer asked as Michael, James and Stella gathered around her. She felt their presence like a shield and stood a little taller.

"I'm afraid I'm not at liberty to disclose that. Just know it might surprise you."

"What does the owner have in mind for the property, then?" James asked in his typical mild manner.

"Why, he told me years ago he envisioned a family restaurant there."

Stella wobbled her head back and forth in a chiding gesture. "Well, if he wouldn't be askin' the moon and stars for it, maybe that restaurant woulda gone in *years ago*."

Bryce didn't even look at her. "Some of us are very particular about the sort of people we have dealings with." He reached out for Jennifer's hand and attempted to pat it, but she recoiled, disgusted by his racially-based dismissal of her friend and his patronizing attitude toward outsiders. "It's better I tell you now it's never goin' to work out. Just don't get your feelings hurt."

Anger overpowered any other emotions as Jennifer replied, "Oh, no worries, Mr. Stevenson. If the majority of good people in Hermon don't understand what a boon to the community an art gallery will provide, it's their loss. I've got no horse in this race. We'll just find another opportunity for Stella's studio."

"Maybe in Lexington," a voice suggested.

Jennifer turned and, with relief, saw Lexington mayor Alton Wilson and his chamber director, Marian Dukes. "Mayor Wilson!" Jennifer exclaimed. "Please excuse me, Mr. Stevenson." She turned away from the councilman and extended her hand to the pair of smartly dressed business people. As she did, she felt a warm hand on her back and knew it to be Michael's. Did she ever love that man! Just so happened that feeling was as new as her so-called identity in Christ.

The silver-sprinkled, dark-haired mayor looked like he could be related to the chamber president, although they just worked together.

Fortunately, both had expressed excitement and support for Jennifer's ideas of revitalizing Hermon at the Summer Gala, to the point of Marian asking Jennifer if she would consider a Main Street director position for the town of Lexington. Even though Jennifer also awaited an interview for her dream job at Savannah Heritage Trust, she'd agreed to meet with Marian. Last she'd heard, Marian consulted with the mayor to finalize the job description.

"Mrs. James, we'd love to have you open a studio and gallery in Lexington should the space in Hermon not work out," Mayor Wilson told Stella. "We have several empty storefronts we'd love to fill. You could take your pick."

"Thank you, Mayor Wilson, that's very kind, and I'll bear that in mind," said Stella. "But of course if I can help bring new life into the community where I live, that would be ideal."

"Of course."

"Excellent presentation, Jennifer," Marian offered, reaching for Jennifer's hand. "I'm so excited about how you folks are using the apothecary for an herbal shop. Your vision of rebirthing Hermon as a trendy future stop on the Rails to Trails route is dead on. Don't let anyone tell you otherwise." She cast a censorious eye over Jennifer's shoulder, where Bryce Stevenson limped away.

"Thank you," Jennifer said, pleased to see not everyone in the county fell under the man's thumb. From what she'd heard, Stevenson used his current home site to block development of the popular biking trail from Athens to Union Point, south of Hermon.

"We'd prefer to redirect your energy and enthusiasm locally, rather than have it run off to Savannah," Alton put in. "I'm sure you folks agree," he added, smiling at Jennifer's group of friends.

"We certainly do," Michael said, causing Jennifer to glance at him in surprise and pleasure.

The mayor nodded. "So along those lines, I finally cleared small town bureaucracy to create an official Main Street director position. We have all our ducks in a row now, if you'd be so good as to sit down with Ms. Dukes and let her share the particulars."

Jennifer blinked. "Well, sure. When?"

Marian raised her elegantly arched brows. "This Friday? I have an opening on my calendar at two."

Jennifer nodded. "I'll be there."

"Excellent. You know my office is located in the Crawford depot. Come see me there, then I'll take you to see your potential space. We want Lexington's main street director in Lexington. We've reclaimed a 1950s gas station on the corner. Right now it houses the office of the Downtown Development Authority, which you'd be working closely with, needless to say."

After waving off the Lexington diplomats and exchanging bemused and hopeful smiles with Stella and the Johnson men, Jennifer went to retrieve her flash drive from the laptop. Grace helped her eject it, and then said, "Jennifer, I am so sorry about my father-in-law. I didn't expect him to come, much less speak up like that."

"It's OK, Grace. It's hardly your fault."

Her shoulders sagged. "I feel like it is. I should have made sure this didn't happen. He's getting more and more ornery in his old age, and someone needs to stand up to him." Her gaze went to her stocky, rusty-haired husband in the back of the room. Jennifer had been told if George Stevenson kowtowed to pressure from his father, he could use his influence at the bank to force council members' votes. Jennifer had never met him, so she had no guess which way that pendulum would swing, in favor of the crusty father or the gracious wife.

"Please don't worry about it," Jennifer said.

Grace squeezed her hand. "Be assured I'll use whatever influence I possess in this situation. I truly believe your vision for Hermon is one we should all embrace. But if Lexington ends up getting you, it's exactly what we nincompoops deserve."

Jennifer laughed and waved a dismissive hand. "Not at all. Thank you for having me, Grace."

"Thank you for sharing tonight, Jennifer."

Michael approached from behind. "Ready?" he asked, gesturing toward the door.

She let out a breath. "Very."

In the parking lot, Dorace, Earl and Stella waited to offer their appreciation for the evening. "You did a great job, honey," Stella murmured in her ear as she hugged her. "And you gave that mean old man a good what-for."

Dorace harrumphed, pursing her lips as she stood nearby with her arms crossed over her purse. "What comes to my mind is what the

Good Book says about pride going before a fall. He best be watching the pavement."

Michael and James laughed, but Jennifer's eyes widened as she asked the James family, "Do you think he could have been playing me about who owns the old store? Do you think he could actually own it himself?"

"I guess it could be," Earl murmured, scratching his chin. "The Stevensons owned property all around in the old days."

That included the empty lot between Michael's house and Mary Ellen's antique store, where Jennifer heard the Stevenson ancestral home stood before Bryce's father Humphrey burned it down rather than have his children squabble about who inherited it. Bryce inherited the tight-fisted mindset instead.

"And not just wood and brick property," Dorace muttered.

"Yes, his attitude toward you really upset me, Stella," Jennifer said.

Stella shook her straight, shoulder-length hair. "Oh, it's nothin' new from folks like him. Some people're just slow to change."

Jennifer pursed her lips. Their discovery about Michael's great-grandmother had made strides toward racial reconciliation in the town, bringing to light that more of the blacks and whites shared blood than they'd even suspected. Still, Jennifer longed to see a thriving community where everyone could flourish by sharing their gifts, talents and knowledge. Maybe that was idealistic, but they'd already come so far by restoring the Dunham property, opening the herb shop, and making over the antique store with a coffee bar serving the baked goods of Jennifer's talented tween friend, Montana Worley. Jennifer had first tasted the homeschooler's mouth-watering muffins out of a basket in the hair salon of Montana's grandmother Rita. She reminded herself that the majority of residents were excited about the changes. They couldn't let Bryce Stevenson stop them. That gutted old store had a vibrant future.

As she often did, Stella picked up on Jennifer's thoughts. "Don't you worry. Even if I end up in Lexington and a restaurant comes instead, those both would be positive changes, wouldn't they?"

"Yes, but no restaurant's going to come at that asking price. That place will remain a crumble of bricks and broken glass forever," Jennifer predicted in a pouty tone.

Of course, she earned Stella's trademark gesture, the finger wag. "If the Good Lord intends it—"

"It will come to pass," Jennifer and Michael finished together. Jennifer rolled her eyes.

"That's right," Stella told them. "Good night, sweet girl ... and gentlemen."

They waved as they got into their vehicles. James climbed in the back of Michael's new F150 extended cab, allowing Michael to seat Jennifer in the front. She thanked him but still felt uncomfortable with gentlemanly gestures. The lack of sentiment in her childhood years had caused her to develop a thick outer shell and the expectation of doing things for herself.

"I kind of think old man Stevenson could own the store," James observed from the back seat. "His attitude about it fits the family profile."

"And his certainty that no one else will ever get it," Michael agreed.

Jennifer sighed. "I just don't get people like that."

"They're the kind who drive slow to accumulate cars behind them, then speed up at a passing zone," James said.

"Renovating the store would be the perfect first job for the new construction crew you're forming here in Oglethorpe County," Jennifer told them. "Even if Stella has another option, you don't."

Michael glanced over at her. "Construction jobs are a dime a dozen."

"Not one like that. That could establish your reputation in the entire Athens area. Set the bar higher for the future."

"We'll just keep praying about it," James said. "And in the meantime, we'll hardly be bored while we're overseeing the reconstruction of the log cabin, preparing the parking lot for Allison, and working on the smokehouse and cook's cabin."

"Right." Jennifer didn't mention that only one of those would command a significant portion of her time. She swallowed. She felt her time here ticking down with the shortening days, and the uncertainty of her future loomed as it had after graduation this past spring. Even if she accepted the job in Lexington rather than Savannah, where would she live? Michael rented the double-wide adjoining his property from a local family as part of her employment agreement.

Would they transfer the lease to her? Would she be able to afford it? And most of all, did Michael even want her to stay?

She glanced over at him in the dim light as the miles between Lexington and Hermon rolled by, framing his profile in moon-touched farm land. Handsome, athletic and self-assured, Michael Johnson represented just the sort of guy she'd skulked away from in high school and college. At first, they'd gone head to head on matters related to historical restoration. Then something changed. She still wasn't sure what about her had captured his interest, or how much she even had. Certainly the make-over Rita Worley forced on her helped. He started staring at her like she'd become a different person after that. But it had to be more than that. He said it was her big heart. It certainly wasn't her sordid past. She still worried about revealing too much to him last month when a visit to his lake house forced memories of her stepfather's abuse to surface. How much dirt could a little make-up and a big heart compensate for?

When they slowed past Montana's family's dairy farm and turned right, into the gravel drive by the white house with red tin roof and high, spindled gables, Michael offered to walk her home.

"Sure," she said, not certain what motivation his offer sprung from. After she said goodnight to James and they started walking toward the row of evergreens separating his property from her rental lot, she drew her sweater closer against the autumn chill and asked, "Worried somebody's waiting to get me?"

He settled a chiding look on her. "Well, considering that since you came to work here, someone has locked you in the shed, caused you to fall and sprain your ankle by pouring oil over the damaged floor in the apothecary, and tampered with the brakes on my truck the day you were driving it to Augusta, that would be a relevant concern."

Jennifer punctuated the air with her finger and joked, "We still have not established the fact that those incidents were caused by a person rather than accident ... or an angry ghost."

"You know I don't believe in ghosts."

"Ah, but you do believe in evil spirits, especially where something evil has happened. I'd say the way Stuart Dunham treated his slaves and his wife before shrapnel hit him in the head, not to mention slavery itself, could qualify as evil."

Michael gave a single nod. "I'd agree with you."

"But you don't think a ghost stalks me."

"No, I do not."

"So you're here to protect me."

Her companion glanced over. "Or maybe I just didn't want to say goodnight to you in front of my dad."

Jennifer tingled down to her toes. She hadn't dared to hope Michael wanted to get close to her again. The night of the coffee bar opening-slash-literature reading, he'd kissed her. Most people would call it a peck, but for Jennifer, half drawn to the man and half terrified of him, it had been perfect. It had happened right after she wrote the letter telling her mother and stepfather she'd accepted the Lord, and the Holy Spirit flowing through her had enabled her to forgive them for years of neglect and abuse. Michael's prayers and presence had also been a big part of that enabling.

Now, he reached for her elbow. "And maybe I wanted to make sure Bryce Stevenson didn't rattle you too much."

She gave a faint smile as they stepped up onto her front porch. "I admit, he did trip my rejection sensors a little bit."

"Don't let him. He's the one who's small, not you."

"I know." She glanced up and smiled again. "I just have to keep telling myself that, or rather, letting the Scriptures tell me that, like Stella taught me."

"That's right. So, no word from your family?" Michael hooked a finger in the loop of his pants and slacked his hip.

Jennifer bit her lip as she dug her keys out of her purse. "Nope. No surprise there."

"Give it time. God had to work on you for a while."

"Yeah. I guess something could be worse than silence. I could get an angry e-mail accusing me of making up things again." That would be from her mother. Roy was the one who had long ago mastered the silent treatment as part of his emotional manipulation arsenal.

"You could, but somehow I don't think you will. Your letter released them, not accused them."

True. Counseling with Pastor Simms helped Jennifer recall memories indicating Roy and her mother both suffered painful childhoods of their own, making their adult actions not excusable, but more understandable. Still, talking about it seemed to shave inches off her stature. She hated that Michael knew what he knew about her.

Seeing her posture slump, Michael reached out. His warm solidness, and the fact that he wanted to hold her again, reassured her. Mmm, but he smelled good. Too insecure to reach around under his coat, she folded her hands against his chest and shivered. She wanted to ask him in, but she feared how that might come across.

"Michael?"

"Hm?"

"How do you feel about my job interview with Marian?"

"I'm glad she finally followed through with it, of course." He pulled back a little to look at her in the glow of her porch light.

"Are you?"

"Of course," he repeated with more emphasis. "I think it's clear you belong here rather than with a bunch of strangers in Savannah. Everyone feels that way."

She belonged here, he said, everyone thought, but did she belong here with *him*, and did *he* feel that way?

He laid his forehead against hers and whispered, "Are you stressing again?"

Their breath mingled, frosty puffs in the night air. Their kiss had started much this same way. But she couldn't kiss him ever again until she knew. "Michael, what am I to you?"

CHAPTER TWO

The jangling of the alarm woke Jennifer the next morning. She slapped around until she located it, frustration from the previous night returning with unwelcome consciousness.

Wrapped in a robe after her shower, Jennifer stood in front of the bathroom mirror and tried to see what Michael saw. With wet hair and no make-up, her petite stature and delicate frame made her appear almost child-like, despite her almost twenty-five years. Yet Michael knew she was no child. He knew Jennifer's stepfather had preyed on the vulnerability of her father's desertion and stripped her of any innocence before she turned twelve. She hated that her appearance reminded her of that, rather than exuding strength.

Then again, elegant curves might be better than strength. Maybe if she looked more womanly Michael would have wanted to kiss her again.

She sighed, pulling back the mouse brown hair Rita Worley had expertly streaked with auburn and snipped into face-flattering layers. Getting out the Mary Kay compacts Rita's daughter Jean force-sold her the same day, Jennifer applied her "five minute face" before completing a quick blow dry and searching her closet for a plaid flannel shirt and jeans. No need for fancy at the old Dunham plantation.

When Jennifer came out of the bedroom, Yoda, the gray female cat she, James and Michael rescued as a starving kitten from under the apothecary, sat by the back deck door and meowed. That meant she wanted to check the nearby field for mice. Jennifer let her out and punched the button on her Keurig. Moments later, the 1980s double-wide filled with the smell of coffee, and Jennifer settled at the table with her mug, muffin and Bible.

She tried to read, but her thoughts kept returning to Michael. She didn't know how to interpret the look that came over his face when she asked her million dollar question. After a pause, he'd answered with one word—special.

Special? She leaned her head on her hand and groaned. Pumpkin spice lattes were special. Humane society puppies were special. Disabled children were special. And special was what you called someone you cared about but weren't prepared to say you loved. And she loved

Michael. His very brokenness and the fact that he struggled with bitterness over his past had made him relatable, allowing her to lower her guard and ask him spiritual questions. But maybe qualifiers existed on the desire Michael had expressed for openness between them. At this point, Michael Johnson might have more walls in place than she did.

Or worse. Jennifer sat up, bit her lip. Maybe he wasn't into her. One could credit most of his tender gestures to sympathy. Sure, he'd exhibited moments of interest like the one in her trailer after the party, but what if after he kissed her, he decided he wasn't feeling it? Maybe unease or disgust over her past overpowered any attraction.

Damaged goods, an old voice whispered in her mental ear.

The coffee in her stomach soured, and she pushed her Bible away. Yet one of the verses written in her notebook popped into her head. "You formed my inward parts; You covered me in my mother's womb. I will praise You, for I am fearfully and wonderfully made."

"OK, Lord," Jennifer sighed. "I hear you. Replace the lies with truth."

At that moment, an explosion of barking caused her to glance outside. Stepping out on the back deck, Jennifer beheld Yoda cowering on a tree branch while her neighbor's lab-boxer mix, Otis, heralded the hounds of heaven from below. She looked toward the dilapidated 1920s bungalow that housed local hermit Calvin Woods and let out a sigh. As expected, although his truck sat in the littered yard, no sign of life stirred.

In her slippers, Jennifer marched across wet grass, up the stone steps of Calvin's house, and knocked on his door. At last the rotund, bulbous-nosed man appeared wearing his bath robe knotted over a T-shirt and sweat pants. The extra pick-up truck on blocks that graced Calvin's yard and the blue cambric shirts he often wore made Jennifer assume Calvin worked part-time at a local garage.

"Good morning, Calvin, can you please come get your dog? He treed my cat."

Calvin stepped around her to the edge of the porch and yelled, "Otis! Get back here." Of course no such thing occurred. Still not speaking to her, Calvin let out a huff and stalked back into the house. Jennifer stood on the porch blinking until he returned with a leash in his hands. She followed him to her back yard. Was it her imagination, or did he move more stiffly than normal, almost with a limp?

Jennifer tried to soothe the hissing feline while Calvin looped the lead over his mutt's thick neck. "Thank you," she called as the annoying duo lumbered homeward. Given the fact that an armadillo-bound bullet streaking across her back porch had provided her first introduction to Calvin, Jennifer hadn't really expected an apology. Still, a muttered word might have been nice. She settled for a backward wave. Huh. Calvin had seemed friendlier ever since Michael paid the man's nephews to exterminate the armadillos tearing up Jennifer's landscaping, just not so much today.

Jennifer finally coaxed Yoda down and carried her back inside the house, stroking the silky body which was not yet full grown but certainly sleeker than in the kitten's early days. Back in her mauve-and-ducks themed kitchen, she set out milk and Friskies as a substitute for field mice and warmed her coffee in the microwave. She glanced at the time. Yikes. Only twenty minutes before she met Michael to ride up to Long Creek. She had to get herself together.

As the mug twirled on the turn table, she pondered the fact that she found herself right where her former professor, Barbara Shelley, warned her not to go. In love with Michael, that was. Barb cautioned her that not only could a romantic relationship endanger her employment status, it could break her heart. Jennifer did not need a man in her life. Her feminist mentor swore that since her divorce, she found all the meaning she craved in her career. But Barbara also rejected the notion of any need for God.

Oh, no. Jennifer jumped with the beep of the microwave, realizing she needed to text Barb. Jennifer's professor planned to come Friday after lunch to stake out the compost and outhouse areas for class excavations scheduled the following week, and Jennifer had agreed to meet Marian Dukes in Crawford at two. Barb's chore wouldn't take long. Jennifer suspected Barb still searched for an excuse to connect, although she failed to understand the middle-aged woman's determination to maneuver from professor to friend. Stella and Michael considered her interest controlling and possibly unhealthy, but Jennifer felt a need to maintain pleasantries since Barbara's influence arranged Jennifer's coveted Savannah interview. But that could wait. She needed to finish her devotions.

She sat back down at the table and pulled the Bible toward her. Since Stella and Michael had helped her come into the family of

God, she'd experienced the first sense of belonging in her life. Jesus said He was the friend who stuck closer than a brother ... which was a good thing for someone whose brother basically sold her out, overlooking the warning signs of his sister's abuse in favor of maintaining his camaraderie with his stepfather. In an effort to repair Jennifer's view of God as a loving Father, one she could trust, Pastor Simms also shared many Bible verses and books with her. Now, Jennifer read in the second chapter of Hosea that God wanted to be like a husband as well.

"I will betroth you to Me forever; yes, I will betroth you to Me in righteousness and justice, in lovingkindness and mercy; I will betroth you to Me in faithfulness, and you shall know the Lord."

Jennifer knew little of faithfulness—everyone abandoned or disappointed, family worst of all. She got glimpses of faithfulness in Stella's friendship and Earl and Stella's marriage, but that felt far removed from the kind of love she yearned for. So God told her He would be faithful. She was counting on that. What about Michael?

In the quiet of the morning, with Yoda lapping milk and Jennifer sipping coffee, she sensed God asking if He would be enough even if Michael wasn't part of the picture. Yes, He would be enough. But Jennifer wasn't sure she could stay in Oglethorpe County if Michael only wanted friendship. The problem was, she didn't really know how to navigate a relationship, either. She'd become adept at keeping guys at arm's length.

God, you've got to take care of this because I don't know what to do. I don't even know how to act when I go over there in a few minutes.

Her mind went back to what happened the night before, after Michael called her special and splintered her heart by kissing her cheek. With new eyes, she saw gentleness and respect in the gesture. And then there was what he'd said after she'd turned away to unlock her door. Before she'd gone in, he'd called her name and, without her turning around, delivered the clincher: "You're the only thing that's made me feel something since Ashley died."

She'd gotten so caught up in what he hadn't done or hadn't said that she'd hardly heard what he had. In fact, she'd been so concerned he'd see the tears in her eyes that she'd only responded with a nod to a statement that must have cost him dearly. Michael cared for her, a lot, and that had to be enough for now. And it could be because she had a

Father, a Friend and a Brother who would never leave. And a Husband, if need be.

Strengthened, Jennifer finished her prayers, rinsed her mug and hurried to the bathroom. There, she texted Barb that she needed to push their plans to four on Friday to accommodate a local meeting. She hoped the appointed hour allowed time to complete the surveying without lingering into dinnertime. She also hoped Barb wouldn't inquire what the new meeting entailed. Jennifer had kept her former professor in the dark regarding the Main Street director position. No need for Barb to think her interested in anything except Savannah Heritage Trust, especially when the other thing she'd warned Jennifer about was stagnating among provincial, religiously backward locals.

No such luck. A text dinged onto her phone's screen just as she stuck the toothbrush in her mouth. "What's the meeting?"

"The chamber president in Lexington. Four should still give us enough time, right?"

While Jennifer gyrated the toothbrush and stared at her phone, it started to ring. Her eyes opened wide when she saw the Savannah number. Oh, my gracious. She spit fast, rinsed and answered in as smooth a voice as possible, "Hello?"

"Hello, is this Jennifer Rushmore?"

"Yes, it is."

The cultured voice of a mature woman said with a slight Southern drawl, "My name is Tandy Sullivan, with Savannah Heritage Trust. I'm callin' regardin' your application for the historic preservation manager position."

"Oh, yes." Jennifer tried to inject the right amount of enthusiasm and professionalism into her tone, despite the galloping of her heart.

"Well, we were very impressed with your application, and also with the recommendation of your mentor and my friend, Dr. Barbara Shelley at the University of Georgia. We wondered if you'd like to schedule a day to come to Savannah to interview with us."

Jennifer propelled herself toward her computer desk and her planner. "I certainly would!"

"I'm so glad. As you know, the job doesn't begin until January 1, so we do still have several candidates to interview."

Jennifer paused with her calendar in hand, open to the month of October. No shoo-ins despite the inside connection. Point taken. She waited until Ms. Sullivan continued.

"Let's see, I'll be travelin' some the end of this month. Would the first Thursday in November do?"

"Yes. Yes, it would. What time?"

"Why don't you plan to arrive at eleven? I can give you a tour of the firm, then we can discuss details and get to know each other over lunch."

"That sounds wonderful."

"Where would you like to go, The Pirate's House or The Pink House? I can make reservations."

"Oh … The Pirate's House, I think." Jennifer had never been to either, but she'd heard The Pink House was elegant. A mental vision of herself facing an intimidating assortment of cutlery made that decision easy.

"The Pirate's House it is. Well, I look forward to seein' you then, Jennifer."

"And you, Ms. Sullivan."

"Oh, Tandy, please. Any friend of Barbara's is a friend of mine."

By the time Jennifer gathered her tools, laced her work boots and arrived in Michael's yard, he leaned against the grill of his truck with folded arms and a grim expression. That might have intimidated her before her devotions and Tandy's call. Now she jogged to the passenger side and slung her bag onto the floorboard.

"Sorry I'm late," she said, climbing onto the running board. "I got a phone call."

"Must have been important. Fig Wilson's going to be sitting by the gate waiting on us."

Jennifer giggled at the log cabin expert's unusual name. "Horace will keep him company." As Michael started the ignition, she took in his jeans and flannel work shirt layered over a button-up thermal and added, "And yes, it was important. It was a lady from Savannah Heritage Trust."

Michael's stubbled jaw dropped. "Did she offer you a job?"

Jennifer smiled. "No, not yet, but she did ask me to come interview."

"But I thought you were interviewing with Marian this week." His straight dark brows hovered close to his blue eyes.

"I am. This won't be until the first Thursday in November. I told you when we went out to eat that time I'd decided to interview for both jobs and let God show me the right path, remember?"

"Yeah. I guess I just thought ..."

"You thought what?"

He looked away from her and put the truck in gear. "Nothing. That's exactly what you should do."

As the truck bounced out onto Highway 77, Jennifer bit her lip. A spark of hope stirred that Michael's reaction meant he thought since they'd gotten closer she might rule out Savannah, but another part of her felt irritated. He'd given her little more than brotherly affection and admiration. Did he expect her to toss aside her career dreams in the simple hope he might want more? That definitely squared with the assuming Michael she'd first met, as did the quiet reserve emanating from the man's muscular frame as they made their way north.

She pulled out her phone. Barb had texted, "Four is fine. What are you doing today?"

Jennifer typed back, "On the way to Levi's cabin to meet the reconstruction expert. And Tandy from SHT just called. Set interview for early Nov."

Ding. "Well, it took her long enough! So excited for you."

Barb's familiar enthusiasm made her smile. After all, their common love of preserving history first put Jennifer on the professor's radar and caused Barbara to become a mentor. That and sympathy for the rough background Barbara knew Jennifer came from.

Michael looked over at her. "That Savannah again?"

"No, it's Barb. You know she's coming Friday to set off the excavation sites. I had to move it to four due to my interview in Lexington. I'm just telling her about the Savannah interview." Jennifer texted "thanks" and pressed send.

"Right."

When she glanced at him, trying to read his tone, he smiled. "Seems like everything is going to work out just like you'd hoped."

"Well, I've not been offered anything yet."

"You will be. They'll both want you, and you'll have to choose." The lines around Michael's mouth tightened as he stared at the highway.

"No," she corrected him, "I'm going to have to figure out which option God wants for me."

Michael turned his head and smiled again. To her relief, he reached for her hand and squeezed. "Let's pray He makes it clear."

Jennifer nodded. She wanted to say "to both of us," but that assumed too much at this point. To her disappointment, the chained fence of the Dunham property with two pick-ups waiting in front of it appeared ahead on the right. She had to release Michael's hand as he eased his F150 into tall grass on the side of the road and hopped out with the gate key.

A minute later, they drove behind Horace and Fig along the two-rut lane leading between low-hanging branches. Early-turning leaves fluttered down onto goldenrod and starry lavender wildflowers. Jennifer sighed.

"What?" Michael asked.

"I just love this. It feels like we're going back in time."

"Yeah, wish we could have seen it before the plantation house burned."

"You're telling me. Even with just the chimneys left, the way the house is situated on the rise reminds me of the Lockwood Plantation."

Michael cocked an eyebrow. "The one you used to visit as a kid?"

Jennifer nodded.

"You'd go there to get away from your family, wouldn't you?"

Nice of him not to say which specific member of her family. "Sometimes I'd spend the night," she admitted in a small voice.

She shouldn't have said that. Michael looked at her with pity, as if he could envision her wrapped up in her sleeping bag in that empty parlor, years ago. "So old houses are more than just interesting to you. They make you feel safe." Surprised at his discernment, Jennifer remained silent. Michael asked, "Didn't your mom come looking for you?"

Jennifer lifted a shoulder. "She knew I liked to hang out there, but never that I spent the night. She assumed I went to a friend's and didn't tell her. She'd rather think me rebellious."

As Michael stopped the truck behind the other vehicles, he said, "Jennifer, when I met your mom at graduation, I could tell she was a selfish and troubled woman, but I could also tell that she does love you. She'll see the light. One day."

"Thanks." Jennifer pressed her lips together and, noticing that Horace and Fig waited for them outside their Dodge Rams, reached for the door handle. She slid out and slung her tools over her shoulder.

While they only planned to discuss relocating the cabin today, she wanted to be able to assess the condition of the logs again. She'd seen the property once before, but that day excitement and Barb's hijacking of the project distracted her. Now, she didn't know why Horace insisted on being present, except Fig was a personal friend Horace had recommended for the job. Maybe historic real estate proved slow these days. And he seemed one of those people who liked to stay connected in the community. For now, he made himself useful carrying Fig's small ladder with Michael.

As Jennifer followed Michael toward the chimneys crowning the rise, she asked over her shoulder, "So, Fig, how many cabins have you reclaimed?"

"Goodness, Miss Jennifer, I've probably lost count." Judging from Fig's full head and beard of snow white, that did not surprise her, but seeing his slender frame move with the agility of a much younger man did. "I've got two on my own property. I've mainly reconstructed Cherokee cabins, so I'm looking forward to an English-made."

"And can I ask where you got your unusual name?"

Fig chuckled. "My daddy says it was on account of my mama wantin' to eat nothin' but Fig Newtons her whole pregnancy."

"Well, that makes sense."

Horace huffed behind them, cowboy boots sliding on the damp leaves as he struggled to keep hold of his end of the ladder while maneuvering through trees and brush. "Most people call him somethin' even more interestin', though," he said.

"What's that?" Michael asked, not winded in the least.

"Spider." He said the word with a Southern twang, like "spid-ah."

Jennifer laughed. "What?"

"Just you wait and see 'im climbin' around on walls and logs, you'll get it. Fig knows what he's doin'. Once he finishes with your cabin, you could move your grandma into it."

"I'll tell you guys what I typically do, and you can tell me if it works for you," Fig offered with a bit more modesty. "Now, if you're lookin' for museum quality, I may not be your guy. I go for simple and lastin', but I do make it look as authentic as possible. I hear you wanna make the cabin into a guest room with a small bath, wired for electric?"

Jennifer bit her lip so she didn't answer instead of Michael. She knew his goals for the cabin centered on livability and solidity, not purism. She'd reined in her instincts for complete authenticity all through his project; she could continue to do so now.

"That's right. Your plan sounds right up my alley," Michael said from the head of the group. "Here we are."

The morning light cradled the rustic structure as gently as the early autumn woods, illuminating the weatherboarding and tin roofing applied after the initial construction. Those afterthoughts probably saved the cabin.

"Oh, this is good, real good," Fig murmured, setting down his tool box. "Good ground clearance remains, and no creepers invaded to trap moisture or encourage termites. What's the length?" he asked Jennifer.

"Twenty-eight."

He nodded with satisfaction. "I think I can manage that without a forklift, which will make it easier on your property … and bill," he told Michael. "Help me set up this ladder so I can inspect the roof."

The man climbed up to the eaves while they waited. "Looks good," he called down. "I'll need to see the rafters from inside, but this cabin's in remarkably good shape." When he returned to the ground, he squatted to examine the stone piers and added, "I like to pour concrete foundations for sturdiness, then cover them with stone, if that's OK with you. My stone mason can use these."

Michael responded just as Jennifer could have predicted, "I'm good with that."

Moving around the structure with Jennifer, Fig admired the single crib construction, commenting on the standard V or full dove-tail corner notching. He agreed with Barbara's earlier assessment that minimal contact between the bottom sill boards and the ground promised less decay, then commented, "Since we're gettin' ready to move'er anyway, I'd really like to pry away a little more of the weatherboarding and see what we've got underneath." He sent Michael a questioning glance.

"Go ahead," the younger man said.

Horace stood with his hands on his hips while Jennifer and Fig went to work with hammer end and pry bar like kids unwrapping a Christmas present. Fig wanted to look right where she did, near the shuttered window, searching for rain damage. Their excited chatter punctuated the autumn morning.

Fig crumbled a loose bit of chinking between his thumb and fingers. "Look at this, mud, rocks and horsehair. That's precious." His terminology caused Michael's brows to quirk but Jennifer to smile in amused understanding. He went on, not noticing either, "I wish we could transport it just as is. Now, I can't give you that, Miss Jennifer, but I use fast-hardening cement and chicken wire that will last real good."

She pressed her lips together, afraid she and the cabin expert were about to have their first disagreement. "Under similar conditions, The National Park Service recommends a quarter part cement, one part lime, four parts sand to an eighth dry color."

Michael shifted his weight. "I'd hazard a guess that mix wouldn't adhere as well to the chicken wire Fig likes to use."

Fig shot him an appreciative look. "That's exactly right, Mr. Johnson, plus cement allows me to add in horse hair, rocks, whatever the client wants. You nail the chicken wire in and smooth your cement on a slight concave to encourage water run-off. But on the inside, we can add some color to the sheetrock putty to make it look like mud, even add some small rocks for an authentic look. That suit?" His small eyes moved from Jennifer to Michael.

"No fiberglass?" Michael wanted to know.

Fig shook his head as Michael and Horace drew closer. Horace's frown, meant to suggest discernment, revealed he possessed no background knowledge on the subject. "I don't recommend it. Messy stuff."

Before Michael could commit to a decision, Jennifer decided to test the older man further. "We want the logs to last without the weatherboarding. How do you treat them?"

"We'd spray on several coats of wood preservative."

Her eyebrows rose. "Most preservatives either change the appearance or color of the logs or contain harmful chemicals. Do you have a plan B?"

Fig tossed a small pick he'd retrieved from his toolbox between his hands, but his movements remained casual rather than agitated. "Well, some swears by borate, but I just don't find it practical. The logs gotta be either green or wet to take to it. Then you gotta add water repellent afterwards. My view is, the preservative I use isn't toxic so far's I know. As to changin' the appearance, it's usually minimal. We can test a small section first and see if you like it. In my opinion, the benefits well outweigh the drawbacks."

Michael nodded. He glanced at Jennifer and said in a moderated tone, "I'm comfortable with Mr. Wilson's plan. I think it's reasonable, Jennifer."

"Fine." She turned to rip off a neighboring board. "Let's move on, then."

She and Michael had butted heads before during the restoration of his house and apothecary, but they'd found ways to compromise and work together. She hadn't expected him to go against her today. She told herself if she ended up in Savannah, she might as well get used to kowtowing to an employer's preference, even if it disregarded her historical expertise or environmental concerns. It occurred to her that she'd have more control and authority if she worked in Lexington.

Michael fell silent as Fig poked the exposed window area with a small pick. "Not bad. We might find some varmint tunnels when we pull these logs apart, but I just leave them as long as they're strong enough."

"If you do have to replace boards," Michael asked, "do you have a source for that?"

"Yep, I've got me a stash of reclaimed logs from other structures. With a single pen, I ought to be able to use those. It won't be hard to notch the ends with a template and my chain saw, then finish by hand with an adz."

"Sounds fun. Need any help, or do you have a full crew?" A faint glow lit Michael's expression, like a boy's when he'd just poured his collection of Lincoln logs out on the floor.

Fig scratched his head. "My son and one other buddy are job regulars. Of course the stone mason comes special. Yeah, most days we can use you. Depends how long you want to stretch this out."

Michael grinned at Jennifer, looking like he barely refrained from winking. "Well, I'm not in a particular hurry."

She offered a faint smile in response to his attempt at reconciliation. It provided some comfort that he wanted her around even if he didn't always agree with her. While she'd always believed in avoiding controlling men, would she really respect one she could boss around? And Michael wasn't really controlling, just sure of himself.

Fig gave them a measuring look, then said, "We gotta get the chinking and daubing done before a freeze, so my goal would be for you to hang a Christmas wreath on the cabin's front door." The older man poked his head in the cabin. "You say it's never been moved before?"

"Not to our knowledge," Michael verified.

"Great. Let me have a look-see on the inside, then we'll follow you back to the reconstruction location. We'll need to talk about access for the trucks and site preparation."

Michael nodded. "Sure."

"You're gonna have a lot of diggin' goin' on out there. You don't want to run into conflicts with too many people on the property at one time," Horace commented, hooking his thumbs on the belt loop of his jeans. His beefy frame belied his time as the county high school's best punter, one who'd possessed the hutzpah to steal the homecoming queen after her quarterback beau shipped out to play football for the University of Florida. He looked at Jennifer. "When's that professor of yours bringin' her class to excavate the outhouse and compost?"

"Next week. She's coming Friday evening to mark the areas." Jennifer grinned. "It should be exciting to see what they find. I was thinking I could display anything interesting in the apothecary shop." Jennifer looked away from Horace, noticing Fig had tuned out the chit-chat and disappeared into the cabin's dim interior. Excusing herself, she followed him.

Spider proved his nickname as he tip-toed around, avoiding rotted floorboards. He verified no previous Roman numerals marked the inside log corners and described his own numbering system, front, back, left and right, using plain numbers on tags starting with one for the bottom logs and working up. He even climbed the decaying steps to the loft, where he exclaimed over the sturdy rafters. Returning to the bottom floor, he joined her to discuss the reconstruction of the chimney, with Horace verifying from the doorway that Fig's friend wielded considerable skill as a stone mason.

"Yep, that's gonna be a big job," the cabin expert agreed. As he spoke, Fig tapped and played with loose stones, particularly one near the top of the surround, above the decaying wooden mantel.

"Well, I'll be hog-tied, this whole thing slides right out," he declared. He held out a river stone for Jennifer to see. "In fact, it don't fit into the hole the way it should at all."

"What do you mean?" Jennifer asked.

"Lotsa folks made hidey holes in these old cabins," he told her. "Y'know, in the days before banks. Look up in there and see if anything's there."

Jennifer's eyebrows shot to the top of her forehead. As much as she shared the desire to satisfy Fig's curiosity, what she expected to find more than anything was one of those "varmints" he described. "You're taller than I am," she pointed out.

The man didn't hesitate to stick his hand right into the void.

"What's going on?" Michael called from the doorway.

"Fig's about to find Levi's hidden gold," Jennifer joked. Then she strangled on her own laughter as her companion's hand emerged holding a blackened leather pouch. "Oh, my stars."

Regardless of the fragile condition of the floor, both men from outside hastened to join them. "Not heavy enough for gold," Fig observed. He slid the stone back in place and opened the bag with his calloused thumbs, ignoring the rotted draw strings. Reaching inside, he pulled out a blackened metal crescent. Bits of ribbon hung from tiny holes on each side.

Jennifer gasped. "I think this was silver, worn as a necklace."

"Is silver," Fig corrected, "just tarnished to high heavens."

"It looks like the gorgets officers sometimes wore during the American Revolution," she observed, voice light with breathlessness. They passed the object around, examining it with wonder, although its current state prevented it from revealing any markings.

"Could it have been Levi's, from the war?" Michael asked. To his credit, he sounded almost as excited as Jennifer this time.

"Could be, but unlikely unless he was an officer," Fig admitted. "Indians wore them, too, as a mark of status."

"But there are no Indians associated with this cabin," Michael pointed out.

"That we know of," Horace corrected. He fixed Michael with a level stare. "There were rumors in the county about Selah Dunham, who spent her life here."

Michael made a scoffing sound. "What rumors? That she was an old maid who scared the local children? I've heard that. Doesn't mean anything. She was Levi's and Verity's daughter. It makes sense she'd want to stay in her own cabin on the plantation if she never married."

"Rumors were that she didn't look anything like their other two children, Comfort and Silas."

Michael started to laugh, but Jennifer broke in, "You know, that old county history book I found in the library when I was researching Georgia Pearl did say that Verity was taken by Creek Indians from the attack on Greensboro in 1787, and that she was returned. I never found anything after that. I wouldn't know where else to look." Her eyes met Michael's.

"Then we'll probably never know," he said.

"Maybe not, but I could give this to Barbara when she comes Friday if you want me to," she offered, taking the crescent and placing it with care back in the pouch Fig held out. "If she can't tell us more about it, she has friends in history and archeology who can. They could clean it up for you, too, if you'd like."

Michael glanced with hesitation at the pouch Fig handed him, as though aware he'd just been given another puzzle piece of his ancestors' history. "Maybe we should just hang onto it for a while."

"They're used to dealing with artifacts. They'd take the best care of it, Michael," Jennifer assured him. Then she reminded him gently, "A lot of good came out of following the clues we found in the house and apothecary, right?"

He sighed and said, "Sure. Why not? We'll see where this takes us."

CHAPTER THREE

Jennifer pressed the gas pedal down as she merged onto the Athens loop Saturday morning, still unable to absorb the phone call she'd received at six a.m.

"I'm a nurse at Athens Regional," an unfamiliar voice said, "and I'm wondering if you can come pick up Barbara Shelley?"

"What?" Jennifer gasped.

"She says you're a friend."

Sitting up in bed, Jennifer pushed the hair out of her face. "Yes. Well, I'm a former student. What happened?"

"It seems someone attacked her as she entered her townhouse last night and knocked her down the stairs. The fall broke her leg, and we kept her for overnight observation due to a pretty severe concussion. She'll be fine, but she needs someone to drive her home, and she's asking for you."

Of course Michael jogged past on his morning run just as she exited her double-wide. His protest sounded in Jennifer's mind as her Civic made quick progress along the empty loop. "I still don't see why you have to go," he said. "Doesn't she have some older friends or colleagues she can call?"

"The nurse said she insists she must speak with me."

The gaze he leveled her with said he thought this constituted more of the manipulation Barbara had displayed over the past few months, but Jennifer couldn't dismiss the urgency she felt. "Besides," she added, "I feel like this is somehow my fault. This happened as she was returning from here."

"And how does that make it your fault?"

Jennifer couldn't explain. Maybe Barb would tell her something today that would. Her mentor had hinted she needed to discuss something with Jennifer even before their Friday plans. And maybe if Michael hadn't hovered like a protective rooster the whole time Barb marked the excavation sites yesterday the professor could have spoken freely. Of course, Jennifer probably didn't want to hear what she had to say. Her interview with Marian had run late enough that by the time Jennifer got back home in her dress clothes, Barb was waiting on her, making it easy for her to ask about Jennifer's meeting. When

Barbara found out Jennifer was considering a local Main Street position, she made no effort to hide her disapproval.

"What type of salary would they offer you?" the older woman asked.

"Thirty-eight thousand," Jennifer answered with a brave effort to not cower.

"Thirty-eight ...?" Barb's eyes looked like they could bug out of her head. "Jennifer, you can make twice that at Savannah Heritage Trust. Someone with half your training could do the job in that little Podunk town. Now, I can see why you might interview just for the experience before going to Savannah, but that's all this was worth. Interview experience. And maybe some bargaining leverage if you mention you've got a standing offer elsewhere. But I trust you wouldn't consider limiting yourself in such a way."

Michael's arrival prevented her from saying more. With him trailing them, Barbara explained the date of the house meant probably at least two outhouse sites existed, the later two-seater building they'd torn down that summer due to its dilapidated, snake-infested condition, and an earlier one that could have become unstable. She used a long, steel probe with a T-shaped handle to investigate any depressed areas of ground about thirty paces from the back door, parallel with the other site. Hitting on an area where the sound and constitution of the soil satisfied, Barb marked a three-by-three area with small red flags.

"We'll let the students shovel test here before we proceed," she said.

The compost heap behind the slave or cook's cabin and the second outhouse site were easy to mark. When James and Michael tore down the outhouse, they'd discovered that someone had poured a layer of concrete into the wood-lined privy vault, presumably to prevent a snake den. Michael used a shovel to scrape away the thin layer of dirt covering the concrete to show Barbara its dimensions and thickness. His half-hearted summer attempt to break the slab with a sledgehammer had left only a crack. After that, Barb advised they leave the site until time to dig, the concrete preserving what lay beneath.

"I've got a jackhammer," he said. "It will be no problem when you're ready."

She nodded. Jennifer helped her measure, and Barbara placed her flags with a stiff demeanor and countenance that suggested she found Michael's continued presence annoying, but she could hardly send him off when he owned the property. Jennifer might have found their ongoing feud amusing had it not been so tiresome. And to think yesterday started out so nicely.

Taking the Prince Avenue exit, Jennifer sighed. After talking at Marian's office, Marian had showed her the already partitioned gas station office, ready for occupancy with a view of Main Street, along with several empty storefronts they hoped to fill. Jennifer would work with the tenants to rehabilitate the buildings according to historic code with the goal of qualifying for grants. They discussed preservation of other old buildings in town and batted ideas back and forth about special fund-raising events. Jennifer had been surprised at how much her high school and college job experience at Westville historic village had served her. Marian and everyone Jennifer met expressed enthusiasm about Jennifer taking the position and bringing fresh ideas to the town as she had in Hermon, and Jennifer herself saw great potential for the "Podunk town" with its late 1800s era jail and courthouse, brick strip of antique stores, and 1785 church, all embraced by antebellum homes as impressive as those Athens and Madison boasted.

When Jennifer arrived, she found Barb parked in a wheelchair in the lobby of the ER, dressed in the same clothes from the night before, hands folded in a resigned position over her purse. A cast covered one extended leg, while a purpling bruise marred her cheekbone. Filled with pity at seeing the normally independent professor looking so vulnerable, Jennifer hurried over to hug her.

"I'm so sorry," Barb said. "I told them to wait until at least eight a.m., but you know how hospitals are. Get 'em in, get 'em out, no matter what the time. I could have called a taxi, but there are some things I really should share with you."

"Of course. Do we have to do paperwork first?"

Barb smoothed her short, salt-and-pepper hair, more ruffled than usual. "Already filled out. I think you just have to sign."

A nurse brought crutches for Jennifer to carry and pushed Barbara's wheelchair to Jennifer's car. After the woman helped Barbara get into the passenger's side, Barbara shooed her away. "All this fuss. I hate it," she said as Jennifer slid behind the steering wheel, the crutches stashed in the back seat.

"I know you do, but you need to listen to them and take a few days off." Jennifer looked pointedly at the lump visible on the back of her former professor's head. "Besides the physical damage, this must have been quite a shock."

"But the dig is next week."

"It's not like we can't postpone it."

Barbara heaved a sigh, and Jennifer noticed the shadows beneath her normally bright eyes. "You may be right."

Jennifer started the car. "I don't know about you, but I could handle some breakfast—and especially some coffee."

Barb gave a weary smile. "That sounds wonderful."

Agreeing on the old IHOP near the library and St. Mary's Hospital, Jennifer wended her way through town. The early morning joggers in Cobbham gave way to the commercialization of the Alps Road area. Once they struggled into the restaurant and a waitress finally filled their white mugs with steaming coffee, Jennifer asked, "So did the police come and take a report?"

"Yes, at the hospital."

"Please tell me what happened."

Barb shook a packet of Splenda into her dark brew. "All right, so when I got home last night, as you know, it was almost dark." Yes, Jennifer knew that. When Barb suggested she and Jennifer catch up over supper, Michael had ever so graciously invited them to join him and James for a pot of his father's chili. James' diplomacy had been the only thing preventing Barbara from choking on it. "I don't have a garage. I park on a little pull-off and take a steep flight of stairs from my sidewalk up to the door of my townhouse. The entrance is on the side, so I didn't see the man waiting in the shadows. Plus, he'd knocked the porch light out. I noticed the glass on the landing, then he jumped on me."

Jennifer shuddered while Barbara stirred in cream. "Did he ask for your purse?"

"Not at that point. He slammed my face into the wall. That's how I got this." Barbara touched her cheek. "I tried to get away. I broke loose and was going to run down the stairs, when he shoved me from behind. The stairs are cement. I felt my leg break just before my head hit the sidewalk. He came and stood over me, then grabbed my purse, took my cash and thankfully … left my credit cards."

"And the gorget?" Jennifer couldn't help asking. The last she'd seen the artifact in its leather pouch, Barb had slipped it into her bag after agreeing to consult university experts.

Barbara patted her purse beside her on the vinyl bench. "No worries, all safe and sound. So clearly the thief wasn't after the historical treasure." She winked.

Jennifer frowned and sipped her coffee. "Do the police think his intention was to break into your house, and you just interrupted him?"

"Something like that." Barb paused as the waitress arrived for their orders. When they were alone again, she continued. "But I think he said something before he ran off."

"What?" Jennifer gasped.

"Well, I was pretty fuzzy, I admit, but it sounded like 'stay away.'"

"'Stay away?' From what?"

Barb shook her head. "I don't know. That's part of what I wanted to tell you. He could have meant my apartment."

Jennifer's eyes shot open wide. "Well, if he did, is it safe to go back there?"

"The police assured me they'll patrol the neighborhood for a while, and the locksmith is there as we speak. I just want to go home," Barb said with the first note of vulnerability Jennifer had ever heard her display. "And sleep."

"I understand." She reached out to pat Barb's hand next to her coffee cup, but to her surprise, Barb grasped on. She raised her eyes to meet her former professor's.

"But I also thought, I'd just left your house. Or rather, Michael's house. What if my attacker meant to stay away from there?"

Jennifer felt the blood drain from her face. "You really don't think someone from Hermon would have a reason to do such a thing? Who would care if you help with the Dunham project?"

"I don't know, but I couldn't help thinking of all the accidents you've had yourself since you went there, Jennifer. This is what I wanted to talk to you about. What if someone doesn't want that property worked on for some reason?"

Jennifer drew her hand away. "But that's crazy."

"Yes, it is. But you can't deny it's a possibility."

Lowering her head to sip her coffee, Jennifer hid her expression. Unease spread like a slow cancer from her stomach upward. Few people had known of Barb's visit yesterday. Then she looked up with hope dawning. "But you said the man was already on your porch when you arrived, so no one could have followed you in from the country."

Barb sighed. "I admit it's unlikely. Did you stay with Michael after I left?"

"No. I went home," Jennifer replied with a little indignation at what Barb implied, then her mind took the next logical step. "Wait, you aren't accusing Michael of this?"

The professor blinked. "Of course not," she protested in a tone too bland to satisfy Jennifer. "But I've noticed a progression in your relationship that concerns me. Yesterday he was stuck like glue. Seemed like more than friendship to me." She sat back from the table as their breakfasts arrived.

Jennifer made a point to bow her head and ask a silent blessing, but when she looked up, Barb still waited with expectation. Reaching for the syrup, she said, "I don't mean to be rude, but that's really private."

"Of course." Make-up free face set in prim lines that declared Jennifer's evasion spoke for itself, Barbara cut her ham. "I'd just hate for that to be the reason you settle for a job beneath you. Who knows if it would even last. Most things with men don't."

Heaven, and Barbara, knew Jennifer could hardly argue from her own experience. The piercing memory of the last time she'd seen her father's semi disappearing into the western sun bound for I-20 and the waitress in Alabama flashed into Jennifer's mind.

"I take this as a sign," Barbara murmured.

"What kind of sign?"

"That it might be time to leave, finish the job in Hermon and move on. Too many bad things have happened. Too much bad could still happen. And you're not the only one with a decision to make."

Jennifer swallowed a bite of harvest nut pancakes. "What do you mean?"

"I was going to tell you yesterday, if your Neanderthal would have given us two minutes, that I also have an opportunity in Savannah."

Bristling at Barb's cutting reference to a man they both knew to be anything but a simple-minded construction worker, Jennifer turned her head and waited, perplexed.

Barb gave another slow blink. "The woman who called you— Tandy?" When Jennifer nodded, she continued, "Her husband is taking a year-long contract position in Italy. She's trying to decide whether to go with him or stay. She's made it clear to me that if I have any interest in filling her position, she could pave the way with the owner of the firm."

"Wait. Are you telling me that if I'm hired as a manager, you could be my director?"

Barb smiled. "Potentially."

"But what about your teaching? You love being a professor. You've done that your whole life."

Barb's smile faded. "That's kind of the point. I might like to try something new before I'm too old to make a change. And I'd love to make that change with my favorite student. We see eye to eye on a lot of things. It would help me to have you as a right hand assistant, and I don't have to tell you how advantageous that could be for you. The article with *Old Houses* could be just a drop in the proverbial bucket."

Nodding to acknowledge the professional advantages of her mentor's proposal, Jennifer stared at her uneaten bacon. It looked far too greasy. Her stomach rolled.

"Well, what do you think? Is the time not right to blow this taco stand? On to bigger and better things?" Barb sat back, cradling her cup of coffee and smiling. She waited while Jennifer looked at her, then cocked her head. "Don't you have anything to say?"

"I don't know *what* to say." When Barb's brows lowered, she hastened to add, "I'm just … surprised—and flattered, of course, that you feel that way. I think I need to process all this."

"It's been quite a morning," Barb agreed. "Well, now you know. I wanted you to go into your Savannah interview informed. Try to go willing to accept a fresh vision, Jennifer. Don't limit yourself to what you see now."

Jennifer nodded. "I can do that," she agreed, but she already knew what her heart was telling her.

When Jennifer slowed her Civic to pull into her driveway, she noticed Calvin Woods sitting on his front porch. His unusual posture, head down and stock still, made her double take. Parking, she peered through the Leland cypress trees Michael had planted to help block her view of the hermit's mess. The shadowy form on the old sofa didn't move.

Jennifer got out and slammed her door, hoping the sound would make Calvin stir. Nothing. What if he'd had a heart attack or a stroke? She never saw friends or relatives come and go from the bungalow. Grinding her teeth, she tried to resist the prompting in her spirit to go check on the man. Exchanges with Calvin never proved easy, and she felt worn down from her rude awakening and Barb's revelations.

To top it off, at the townhouse, her former professor invited her in. Barbara remained uneasy after the attack, which was certainly understandable. Unable to shake her awkwardness, Jennifer made excuses after helping the older woman up the stairs.

Now, she blew out a breath and crossed the border. When she set foot on the bottom step of the porch, Otis, lying at his master's feet, raised his head and woofed. Thank goodness, Calvin looked up, too.

"Are you all right, Mr. Woods?" Jennifer asked. "I saw you sitting so still when I came home that I was worried."

"Oh, I'm fine, just wore out," Calvin replied. He studied her a minute. "You really came over just to check on me?"

"Well, yes."

"Huh. Since you're here, you want a beer?"

Jennifer opened her eyes wide and blinked. "Oh. No, thank you. I don't mean to interrupt your morning." She glanced at the plastic table between the old hunting print loveseat and the rocker, relieved that no alcohol cans or bottles littered it at this hour. Just a scraggly plant and some peanut shells resided there and brought back memories of trailer park living in Stewart County.

"When nothin's goin' on you cain't interrupt, young lady. Have a sit. How 'bout a water?"

"Thanks, I just had breakfast. I'm good."

Sit down.

She froze with one foot on the top step. Last time she'd heard that voice, God revealed He felt about her much like she felt about the bedraggled kitten she pulled out from under the apothecary. The Father sure chose to speak in unusual moments, but she'd already learned one was wise to listen. She tip-toed over to the rocker and lowered herself down.

"So, what you been up to?" Calvin wanted to know.

"Well, I just visited my former professor, the one who plans to excavate the Dunham outhouse and compost heap with a class from UGA. She just got out of the hospital. Someone attacked her when she tried to enter her apartment last night."

Her neighbor eyed her from under a bushy brow. "Now that sure was rotten luck. Is she OK?"

"She got a broken leg and a concussion, and they're going to have to delay the excavation so she can be present, but she'll be fine."

"Did she get robbed?" Calvin reached a plaid-clad arm down to rub Otis' dark head.

"The attacker took some cash, but that was all. She … seemed to think the incident could be connected with her work here, but I don't know." Jennifer glanced over. "Does anyone come to mind who might not want us working on Michael's property?"

Calvin frowned. "Why would anybody care? 'Cept maybe old man Stevenson. He don't want anything done anywhere, 'less he's doin' it for his own benefit. An' somethin' tells me he's in no shape to go attackin' anybody." He let out a rough chuckle.

Jennifer smiled but thought one often noticed flaws in others that one possessed oneself.

"I gotta say I had my doubts, but what you all done on that property looks real good," he continued.

She blinked in surprise. "Why, thank you. I appreciate hearing that, especially from a neighbor. So you've never seen anything suspicious?" Her gaze went to Calvin's hands. He rubbed one over the other, and the knuckles bore various scratches and rough spots.

"Naw. Back in the day Horace managed the property, kids used to sneak in there sometimes, you know, up to the mischief they'll get up to. I'd see lights, hear voices, but I never thought much about it. Why?"

"Well, you know I also had several accidents on the property."

Calvin's hazel eyes met hers. "Well, an accident's an accident, ain't it?"

She smiled. "Yes, I suppose. Probably just coincidence."

Another chuckle, and more rubbing. "If you're accident prone."

"Mr. Woods, your hands, are they bothering you?"

He held them up and flexed his fingers. "Yeah, just got me a bit of arthritis."

"I'm sorry. Do you work with your hands? I noticed the clothes you sometimes wear. Are you a mechanic?"

"Been one my whole life, ever since my daddy had a heart attack right after my high school graduation. Had to find a job fast, and I was always good under the hood of a car."

Jennifer fought revulsion at the memories Calvin's words brought up. Roy owned his own automotive shop in Stewart County, where her brother Rab now worked as well. Her early efforts to hone in on their camaraderie meant she now knew her way around an engine as well, along with other things. She pushed that aside. Calvin bore no fault for her painful past. "Do you have a family?" she ventured.

"I had a wife. She left me when someone better came along. I had bigger plans, but I took too long makin' 'em happen, I guess."

"I'm sorry to hear that," Jennifer said, and meant it. "No children?"

As he shook his head, the sunlight glinted off the spot not covered by the swipe of his thinning, tawny hair. "Just Otis. My nephews come to see me once in a while. Sometimes we go hunting."

What a lonely life. It occurred to Jennifer that Calvin's solitary state might not be of his own choosing. "Do you work a lot, then?"

"I did. Lately the arthritis's gotten so bad I cut back my hours. I get it in my knees, too."

Watching Calvin's scaly hand rub the bend of his jean-clad leg, the unease Jennifer experienced earlier talking to Barb stirred. Barb's attack, the loose bleeder screw, the oil on the floor of the apothecary, and the locking door of the shed all made a lot of sense traced back to Calvin Woods. Suddenly Jennifer wanted to leave, and at the same time, an excuse dawned.

"You know, I think Allison Winters is at the apothecary today stocking items for her opening. She has some cream that's supposed to be wonderful for arthritis and gout. Why don't you let me go pick some up for you?" Jennifer offered.

Calvin looked amazed. "You don't need to do that."

Jennifer stood up. "I want to."

He shook his head. "I've tried every cream under the sun, and medicines, too. Nothing works. Just gives me other problems."

"Well, this is all natural. If you let me get it for you, it will be no loss if it doesn't help."

Calvin spread his feet and pushed with the heels of his hands to get off the thread-bare sofa. "No, ma'am, I don't take no charity. Come in 'ere a minute and I'll get you some money. How much you think it'll take?"

"Uh, probably a ten would cover it." Jennifer hung back, holding the screen door open as Calvin waddled over his threshold. "I'll bring you change."

He turned and looked at her. "Come on and I'll show you a picture of my sorry wife. Oh. You don't wanna come in. Guess that ain't proper, is it? Well, hold on there a second."

Jennifer's mouth dropped open as she watched her neighbor shuffle down the straight hallway into a kitchen. She never would have guessed Calvin Woods would stand on propriety. She surveyed a mish-mash of junk and antiques, including an antique hall tree, the kind with places to hang coats, canes and umbrellas. Then she noticed Calvin, with his back turned, opening a tall tin canister. He pulled out a considerable wad of cash and peeled a bill off. The man probably kept money stashed all over his house while it went to pot around him, not unlike the chimney hidey-hole, she mused in amazement.

On his way back, Calvin took a detour through his living room. When he returned, he carried a wooden picture frame. He held it out to show her a photograph of a young woman with a milky complexion, a swirled and sprayed up-do and a loud floral print shirt of the 1960s.

Jennifer tried to keep the surprise out of her voice as she said, "Wow, she's pretty."

"Yeah. Too pretty for her own good." The words accused, but the tone softened as Calvin glanced at his former wife.

Touched, Jennifer took the ten dollar bill. Could a man who pined for a woman half a century be capable of harming someone? And for what? What motive could Calvin Woods possibly have to frighten or harass her? And when would she learn that her first assumptions about the people of this county usually proved wrong?

When Jennifer returned with the arthritis cream, Calvin waited on his porch, a fresh glass of iced tea on the table. After stuffing his change in his pocket, he grunted, unscrewed the lid and sniffed the contents. "Huh," he said. "Good strong smell. Seems promising."

"Well, I hope it helps," Jennifer said, and, on a whim, added, "You know, you should come to the opening of the apothecary on Halloween. We'll have all kinds of samples available then. You might enjoy seeing what we did with the place."

Calvin paused in rubbing the cream over his knuckles. "I just might, then."

"Good. OK, have a nice afternoon." Jennifer raised a hand and started to walk away, but her neighbor's voice stopped her.

"Did you see the Stevensons there today?"

She turned back around. "The Stevensons? Where?"

"At the hospital."

Jennifer tilted her head and frowned. "No, why would I?"

Calvin gave a shrug. "I still hear things, y'know. When I said earlier old Bryce was in no condition to attack anyone, I wasn't kidding. I guess George finally stood up to his old man and told him to stop being such a horse's rear about progress in the town. That would be his wife's doing, I expect. Anyway, the shock musta been too much for 'him. He had a stroke. They took him in this morning."

CHAPTER FOUR

O
n opening day, a festival atmosphere at the apothecary prevailed between ten and four. Inside the shop, herbal expert Allison Winters from nearby Wolfskin District presided over her hand-crafted assortment of candles, lotions, honey, soaps, creams, bottled herbs and teas. Her husband manned the outside herb sale with plants brought from their farm. Next to his tent, Michael and James assisted with a wheelbarrow in an improvised pumpkin patch dotted with potted mums of rust, yellow and purple, courtesy of local growers. Teenagers from Hermon Baptist, the church James attended with the McWhorters, staffed a messy pumpkin-carving table.

Located only steps away, Mary Ellen's antique store cashed in on the action. Her two umbrella tables on the sidewalk hosted Stella, providing face painting for children, and Montana Worley, with her baked goods for sale and free candy from Mary Ellen. A rack to her right displayed a collection of pre-owned Halloween costumes for procrastinators. Mary Ellen had arranged her vintage clothing, marketed as also suitable for Halloween, on a circular display front and center inside the store. That captured more adult interest as kids, many already costumed themselves, begged their parents to join them dressed up for trick-or-treating that night. Now adept on the latte machine, the store owner steamed coffees, while she enlisted Jennifer's assistance producing samples of the herbal teas sold in the apothecary.

After her plummeting sense of usefulness the past couple of weeks, Jennifer didn't mind the rush. True, she'd spent some time online and made a trip to Madison in search of medical items for the apothecary, and she'd put some hours in on the grants for the Gillen store in case the renovation proceeded, but she'd felt like a fifth wheel in the relocation of the log cabin.

As the first step in that process, Michael ran a back hoe clearing and leveling the chosen area in the pecan grove. She helped James and Michael measure and mark the dimension of the cabin. Then the stone mason arrived to pour the concrete footers.

Fig went to work deconstructing at Long Creek. Jennifer tagged boards while the men stripped the tin sheets from the roof, smashed the "precious" chinking, and moved the heavy logs, rafters down to sill, by hand. Unable to manage that type of weight, she piled tin, made lunch runs and collected debris into burn piles. Finally, strapped onto a flatbed, the tin and logs rattled down Highway 77. Now, the lonely bones of wood waited for Fig's crew to reconstruct their skeleton on the Dunham lot.

A stout figure bumping up against Jennifer in the close quarters behind the coffee bar interrupted her reverie.

"Sweetheart, I hate to say it, but I think your fliers worked a little too well," Mary Ellen whispered, turning to her and swiping a strand of thin brown hair from her forehead. "Don't get me wrong, I'm tickled pink about all the sales today, and the increased business since we opened the coffee bar, but I'm about to run slap out of pumpkin spice flavor. You wouldn't believe how grumpy folks get when you don't have what they want. It's not like I'm Starbuck's, y'know."

Jennifer grinned. "You're doing great, Mary Ellen, but you're right. I'm afraid I'm going to have to sneak next door and get some more vanilla chamomile from Allison's shelf. Can you hold the fort for just a minute by yourself?"

"Sure thing. If it gets too bad, I'll just hide under the counter." Chortling, Mary Ellen greeted a customer at the bar.

Jennifer laughed and darted for the door, secretly glad of the opportunity to see how things progressed in the apothecary. She waved at Michael, who stood with arms folded against a backdrop of rust-colored maple leaves, looking handsome and manly in a corduroy over shirt, jeans and work boots as he talked with several other waiting men.

To her delight, women and children and the occasional gentleman crowded the shop, sniffing seasonal candles and rubbing on lotion. The refurbished shelving and wide heart pine flooring glowed. Allison had even stuck clusters of fall leaves among her displays. The proprietress, her graying hair drawn back in its typical ponytail, wrapped purchases in tissue paper and placed them in checked paper bags with handles. Her calm nature remained unruffled by the line that formed in front of the dark green compounding desk with its mustard yellow, inset panels.

As Jennifer sorted through the tea bin, a woman snapped a photo of the shop's interior, then turned. Jennifer startled when she realized it was Barbara, balancing her weight on one of her crutches.

"Oh my goodness, Barb, I didn't expect to see you today!" Jennifer exclaimed.

"Did you really think I'd miss this?" Barb smiled and slid her phone into the pocket of her khaki pants. A tailored, plain Oxford hugged the slender curves of her middle-aged body.

Jennifer glanced pointedly at the crutches. "Well, yes, given the struggle it must have required to get in here."

"Nonsense. I'm going to send my photos to Tandy. She ought to see your success."

Jennifer didn't know what to say. "Thank you. You do too much for me, Barb."

"Remember, it's also for me."

"Hi there, neighbor," a deep voice said from behind.

Jennifer turned to behold Calvin Woods, looking out of place in the trendy shop, although he'd made an obvious effort at looking presentable. His hair slicked neatly to one side, and while his shirt-tails hung out, he wore a button-down cotton shirt with gray pants. Scuffed loafers replaced the standard work boots.

"Calvin!" Jennifer touched the man's arm in greeting. "I'm so glad you came by! Did the cream work?"

His eyes sparkled. "Like a charm. Ain't never had anything work so good. I came to buy another bottle and see what else is in here."

"Oh, that's wonderful." Jennifer paused, realizing introductions were inevitable. Barb surveyed the rustic newcomer with a dubious eye. "Calvin, this is my former professor, Dr. Barbara Shelley. She taught me much of what I needed to know to restore this place. Dr. Shelley, this is my neighbor, Calvin Woods."

Barb's eyebrows hit her feathery bangs. "The one who owns the bungalow on the other side of Jennifer's double-wide?"

"That'd be me." Calvin offered one of his large, work-roughened hands.

Barbara shook, limp fish style. "Have you ever considered restoring it?"

"What's to restore? It's in perfectly good shape."

Jennifer muffled a laugh at Barbara's blank expression. "Uh, Calvin, look here. Allison has a tea she's packaged special for arthritis and gout, called Queen of Teas for the Queen of the Meadow in it." She held up the tea bag.

"I don't reckon I need anything queenly," Calvin protested.

"That's just the name. It's for men, too." She flipped over the pouch to read the tag. "Active ingredients include Queen of the Meadow, cleavers and hydrangea."

Calvin's pursed lips relaxed only when Allison, overhearing them, leaned toward the end of her counter and offered, "Joe Pye Weed, Mr. Woods, sometimes known as gravel root."

"Oh, gravel root I did hear of from my grandma."

Allison pointed a finger at the item in question. "That tea works great, Mr. Woods, but if you want to sample it first, have Jennifer take a bag down to the apothecary and fix you up some. Put a good splash of honey in." Nodding, she turned back to her next customer.

At that moment, a small girl dressed as a blue fairy knocked the crutch out of Barbara's hand. Jennifer caught it and suggested, "I think we better all get out of here. Why don't you both come down to the antique store? Let me fix you a cup of tea. You can sit down and see what's changed in there."

"All righty then." Calvin sounded satisfied to be included, causing Jennifer to glance at him in surprise. She'd never seen the man in such good humor. In fact, he held the door for Barbara, nodded and smiled. She acknowledged him with a befuddled frown and a muttered "thank you" before hopping down the steps.

Walking behind her guests, Jennifer sent Michael a fake, bright grin when he gaped at the unlikely little group.

"How's it going, Montana?" Jennifer asked her young friend as Barbara stopped to admire the display of baked goods, warmed by the autumn sun.

The young girl jumped around the side of her table to hug Jennifer. "Great! I'm almost sold out of my pumpkin streusel bars, and the Woman's Club just placed an order for two dozen cheesecake scones for their Christmas tea!"

"That's awesome." Jennifer tugged a braid, then tucked it behind Montana's ear. "Your hair's growing out."

"Thanks. I'm thinking layers. You inspired me!" Grinning, Montana ran a preening hand over her head.

Barbara held up a tan triangle wrapped in plastic and sealed with a fall leaf sticker. "Is this the cheesecake scone?"

"Yes, ma'am."

"Well, that sounds like something I have to try." Barbara fished in her pocket for change.

"Montana, this is my former professor from UGA, Barbara Shelley," Jennifer said.

The girl paused her digging in her money box and asked, "Oh, the one Jennifer had to meet the day of my booth at the Fourth of July festival?"

Barbara's eyes widened, then she laughed. "That would be me, the mean professor."

Montana shrugged. "You don't look too mean. I can forgive you, anyway. Jennifer set it up so that I take regular orders now, and Mary Ellen sells my merchandise every day in her shop. We're making a killing."

As the group laughed, Calvin said, "You got anything chocolate? Yeah, that brownie. I'll take one of them, honey." He handed her a five and insisted she keep the change, making her eyes shine.

To Jennifer's dismay, only one small table for two remained open in the clearing in front of Mary Ellen's counter. She situated the strange duo there and hurried to fix their tea, expecting both to sip and quickly exit, but when she returned with their cups, she found them deeply engaged in conversation. Surprised, Jennifer set the cups down next to the open hardcover coffee table book on architectural styles, noticing the partially eaten goodies and plastic wrap shoved to one side of it. Barbara pointed at a picture of a nineteen-teens home similar to Calvin's as she discussed the merits of early Craftsman style.

Her former professor looked up as Jennifer placed tea in front of her. "Oh, Jennifer, don't let me leave without returning the gorget. I have it in my purse in the car," Barbara told her. "My colleague cleaned it and verified it's from the late 1700s."

"Cool. Thank you so much. So there were no markings on it?"

"Actually, there was something," Barb said, stirring her tea and lifting the cup to blow across the surface. "Someone etched a thunderbolt on the front."

Jennifer's eyes widened. "That's fascinating. I wonder why."

"Probably a declaration of military prowess or some such nonsense. My colleague thought that denoted it was more likely Native American. It could bring up to a thousand dollars at a good auction site or relic show, though I imagine with it being a family heirloom, Michael wants to keep it."

"I'd think so," Jennifer said. She turned when she felt a hand on her back and saw Amy Greene, sparkling with an autumn-colored, glass-beaded necklace that complimented her burnt orange shirt, dark denim jacket and jeans and highlighted, ash-blonde hair. Jennifer turned to greet and hug Horace's wife, then introduced her to Barbara.

"Such a pleasure to meet you at last," Amy said, extending her hand with perfect gel tips to the no-fuss professor. Barb looked surprised until Amy clarified, "You know my husband, Horace. He's your university contact for historic properties and managed the Dunham place as a rental before Michael came."

"Oh, yes," Barb agreed, "a very knowledgeable man. It's nice to meet you, Amy." Her unblinking smile gave no indication of the disdain Jennifer knew she harbored for the bling and Southern charm Amy exuded.

Jennifer, however, now knew Amy not to be the shallow cheerleader-type she'd originally assumed. True, Amy responded with warmth to Horace, who treated his wife like the queen of the county, but during the restoration project, Amy had shared with Jennifer her heartbreak over her high school love, former Oglethorpe County quarterback Chad Fullerton.

Chad Fullerton had disappeared—not just from Amy's life but from life in general—after telling both Amy and some of his fellow students he might move back to Athens when an injury left him unable to complete his football contract with the University of Florida. People generally believed that a depressed Chad fell back into drug use. For Amy, Horace stepped into the gap of Chad's absence, and the then-scrawny high school punter won the girl. It worked out well for Horace, whose courtship of Amy had been threatened by the athlete's plans to move home. But Jennifer sensed Amy had never completely moved past her lack of closure over Chad.

However, Amy was not the sort to let uncomfortable personal feelings override politeness, then or now. With a nod at Calvin, who looked grumpy at the interruption, she continued, "You sure did teach Jennifer well. I got to supply the paint for the house and apothecary, as well as order and install the authentic window treatments. I'm an interior designer. Since I specialize in historic homes, I really enjoyed this job, and working with Jennifer. She's quite a perfectionist, isn't she?"

Barbara smiled at Jennifer in a way that excluded everyone else. "She comes by that honestly," she murmured, tone warm.

Jennifer flushed.

"Well, it's positively fortuitous you're here today. Horace was tellin' me about the dig you plan to have some students do on Michael's property. I told him how much I wanted to hover that day if I could. I find archeology just fascinatin'. I've even read there are some folks who specialize in excavatin' privies. Who would've thought?"

Barb pinched her lips together in disapproval, then said, "Professionals call such people looters. Michael is going about things the right way, calling in qualified archeologists to conduct the dig."

Amy smiled. "Yes, he's done everything the right way. I guess you can when you have the money. Anyway, Horace said I should ask Jennifer what day the dig is scheduled for and if it would be OK if I came, but now I can go straight to the source."

"Of course it would be fine for you to observe," Barbara agreed. She went on to provide the date, then clarify that the dig depended on a stretch of warm weather. Her archeology professor friend had been gracious to insist Barb help, but the rescheduling due to Barb's injury played havoc with the full agenda of her class, causing them to press close to a potential freeze that could render the soil too hard. As she spoke, Calvin shifted uneasily, gazing at Amy from under his eyelids like he wished she'd go away.

"We're also running a risk with daubing the cabin," Jennifer admitted. Like Calvin, she hoped Amy would wrap up. She felt Mary Ellen's bustling anxiety behind her and knew she needed to return to her station.

"Well, we'll just cross our fingers and pray that you both get all this done before a cold snap," Amy said, twisting two of her fingers together and winking. Then, finally satisfied, she asked if Jennifer could make her a café mocha.

Jennifer nodded and ushered her toward the counter. "I'm on tea, but Mary Ellen can."

She'd hardly gotten her sentence out when she noticed Barbara turn to Calvin and say, "So tell me more about your family home, Mr. Woods. You said your grandfather built it?"

Astonished at Barb's polite attention to the crusty old man, Jennifer returned to Mary Ellen's side, passing the next hour making drinks and chatting with customers. She felt like her former roommate Tilly working at Jittery Joe's. She'd never guessed she could enjoy a social job this much. Of course, she wouldn't in Athens, where strangers constituted most of the clientele, but here in Hermon, she had developed enjoyable bonds with this small, tight-knit community.

Her surprise rose when she noticed Barb and Calvin still talking as closing time approached, then doubled as she realized that Grace Stevenson and her husband George stood before her, clad in tweed coats and dress shirts. Grace smiled and reached out to hug Jennifer over the counter.

"This is lovely, Jennifer," she murmured.

"Grace! I'm so surprised to see you. Hello, Mr. Stevenson," Jennifer added in what she hoped constituted a respectful tone. "I was so sorry to hear about your father. How is he doing?"

"Thank you," George replied, stiff but not unfriendly. The proper banker sort, she thought. "We brought him home last week."

"Is he going to be fine, then?"

Grace cut in, placing a hand on the counter. "If you're slowing down a little, would you have a minute? We came late in hopes of talking with you."

"Of course."

Jennifer excused herself from Mary Ellen and led the couple to the table for four now open next to her professor and neighbor.

"I hope you don't mind, we've taken the liberty of asking Stella and Michael to join us," Grace told Jennifer, fingering the vase with a single golden mum that sat between them. "They should be here in a minute. This is something all of you should hear."

Jennifer nodded, her heart beating fast with the fear that Bryce had made some trouble. Cleaning up, Mary Ellen cast her curious, surreptitious glances, while Montana darted in and out, stashing her remaining baked goods in the display case. As Calvin thumbed through another book, Barbara watched as Michael and Stella came in and sat down, Michael moving with a stiffness that evidenced two weeks of hard physical labor. Jennifer offered the professor an apologetic smile, hoping the impromptu meeting didn't delay Barbara's need to leave. Barb raised a hand and smiled to show her everything was fine.

Michael shook hands with George. "Mr. Stevenson, how is your father?" he immediately asked, removing his ball cap and placing it on one knee. Jennifer noticed his ruffled hair and refrained from reaching out to straighten it.

"Thank you for joinin' us, Michael, Stella. Miss Rushmore. To tell the truth, my father will never be the same. The stroke has rendered him in need of a nurse's full-time care, and impaired his mental faculties. We've taken him in to live with us."

"Oh, no," Jennifer said as they all offered their condolences.

"You may have heard this came about after a conversation we had with Daddy Stevenson," Grace admitted, placing a hand on her husband's arm. "And that would be true. Right before the stroke George and I discussed some things with him that we felt needed to change, in both our personal lives and the community life. I'm afraid he didn't take it very well."

"I hope you folks aren't blaming yourselves," Stella murmured.

George sighed. "No, although I do regret not standin' up to Daddy years ago. If I had, this might never have happened. But that conversation did need to take place. Daddy took far too much delight in controllin' other people his whole life. It was time he released the reins. Suffice it to say, I have power of attorney on his behalf, and I agree with my wife that that biking trail should not be prohibited from going through on account of us, and the Gillen store would make an excellent community resource and art gallery. Without my father standin' in the way, both things can now happen. That is, if the owner of the store accepts the purchase price the town council voted last week to offer."

Jennifer laughed in amazement as Stella leaned back and clapped her hands. In the hush of the closing store, she felt sure Barbara and Calvin heard everything. Even Mary Ellen at the counter moved awful slow with her dish cloth, shushing Montana whenever the child burst into conversation.

"Now then," George continued, serious next to his smiling wife, "as long as that happens, the council would like to accept the bid of Johnson Construction for the building's renovation."

Michael grinned in surprise. "Well, thank you, sir. That's great news."

The councilman turned to Jennifer. "And young lady, we wondered if you might agree to oversee the project as historical consultant, as available alongside your work for Mr. Johnson, of course. On an hourly rate commiserate with your proven skill."

Jennifer blinked. "Oh. My. That would be wonderful." Her brain went to her outstanding student loans and the costs of a potential move. How amazing that God would fill in her time and financial blank in this manner. Then she glanced at Barbara and added with hesitation, "Although … if I take a job in Savannah, I might not be available past December."

"We understand," Grace assured her. "But you'd agree at least through then?"

She glanced at Michael. "If it's OK with my current employer," she said. When he nodded and smiled, she added, "Yes!"

"Wonderful, then," Grace said. "We'll be in touch just as soon as we get word."

As Stella clasped Jennifer's hand in a happy squeeze, Mary Ellen appeared next to their table, holding a tray full of steaming cups. "What's this, Mary Ellen?" Jennifer asked.

"Why, a toast, of course! I used the last of my pumpkin spice to make you all a little treat," she said as she passed the coffees around. "We have to celebrate this good news. But no worries, it's decaf!" She chuckled as she included remaining guests Barbara and Calvin in her generosity, then held up her own cup. "To a thriving downtown!"

"To a thriving downtown!" everyone echoed with enthusiasm.

They all laughed at Calvin's expression of trepidation, then grudging approval, as he sipped the brew. Jennifer guessed this constituted his first taste of anything fancier than plain black coffee. "I'd best get on over to that apothecary before that hippy woman shuts it down," he announced, rising with slightly less stiffness than pre-cream, now about equal to Michael's. "Can I help you out, Mrs. Shelley?"

Jennifer cringed at Calvin's misuse of the doctor's title, but to her surprise Barbara brushed off the mistake. "I might take you up on that," she agreed. "And do give me a call if you decide to pursue a make-over for your home and have further questions. With all the renovations going on in town, right next to you, it's a perfect time to spruce things up a bit."

Jennifer closed her gaping mouth as Calvin shot her a hopeful look. "Maybe this one'd come over and help me out. After all, I did help with your armadillo problem, young lady," he said, pointing a gnarled index finger at her.

"That's true, you did," Jennifer agreed with a smile. She refrained from reminding Calvin he'd retreated to his house to watch "Mountain Men" while his paid, camouflaged nephews took to Michael's yard with their hunting rifles.

Barbara pressed her lips together, balancing on her crutches, then said, "Remember, she'll likely relocate after the holidays, but I can send someone qualified to help you."

Looking away from Michael's frown, Jennifer thanked the Stevensons again. As Stella initiated a conversation with the couple by promising to pray for Bryce, Jennifer offered to walk out with Barb to get the gorget. After Calvin helped the professor into her Explorer and shuffled over to the apothecary building, Barb reached in her purse for the leather pouch, which she'd enclosed in a large plastic Ziploc.

"Here," she said, "I'm glad to give it back. I couldn't help thinking this thing brought me bad luck."

Jennifer quirked her brows, looking up from her inspection of the now-smooth and shiny silver piece. "It's beautiful, thank you. But it's not like you to be superstitious." She ran her finger over the cool metal, drawn by the mystery it represented. She'd dug until she'd found the truth about Georgia Pearl and Charlotte. She could find the truth about Verity, too, whose name, after all, *meant* truth.

"Well, maybe I was wrong," Barb joked, then said, "In all seriousness, Jennifer, I admit I may have been a little judgmental about this place. I still find the people rustic, almost like they're stuck in the 1980s or something, but I can see now this experience has been good for you in more ways than professionally."

"Really?" Jennifer asked in surprise.

Barb nodded as she slid her seatbelt over her lap and snapped the buckle. "Yes, I watched you today, and it's clear they all think very well of you. You needed that. You've matured here. But I consider it a stop gap measure meant to fuel you with confidence and experience for Savannah. I hope you'll take it for what it's worth and move forward from here."

Jennifer merely nodded and waved as Barbara drove away. She'd go to the Savannah interview because she never wanted to regret failing to explore that option, but she expected the trip to confirm the coastal town could never feel like home, because home felt like Hermon. She could not replace the people here, their realness and enthusiastic acceptance of her, a loner, an outsider, as one of them. And now with the promise of good things happening with the Gillen store, due to the admirable way George and Grace had shaken off the control of his father, the future here looked more secure than ever. Considering how clearly God seemed to be illuminating her path, Jennifer allowed a satisfied smile that transcended her professor's opinion or approval.

A glance down at the bag in her hands and the memory of Barbara's words about the gorget being unlucky erased that smile a moment later.

Winter 1788

Even in my fevered frame of mind, I recognized that Tenetke prepared for a journey. He fried cornmeal balls, packed jerky and beans I boiled before I had become too weak to cook, gathered blankets and bear skins and stuffed his tall deerskin moccasins with hair and leaves. His trade fusil with metal side-plate engraving depicting a coiled serpent leaned against the pile by the door. But when I asked him where he was going, he wouldn't tell me, only cast me a pained look.

He had brought me to this cane-lathed house outside a village which I guessed to be in extreme western Georgia or even over the line in Alabama following the brutal summer attack. Clay packed the walls, while the wooden shake roof pitched from a ridge pole. One door led in and out. Corn, sweet potatoes and pumpkins grew down to a river.

At first I had been glad of our semi-isolation. The violent braves frightened me, and I expected the women to treat me harshly, perhaps like a slave. Tenetke only took me into the village for the *boosketah*, or feast, held not long after I arrived. In the town square, the men danced and drank the black drink. Tenetke explained this provided their time of spiritual cleansing, new beginnings, marriages, and, at the end, a feast of thanksgiving for the corn harvest. The people extinguished the town fire and started a new one using the traditional method of rubbing sticks together. After several days, we took some of the village fire home to our own hearth, my attempts to connect privately with the other captives foiled at every turn. Tenetke kept a close eye on me, keeping me with him in the village and leaving me in the company of a young boy at the rectangular hut when he attended councils, assisted with the harvest, or checked his trap lines.

Gradually I realized my life shrank to the walls of my new home and the tattooed body of my new husband. My whole world revolved around working in his garden, preparing stews and *sofkey*—cornmeal cooked with lye and water and left several days to sour—drying and storing hominy and autumn apples, feeding Tenetke's horses and hogs, and tending Tenetke's physical needs. Despite his thread of European ancestry, which I learned through the brave's French and broken English came from a French soldier grandfather, he made no excuses or apologies for expecting marital intimacy. Neither was he rough. Indeed, had he been, I could have hated him for it. That would have been easier than slowly falling under his spell. There were moments when he held me and stared at me with those gray-green eyes that I thought he loved me.

But now he appeared ready to abandon me. Now, if he did not call the boy, he could leave me and I could die here. Was that what the Upper Creeks did when their captured wives failed them through weakness and infirmity?

I knew the moment had come when he placed the belongings by the door in a bedroll. I reached out a hand from the pallet where I lay, but my attempt to call him resulted in a fit of coughing. My breathing sounded like the wings of the dragonfly hovering over the Oconee on a brighter summer's day. A tear slid down my face as he left the hut without looking at me.

But to my astonishment, he returned a moment later and scooped me up into his arms.

"You are taking me," I whispered.

"To get help. A long journey," he told me in French.

Satisfied, I nodded, assuming a better *owala* must exist in a nearby village than the one here who had concocted a brew of roots and herbs, singing over and blowing into the liquid with a straw, then forcing me to drink and rubbing the medicine on my chest. Sweat baths had not helped much, either.

Tenetke cradled me in front of him on his stallion. Our pace varied between a walk and a trot, the most I could handle without falling off. Even so, I slumped against him, and his hard arm held me up. Despite the scarf he wrapped over my lower face, the cold air bit my lungs and caused me to cough. Sometimes the fits lasted so long I thought I would pass out. I shook with chills, then raged with fever.

When we camped that night, the fire, cave shelter, bear skin and warmth of Tenetke's body barely broke the cold. "S-s-s-sorry," I managed to get out.

"Do not apologize, *vpueke*," he murmured and stroked my hair. His word for a tame animal, a pet. He still cared for me. I slept in the security of his protection.

But days later, I questioned his plans again. I'd endured the hours in the saddle through a daze of delirium. Sometimes I thought myself back home in Augusta, before Mother had passed away. She stood on the other side of the river, calling me. Now, Tenetke laid me under a shelf of rock in the forest and told me he'd return. Or did he? Did I dream that? The wind soughed through the bare tree branches a mournful song, mayhap one of my demise. For all I knew, Indians left their dying kin outdoors in some sort of parting spirit ritual.

The next thing I realized, I labored for breath and consciousness. Something icy touched my forehead, then my chin. My lashes fluttered open. Against a purpling evening sky, snowflakes descended. Beautiful. Someone carried me through the forest. And I smelled ... wood smoke. My captor, my savior, lowered me until my back touched something hard.

Tenetke's face came close to mine. Sorrow filled his eyes. "Hear me, *vpueke*," he said in French. "*Esaugetu Emissee*, Master of Breath, has not seen fit to return your breath to you. Our healer can do no more. He believes your second spirit wanders at night, returning here, in search of the one you lost. So I must return you in body. Perhaps his medicine can save you."

"No!"

"I cannot let you die."

He really was leaving me now. Wait. Only through him had I survived thus far. I couldn't survive without him. "Tenetke, no. No, please, you musn't leave me." I pushed the words out past the incredible weight on my chest.

His finger touched the gorget around my neck, then pointed upward. "Thunder," he said. "When you hear it, think of me, Tenetke."

Then he was gone, the sky dark in his place. Snow kissed my face, but he did not. Liquid burst from my heart and filled my lungs with pain, suffocating me. From a distance, I heard a sound like the shot of a gun. In response a moment later, a square of light opened above me, and a tall, slender form with broad shoulders, clutching a hunting rifle, appeared. I looked on a face I had almost forgotten as Levi cried, agonized and amazed, "Verity!"

From the cleavers-stuffed pallet next to the fire where I'd slept since Levi took me in that first night, I watched him climb into the rope bed against the chinked cabin wall. At first my location served to ward off chill and allow him to mix and heat his medicines and serve them at my side. He plied me with constant teas, tonics and rolled pills, explaining in my lucid moments that the cinchona bark, Dover's Powders, butterfly root, white plantain, mullein and elderberry aimed to break my fever, open my lungs and breathing passages, and cleanse my body of sickness. Levi added licorice and peppermint from small glass bottles in his cabinet to prevent me choking on the bitterness of the drugs and herbs. He constantly pressed his ear to my chest and rummaged with desperation in the black medical bag he'd brought from Virginia.

Now, my fever had abated and my breathing returned almost to normal, although the continuing weakness forced me to limit myself to the lightest of chores between periods of rest. Levi never suggested I join him on the rope bed. I did not think I could have, but the alienation I continued to feel from him convinced me we would never return to the newlywed bliss of last winter. I shuddered at the memory of the questions he had asked me as soon as I had been well enough to answer. How had I survived the attack?

Who had taken me? Was it the same man who returned me? Had I been a slave, a wife? Had he abused me, forced me into unspeakable acts? Had I tried to escape? And worst of all … how did I feel about him?

I stared into the fire crackling on the stone hearth. How could you love and hate someone at the same time? Love him for saving your life and treating you with respect and tenderness that contradicted hate for the atrocities you had witnessed and the stripping away of all your rights and choices, making you feel less than human? How could it feel like an invisible tie still bound you to him, across the miles, pulling, pulling, a searing, bleak emptiness in your soul reminding you at every moment, both waking and sleeping, that you still belonged to him? Self-hate, confusion and yearning warred within, almost rousing me to a spirit of violence at times. And how could you possibly explain that to the man, the lawful husband, who said he had ridden out three times in search parties, following to the very edge of Indian villages before being turned away by hostile natives? Who laid awake every night crying and praying, and by day entreated the new governor, fellow Revolutionary War officer from Goosepond, George Mathews, to treat with the Creek Nation for the return of the Greensborough captives? Whose eyes told of sorrow and longing but whose face twisted with loathing as I answered his questions as best I could?

And now, I had a new reason to expect Levi's loathing. I had no choice. I had to attempt to return to Tenetke.

Could I even remember the way back to his village? No memory remained of my recent journey, and those of the summer route west proved vague, fogged by trauma and fear. But I'd heard the name of the village. Perhaps if I gave it to the first Indian I met west of the Oconee they would take me there rather than kill me. Unlikely. Levi said arsons and scalpings continued after my capture, and the Creek had further reason for fury following their defeat by Colonel Elijah Clarke in September at the Battle of Jack's Creek. But I reasoned death would be better than the life I pictured ahead.

Trouble was, I must have a horse to even give me a chance of survival. Levi possessed only one, which he used to call on neighbors. He had scarcely left my side over the past six weeks, but the other settlers knew of his medical training. Even though he had not finished his course of study, many frontier doctors practiced only from a textbook, so Levi offered rare training by compare. He told me his neighbors on Long Creek—a Lumpkin father and son, and the Brewers who established a mill and blockhouse—prized

Levi's skill. Settlers in Scull Shoals on the Oconee—a French and Indian War officer named Vines Collier cultivated a number of acres with a large family and some slaves nearby, and six Presbyterian families who worshipped at a flint fort with a renowned minister of their faith—also called on him when necessary. That meant I must make my escape at night. Tonight.

I waited until Levi breathed evenly, then tip-toed to the door, where I slid my feet into my unhooked leather boots. I mustn't chance waking him by dressing in the cabin so, taking my cape off its hook, I slung it around my shoulders and rolled my bodice and skirt under my arm. Pierced tin lantern in hand, I unlatched the door and slid out as small an opening as possible.

Once in the shed, I located the bag I had packed earlier and hidden in a heap of straw. I used a flint to light the lantern's candle and stuck its base on the inner prong, closing the metal door to protect the flame. The milk cow watched with mournful eyes as I hurried into my dress, my breath issuing in frosty puffs. I moved around to the stallion's stall, taking a moment to stroke the muzzle of Levi's mount. The stallion snorted at my unfamiliar smell and uneasy approach. But I didn't have time to waste. If Levi woke up and noticed my cot empty …

My heart hammered as I attempted to lift the heavy leather saddle off the rail where Levi had hung it. My arms felt like jelly. The lung sickness had rendered me as weak as a child. At the opening of the stall, I faltered under the saddle's weight and dropped it on the dirt floor.

The door to the stable banged open, and Levi's form darkened the threshold. "What in heaven's name are you doing?" he yelled.

I righted myself and trembled before him. When I did not answer, he grabbed my forearms and repeated his question. The horse behind me nickered. "Leaving," I answered in a small voice. "And you must let me."

"In the middle of the cold night? With you barely strong enough to stand? Are you tetched in the head?" Agony mingled with accusation in my husband's voice.

But I did not think of him as my husband, not anymore. Tenetke had claimed me, and nothing Levi could do could remove the stamp of his possession. "Yes. I am tetched in the head. I do not belong here and cannot tarry. My life as I knew it ended last summer, when savages killed my whole family and took me to live as one of them."

"Yet I am alive, Verity. I am your husband. You belong with me." Levi attempted to draw me into his arms, but I pulled back.

"No, I don't, and pretending that I do merely kicks against the pricks. We both know I am not the same. I see the way you look at me. I am ruined, damaged."

"'Tis not how I see you—"

"I cannot show my face among decent white society ever again. I have better standing as Tenetke's captive wife."

"That is where you were going, back to him?" Levi's voice sounded like it ripped from his chest.

I turned my back and wrapped my arms around myself. I must speak the awful truth, but I could not do so while looking at him. "I cannot live another day without him. The pain is too great. And you will let me go when I tell you, I am to bear his child."

"No!"

Levi's cry rent the air with tangible pain. I cowered as tears flowed down my face. Then, when I heard nothing but a shuddering, tear-laden breath, I bent and slid my arms under the saddle. But before I could rise with it, Levi's arms came around me, and he pressed his face into my neck.

"No, no, my Verity, no," he murmured, trying to draw me against him as if to absorb me and mayhap the unborn child into himself, as if to erase its existence. I felt his lips touch my ear, his tears wet my hair. Trained now to respond to another, I recoiled. "I cannot let you go. No matter what he did to you, Verity, you do not belong with him. With them. Don't you understand? I love you! It's a miracle you came back to me, and I never mean to let you go. God will take care of this child."

At Levi's words, disgust for myself—disgraced and impregnated— and disgust for him, flooded me. His determination to keep me seemed pathetic and controlling. But wait, was that not backwards? I rejected both notions as panic surged through me. The cord around my heart drew me to Tenetke with insane intensity, undeniable.

"Don't you see, I have no choice?" I cried, trying to lift the saddle again. "Something unseen holds me to him and makes it impossible for me to belong to you ever again. My heart and spirit are his, and you cannot alter that!"

Levi knocked the saddle out of my arms, causing the stallion to snort and paw in protest. He whirled me around and clawed at my neck, untying the ribbon that held the gorget in place. What I had first identified as a slave collar had become my mark of protection and connection among the tribe. Levi honored my request to leave it where Tenetke had placed it all these weeks, but now he flung it on the ground. I flew at him with the last of my strength, beating his chest with my fists.

"Let me go! Let me go!" I screamed.

"You will cease! You are hysterical!" Levi commanded. His deep voice now became that of a doctor. He bent and slipped his arms under me, carrying me out of the stable and back toward the house, pausing only to blow out the lantern. Inside the cabin, he laid me on his rope bed and went to slam the door and throw the bolt. Ignoring my weeping and pleas for Tenetke, Levi built up the fire, the aristocratic angles of his face sharp with determination. He knelt beside the bed, pulled loose the laces of my bodice while I cowered away from him, then slid my skirt and shoes off. Covering my shivering, shift-clad body with a quilt, he went to work over the fire, simmering a brew using herbs from his medicine chest.

"Please let me go," I begged when he returned with a steaming tin cup. "I am not worthy of you now."

"Hush," he said. "The fennel and ash bark will calm you so that you can sleep."

When Levi slipped a hand behind my head to raise it, I turned my face away. "I do not need your drugs."

"You are beside yourself, and understandably so. I would never give you anything that would harm you."

I sat up and smacked the cup from his hand, screaming, "Will everyone stop trying to control me?"

Levi stared at me with sadness pooling in his dark brown eyes, the tea he had prepared with such care using his precious medicines staining his wool knee-breeches and creating dark spots on the floor. The hand-hewn floor he had raised blisters on his doctor's hands installing for me so I wouldn't have to sully my feet on dirt like most settlers. And instead he had gotten a sullied wife. I turned away from him and curled into a ball, fighting the overpowering urge to scratch off my own skin. The darkness pressed close around me, suffocating me, despite the false cheer of the fire's crackle.

I heard him moving around the cabin, cleaning up. When he slid into bed beside me and placed a hand on my shoulder, I stiffened. *No.* He had best not make the mistake of touching me. But then I heard him whispering.

"'The Lord is my rock, and my fortress, and my deliverer; my God, my strength, in whom I will trust; my buckler, and the horn of my salvation, and my high tower.'"

He quoted Scripture! I had not heard Scripture since my father's reading the night before the Greensborough attack. At first, when I realized the Indians worshipped animal spirits, I had tried to speak to Tenetke of spiritual matters, but he insisted *Esaugetu Emissee* was the same as my God, and the lesser gods would grow angry if he did not honor them. Tenetke made it clear the topic was not up for discussion, and the scalps that hung from his war belt served as a visible reminder that while my captor might be kind, he could also be cruel.

Now, even though Levi's words bristled the hair on the back of my neck with a strange resistance, I also felt safer. He would not accost me while reciting God's Word, would he? And perhaps I could sleep. The words produced a calming effect as sure as if I had drunk the tea. I could not remember my last night of good sleep free from fitful tossing and nightmares. At night, what my memory did not regurgitate it imagined, like the death of my brother, whom Levi verified had perished defending the fort.

"'He delivered me from my strong enemy, and from them which hated me: for they were too strong for me. They prevented me in the day of my calamity: but the Lord was my stay. He brought me forth also into a large place; he delivered me, because he delighted in me.'"

My body sagged in exhaustion.

"You may not feel it now, but He did deliver you, Verity," Levi whispered in my ear. "He delivered you in body, and He will deliver you in soul, too, when you are willing."

What did Levi mean, when I was willing? Did he think me rebellious? Did he not understand the anguish of spirit I endured with each breath? That it was not rebellion, but pain, that pulsed through me?

Determined to convince him of my balanced state of mind, I rose and dressed the next morning and made mush and milk sweetened with molasses. In a show of interest, I asked questions about all that had happened in my absence. He told of our neighbors and how he supplemented farming with doctoring. Most settlers paid him in food and goods, but some had coin. Today he had to go hunting, "and I will take the horse with me," he said with a firm eye on me. "I shan't be far away. You do understand, do you not, that the Indians torched other forts after the attack on Greensborough, and continue to strip the pates of white settlers on sight?"

I nodded, rose and started to gather the wooden trenchers and spoons.

"I wish you to lie down after breakfast," he directed, then he hesitated before speaking again. "After the attack, everything was in chaos and ashes. The soldiers who came turned out their horses to graze among the remaining crops in the fields. Local men pursued the war party to no avail while those from nearby farms tried to help the wounded, some of whom were grievously mutilated. Little from the town proved salvageable, but one of your neighbors did find a few items that she identified as from your cabin. I thought to wait before stirring those memories, but I am afeared that was a mistake. I hope the things will remind you of who you are."

Responding to my expression of amazement, he jerked his head toward a chest in the corner. "Tis in there."

As soon as Levi vacated the cabin, I hurried over to the piece of furniture and unhinged the lid. Pushing it open, I discovered several familiar but dirty items, some blackened with soot, lying on top. There was my father's shaving kit in a wooden box with a leather top, used for sharpening his straight razor. When I saw my childhood rag doll with knotted yarn hair, I held it to my heart. Patience's blue and white, prized Delft tea pot that we had poured from while dreaming of our futures, the handle now broken, made tears drip down my face. And in a leather pouch, I discovered my mother's carved ivory cameo on a ribbon.

I slammed the lid of the trunk down. I could not stand to look any more. Those treasures reminded me of the happy, innocent, pure girl I had been and, of a life burned to ashes in the Georgia wilderness. We had stupidly thought we could bring civilization with us, forging inland from the coast. What would my family think of me now, a harlot yearning for a heathen, carrying his child, caring nothing for the laws of God? What shame would I bring upon their name, bearing a dark-skinned infant and trying to pass it off as Levi's? What shame upon Levi?

Levi's words about the baby came back to me. "God will take care of this child." I took that to mean God might favor me with a miscarriage. If Levi meant to prevent me from returning to a tribe where such a child would be accepted, it would be better to not be born—better for all of us. Levi would never forget so long as such a child lived.

My gaze swung to Levi's medicine cabinet, which he kept locked. But I knew where he secreted the key. And I had heard some women in Augusta say that a tablespoon of brewer's yeast mixed into pennyroyal tea could rid a woman of infidelity's evidence. Did Levi have pennyroyal? He took pride in his bottled and corked collection of herbs that he had brought from his father's Virginia medical office. Some boasted exotic origins. Some he replenished locally. If he possessed the European herb, it would be labeled like all the others in his neat, looping script. The question was … did I have the courage to do it? And if I did, would a God I now doubted show mercy on my woebegone state?

CHAPTER FIVE

Jennifer loved the way the morning autumn sunlight highlighted the variations and grains in the wood of the cabin. She loved the simple rectangle the stacked logs created, neat and clean. She even loved the growl of chainsaws and the smell of sawdust. She heaved a sigh. She was definitely not the typical girly girl.

She stood in Michael's back yard admiring Fig's construction crew at work. The sill logs sat eight inches off the ground, front log flush with the piers, measured as perfectly even to prevent gaps in the dovetail notches that would let in water. They drilled a "course" through each log for electrical wiring. The men were almost ready to drop in the joists for the loft when they discovered a replacement log didn't fit right. Spider, toes of his boots appearing Velcroed to the top logs, called to his son, Randy, to help lower the log to Michael. Spider scrambled down.

"Now I coulda went to this with the saw, Michael, but I can tell you're itchin' to get at somethin' with your ax, seein' as how you turn up every day with it," he said. "So show me how to do it the pioneer way." Fig handed Michael the tool from Michael's belt on the ground.

Michael's breath puffed in the cool air as he asked with raised brows, "You trust me to do that?"

"Sure, it's your cabin." Fig chuckled. "Just level 'er out about half of an inch. Remember how Randy did it yesterday."

Glowing with enthusiasm, Michael glanced at Jennifer, making certain she watched what was sure to be an impressive, muscle-flexing exercise. She nodded, then smiled as he chiseled the wood horizontally with carefully aimed shaving motions.

"Whoa, that's perfect!" Fig yelled.

Grinning, Michael dropped the ax and helped the third man on Fig's crew elevate the log to the cabin expert and his son. Once they pronounced it a perfect fit, Jennifer knew she needed to speak up. They'd had no time alone together lately, partly because the owner of the Gillen store had accepted the town council's purchase offer. While that provided cause for celebration, it also meant that she, Michael, James, several new guys on the Johnson construction crew, Stella, Earl, and their teenage sons, Gabe and Jamal, added clean-up of the building's rubble-filled interior to their other tasks. Today, Jennifer had no intention of squandering a rare outing with Michael to chain saws and sweaty men. As everything fell into place for her to stay in Hermon, one puzzle piece remained missing, and that was to determine what kind of future Michael envisioned.

"I'm sorry to interrupt your fun, but Michael and I have to get ready to go. We promised Stella and Earl we'd join them at Watson Mill Bridge State Park for their church outing."

Michael looked at her with poorly veiled dismay. "I thought we didn't have to be there until this afternoon."

Jennifer put her hands on her hips. "They're expecting us for lunch, and from the looks of you, you haven't even showered yet."

"Whoo-hoo," Fig hooted, owl-like, from above. "I guess you better listen to the missus, Michael." The other men joined him in laughter.

Jennifer felt her face flush and watched Michael struggle to hide his discomfort. "I'll be leaving you too short-handed," he protested.

"Nonsense, we can finish up on our own," Fig called. "Besides, I've got my marchin' orders, too. Randy's son's got a cross country meet this afternoon we're all supposed to attend. We'll get the floor joists laid, then see you bright an' early Monday." Looking like a sentry on top of a fort, he gave a smart salute.

"Let me guess," Jennifer joked, "You'll be ready to raise the roof."

Fig pointed at her. "That's exactly right, Miss Jennifer!"

"Fine," Michael agreed. "See you then." He turned to Jennifer and flapped the tails of his flannel shirt. "You're right. I do need a quick shower, and you look ready."

Jennifer nodded and glanced down at her rust-colored, corduroy high-waisted dress, worn with muted print leggings and dark sneakers. While shopping with Montana had modernized her style, she found some elements of vintage and SoHo remained. She aimed to stay true to herself while updating with an air of professionalism, but she'd thought the eclectic outfit appropriate for a church outing to a park. She just hoped Michael found her cute rather than frumpy. She felt reassured as he took her arm and smiled, walking away from the construction site.

"Why don't you wait in the house for me? I'll be quick. Dad's working in the office."

"OK. What's he doing?"

"Hanging pictures, I think."

Jennifer found James doing exactly that, humming to praise music while the smell of his morning pot of coffee still permeated the house. Before joining him, she peeked into the parlor to admire the golden-brown velvet upholstered, flamed mahogany American Empire sofa and Gothic Revival side chair they'd bought from Myrtle Dee's antique store in Lake Oconee. She smirked at how perfectly they complimented Stella's restored faux wood grain on the unusual triple baseboards and Amy's gold-brown paint and satin laine curtains. Providing perfect light for reading, the bay windows now embraced a Gothic Revival table flanked by armchairs.

"Yeah, I often do my morning devotions there," James said when Jennifer complimented the arrangement. He marked two spots on the wall for pictures to hang one above the other, then reached for his hammer.

Jennifer heard the shower turn on in the bedroom off the parallel hallway. "Can I help?" she asked, reaching for a framed double photo. Looking closer, she realized one featured a professional shot of Michael's head, shoulders and arms coming out of a pool lane in butterfly stroke, and him clasping a medal around his neck on a podium in the other one. "Oh, high school state?" Michael had told her about how he'd won two swimming individual and two relay events as a senior, partly to please his mother who was dying of cancer at the time.

"Yes, where he won gold in the 100 fly and 200 freestyle and set a state record in the free." Looking at the picture, James glowed with pride even years later.

Jennifer handed it to him and picked up the other print, a framed newspaper article about two Emory University students who made national cuts for USA Swimming. Michael Johnson was one of them, pictured in a Speedo warm-up jacket. She blinked. "Uh, wait, he made nationals?"

James turned from adjusting the picture on the wall and reached for the framed newspaper article. "Yep."

Jennifer couldn't keep her eyes off the likeness of the young Michael with his gelled and spiked hair. She swallowed. "I don't know a lot about swimming, but that sounds big. Could he have gone to the Olympics?"

"At one time, the thought crossed our minds. But when his last chance came for an Olympic Trial cut in the 200 and he swam two-hundredths off, it kind of took the wind out of his sails."

"Oh, how awful. He didn't quit?" Jennifer asked in exasperation.

James hung the picture and nodded. "Not long after."

"But why? Who would quit when they were that good? Couldn't he have tried again the next year?"

"He could have, but practices and competitions consumed so much time and focus, it interfered with his education. He made a choice to concentrate on academics."

Jennifer studied the older man's face. "And that made you sad," she observed.

He gave her a faint smile. "Watching Michael swim was one of the greatest joys of my life, but seeing him become what God called him to be was greater. I couldn't be prouder than when he graduated from Emory." James moved a box of towel-wrapped, framed prints from the floor to the computer desk.

"Michael said his grandmother Gloria told him about the doctors in his family line and wanted him to follow in their footsteps, but he also said that didn't work out. I hadn't realized he graduated." Jennifer shrugged, trying to appear nonchalant about her lack of information. "I'd assumed he'd not finished at Emory and decided to work for your construction company, maybe that he found the course of study too demanding."

James pulled a framed undergraduate degree from the box, brushing it off for her inspection. "Oh, he finished, and with honors. Thought I'd hang this over the mantel. Michael aimed to be an oncologist, on account of what happened to his mother, see," he told her. "But that takes a long time, an M.D. after this one, then three years internal medicine residency, then three years of an oncology fellowship."

"That begins to make sense of letting swimming go," Jennifer murmured, hand on the box of pictures. "Michael seemed hesitant to talk about that time in his life. I know between the death of his mother and his wife it was very painful, but there's so much I don't know." In minutes, though, she would. James would unwrap these pictures chronicling Michael's university years and, recognizing the progression of his son's relationship with Jennifer, offer her answers.

The scent of aftershave preceded the man, wrapping around her before Michael's hand fell over hers from behind. Jennifer's heart sank at how fast he took a shower. As much as she wanted to leave with him, she wanted to unravel his mysterious past more, and she stood a better chance of doing that with James than with Michael himself.

"If we're in as much hurry as you say," he told her in a teasing voice, "you don't have time to hang pictures. Let's go. Dad, I just want that outdoor print over the mantel, OK?"

"Son—"

Michael pulled Jennifer from the room and said over his shoulder, "Just put that stuff in the closet. I'll help you with it later. Since I had to leave, the guys could probably use a hand outside right now." Not waiting on a response, Michael tugged Jennifer down the hallway and out through the kitchen.

As they buckled into Michael's truck for the half hour drive through Lexington and north on Georgia 22, Jennifer tried to stifle the burning sense in her chest that Michael did not want her to learn more about his past. Finally she could no longer stuff down the questions that bubbled up like effervescent intruders.

"Michael," Jennifer asked, "how do you feel about me staying here?"

He hung a hand over the steering wheel and glanced at her with measured impatience. "Why do you keep asking me that?"

"Because I don't feel like you've answered it."

"I have. I told you that we all think you belong here, not in Savannah."

"Yes, you told me where you think I belong, but … I don't know how you really *feel* about it." She shifted her feet beneath her and stared at her sneakers. When she chanced a glance, Michael's pained expression looked like she'd suggested a root canal. Guys hated that particular word, "feel." Typically she avoided it, too, preferring to keep a shield around her heart, but she could no longer afford ignorance. Not when her whole future and all her dreams hung in the balance.

"Jennifer, you're not making sense. I want you to stay. Can I be any plainer?"

She folded her hands. "Yes. I think you can," she said in a small voice.

His tone gentled as he picked up on her vulnerability. "OK. How? What do you need to know?"

"Michael, I appreciate your friendship and support. I do. But times like today make me feel you really don't want to go any deeper. I've opened up and shared a lot with you that wasn't easy, but I feel like you're stone-walling me. You don't even want me to know what happened in college, why you quit swimming, why you quit your studies, what happened with Ashley. It seems to me you just quit a lot of things, and now you don't want to talk about them. At all. So what else am I supposed to make of that besides that you don't trust me, or want to keep me at a distance?" Jennifer swallowed and forced the last fear out. "And if I stay here, thinking there's some sort of future for us beyond friendship, what if you quit on me, too? So I guess if friendship is what you have in mind, I'd rather you tell me that now."

Michael drew in a deep breath and then let it out. He reached over for her hand, making her heart beat fast with hope. "Tell me what makes you think friendship is my goal."

She gave an abrupt laugh. "Seriously? Besides this being pretty much our only date, if this is even a date? I mean, you probably conceded to this cookout just to satisfy Stella."

"I conceded to this cookout because I wanted to be with you, and we needed to get out for the afternoon."

"Agreed."

He squeezed her hand. "Look, I'm sorry I've allowed work to crowd out time to get to know you. I guess I figured there was no better place to do that than living real life side by side. But girls like to do special things occasionally, right?"

Jennifer smiled. "I guess. I'm not exactly an expert on dating."

"Well, I'm a little rusty at it, too. But yes, I'd like to go out with you, if you agree. Forgive me? Give me another chance?"

She nodded. She felt he still evaded a deeper issue, but couldn't pinpoint what. She muttered with her face turned toward the window as though she studied the passing scenery, "So you think there could be more than friendship in the future..."

An excruciating moment passed before Michael answered. "I've told you I have feelings for you. You're smart, funny, pretty, and you

84

make me feel things I thought I wouldn't feel again. Not to mention you're about as stubborn as a stripped screw." He paused while they both laughed, the tension easing. "But I've got to be honest with you, not only am I still working through some things, at times I think I see you struggling with your past, too. I don't know how ready either of us is for a relationship. God kind of told me to take it slow with you."

Her head swiveled to her left. "He did?"

The gentleness in Michael's expression surprised her, and caused her to admire him more. "Yeah. We're both in a healing process, wouldn't you say?"

Jennifer nodded. "But I'm not scared of you." She intended the statement to be bold and reassuring, but it sounded like a child making an announcement to the monster she believed lurked in her closet.

He cut an eye at her. "You're not?"

She jutted her chin out a fraction. "No."

To her surprise, as Michael turned into the state park, he pulled the truck over onto the grassy side of the road. Her eyes widened as he shifted the vehicle out of gear and turned to her, touching the side of her face as he made eye contact, letting her know she had his full attention.

"Thank you for trusting me," he said. "I know that's not easy for you. I'm not even sure what I've done to earn that trust, because you're right, I've stuffed things inside for so long I don't know how to reciprocate and talk about them. I do need to talk to you about some things, but not right now, OK? Stella and those folks are expecting us, and I don't want to ruin the day. Can we just have a good afternoon for now?"

Jennifer nodded. She'd learned some secrets needed to be exchanged for emotional intimacy, trust and healing, but the transaction still carried a price tag. The sharing of dark things could bring misunderstanding, pity, the realization that you'd become a burden, or all three. "But I'm going to hold you to it," she warned with a frown that pretended to be stern.

"OK." Ignoring a passing car, Michael cupped her face and pushed back her brown and russet locks. "I don't want to mess this up," he confessed in almost a whisper, "because I really do like you, Jennifer Rushmore."

And I love you, she thought, but bit her tongue. She'd already gambled far too much today. No way would she tell Michael that first. Her stomach dropped. Maybe he still was in love with Ashley. Maybe her fears of never being able to compare to Ashley's sweet, spiritual beauty rested on reality.

His next question put all thoughts of Michael's former wife from her mind. "Can I kiss you?"

Her eyes wide, she nodded, touched that he requested such a smaller liberty than others had taken over protest. As they both leaned in, Jennifer could hear her breath coming fast and felt his fan her face as he studied her reaction before sealing her lips with his once, twice, three times, slow and sweet but brief. When he pulled back a fraction, the result resembled getting just a whiff of a cinnamon dolce latte or merely licking the outer shell of a Godiva chocolate.

"See? Not scared," she whispered.

His soft lips met hers again before he whispered back, "Your hands are trembling."

She looked down onto the seat between them. Blast it, he was right. She stuffed them into her lap, but the atmosphere altered. Michael leaned back with a smile at her and put the truck in gear. Arguing the trembling stemmed from anything besides fear would look worse. Her mother would already say she'd been forward today. A string of three husbands never kept Kelly from voicing her criticism of any perceived attention her daughter paid men.

Jennifer sighed. Her father's abandonment created a pocket of longing inside her to be held and loved that Roy had taken advantage of. For a long time after that abuse, she shut down that part of her, but now, Michael's gentleness pried the lid off the void. True, she felt God's love in so many new ways. Lots of the recent occurrences where things fell into place stemmed from that sense of His favor on her and caused her stop, smile over her Creator's attention to the details of her life, and say a prayer of thanks. Yet the desire to be cherished by a man remained.

CHAPTER SIX

S ight of the 236-foot, 1885 covered bridge spanning the waters of the South Fork River broke Jennifer's musing and caused her to sit forward and say, "Oh!"

Michael grinned over at her as he pulled into a parking lot. "Quite a work of craftsmanship, yeah?"

"Definitely." She slid out of the truck and took off for the historical marker set in stacked stone, the rushing of water over the low dam on the other side of the bridge and the distinct savor of meat cooking seasoning the cool air. Michael joined her as she read about the town lattice truss system held by wooden pins and designed by W.W. King. "I read before we came here that he was the son of a freed slave and another famous covered bridge builder, Horace King," she said to Michael.

They eyed the long, weathered span of gray wood broken only by one horizontal window in the middle. "Wanna go check it out?" Michael asked.

"I sure do." She glanced past the river to a shelter where a number of African American people moved around grills and picnic tables. "I think that might be Harmony Grove on the other side."

"Come on."

The bridge looked even longer when they entered its shade. Michael cupped his hands and called, "Halloo!" They laughed when the sound seemed to echo, walked on one of two wooden tire treads, and paused at the windows to view lazy brown water on one side and lively white spray on the other as the South Fork plummeted past the dam and remains of a power plant, rippling over rocky shoals into the distance.

Stella stood at the other end of the bridge, arms akimbo, wearing a butterfly-sleeved rayon blouse and dark denim jeans. "Is that you, Michael Johnson?" she called. "Are you lost, boy?"

Michael played along. "Yes, ma'am, can you direct me to the Harmony Grove picnic?"

She swatted him and grabbed his arm. "Get on over here. Earl's got your burgers on the grill. We better hurry before he burns 'em up. Mama brought her potato salad, and honey, I made my fresh pear cake. Come on, Jennifer. Don't you look cute today?"

Jennifer returned Stella's embrace, saying, "Thank you, but I wish you'd have let me bring something for the meal."

"Oh, shush, girl, you've been so busy lately, I was afraid if you had to add one more thing you wouldn't come."

"Of course I'd come! I've been looking forward to this all week."

She and Michael followed their friend, Michael's distant cousin, toward the gathering. Michael's fingers curled around Jennifer's, causing her face to heat and her mind to race in amazement that he wanted to declare the status of their relationship. Stella turned back around to say something, noticed their joined hands and slapped a flattened palm over her heart. She declared, "Well, is that how it is? My, my, I thought it would never happen! Boy, you sure took long enough. I thought you'd let this girl get off to Savannah and leave us."

"Frankly, I've been hoping she'll just cancel the interview."

As Michael studied Jennifer with a faint, expectant smile, Stella looked back and forth between them, making a sound of amazement. "Sounds good to me!"

"Stella, come see if these burgers are done!" Earl called from a cloud of smoke over a large, open grill.

Jamal stood over him and did not hesitate to offer his unwanted opinion. "Daddy, if it's any more done, they'll have to gnaw it like jerky."

He got an elbow in the rib. "Just you hush, boy. It's not like you ever once grilled anything."

Stella rolled her eyes. "We better rescue your lunch, but after you eat, you two should go canoeing or take a walk, get in some alone time, before Pastor Simms gives his homily."

Michael cleared his throat. "Homily?"

Stella just chuckled, her shiny brown boots picking out a sure path over the loose gravel. "You should know by now we don't do any church function without a homily."

While the James family surrounded one table under the loud and crowded shelter, talk over lunch centered on plans for the art gallery. Jennifer and Michael described the floor plan that would allow for meeting rooms, class rooms and gallery space featuring hardwood floors, exposed brick, white sheetrock walls and can lighting, a mix of modern with historical.

"What you gonna call it?" Stan, Stella's brother and the sheriff of Oglethorpe County, wanted to know. He pointed a pickle spear at Stella. "It's gotta be catchy, not something lame like Hermon Art Gallery."

"It should have my baby's name in it," Dorace insisted.

Stella waved a hand at her. "No, Mama, that'd be promotin' myself."

Dorace dug into her potato salad and asked, "Well, don't you wanna promote yourself?"

"Yes, but I do that by advertising."

"What about using the name of the general store?" Jennifer suggested. "The Gillen Gallery?"

"Oh, I like it," Earl agreed. "What you think, Stella?"

She nodded slowly. "I do, too."

At the end of the table, Jamal crunched a chip and said, "I agree with Grandma, but I think our last name should be on there."

"Boys, this isn't about us. The good Lord has blessed us with an opportunity, but it's about the community. And nothin' means more to a community than its history," Stella said.

"I'm hopin' nobody gets it into their mind to start messin' with work on that building the way they have with Michael's property," Stan observed. He shook his head. "It gets under my skin that we can't figure out who's been up to tricks or why, and by now there have been too many to dismiss them all as accidents or coincidence. I feel like a failure, Michael. I've talked to all the neighbors and anyone I can think of with any possible desire to stop progress in the town."

Michael shook his head. "Don't feel that way, Stan. We know you've done all you can."

Dorace perked up. "Do you think it could've been that old Bryce Stevenson? He was a rotten egg if I ever smelled one."

"Grandma, that old man's laid up in the bed," Gabe pointed out, his basketball player frame looming over her as he reached for a thick slice of pear cake. "And even before his stroke, he used that cane. It's not like he coulda crawled under Mr. Michael's car to mess with the brakes, or attacked Miss Jennifer's professor in Athens."

The older woman pursed her lips. "No, but he coulda paid someone to." When Stella gave a pointed glance to the people behind them and widened her eyes at her mother, Dorace punctuated the air with a finger and announced, "Now no one needs to go repeatin' that I'm makin' slanderous accusations. I'm just observin' that he was the most outspoken against the Firefly Trail and the Gillen store renovation." She fixed her son with a stare. "Did you talk to him? Or were you afraid to ruffle his feathers?"

He gazed back at her with a blank look. "Mama, why would that man care if Michael fixed up his own house?"

She blinked. "Well, I don't know, I guess that's what *you're* supposed to figure out."

Stan shook his head and turned to Jennifer. "How's your professor? Has the class come out yet?"

"She's doing fine, thanks, and they're slated to come midmonth."

"I'm thinkin' it wouldn't be a bad idea for me to be on site that day."

"You're more than welcome," Michael told him. "Thank you."

After lunch, Michael suggested taking the nature trail by the river could help walk off their soreness from the week's labor. Stella pressed her lips together to stifle a smile and turned away to cover the food. When Jennifer tried to help her, Stella shooed her off. "Just be back by three," she said.

They walked out on the large rocks, worn smooth by years of erosion, to the edge of the river. Michael threw a large stick into the current and watched its progress. "So when's the interview in Savannah?" he asked.

"This Thursday. I was thinking I'd drive down Wednesday night to have a little time to see the city and rest up."

He nodded. "You've been to Savannah before?"

"Yes, I participated in a UGA field study there. It was in my resume, remember?"

"Oh, that's right."

90

She grinned and poked his side with her own stick. "You didn't read it."

He threw a smirk over his broad shoulder. "I knew you'd be gold. You liked it there?"

"Loved it."

"It has a lot more to offer than Hermon."

What would he say if she told him Barbara now might be tied up in the Savannah package? Jennifer allowed the rushing of the water to fill the silence a moment. Then she grew brave enough to say, "It doesn't offer all the people I love here."

Once the words escaped, she could have clamped her hand over her mouth. She hadn't meant to say "loved," and sure enough, Michael picked up on the potential implication, turning and spearing her with his gaze. "Then don't go. Call and tell Marian you accept the position in Lexington."

"She hasn't offered it to me yet. The position had to be listed in the required places for the required time."

"But she will."

"I think so, but something strange could happen."

Michael started walking back toward the trail. Tossing her stick away, Jennifer scurried to keep up with his long strides. "Wait, are you mad at me?"

He slowed down near a covered foot bridge. "No, of course not. I get that it would be irresponsible of you to not check this out. I guess ..." He paused and covered his lowered face, then ruffled his hair. "I guess the reality that you could still go to Savannah just hits me sometimes. In my mind, you've grown synonymous with living here."

Jennifer gathered the courage to reach for his big, calloused hand. "I'm glad that bothers you. It helps me to see it." As she spoke, she opened his fingers and ran her own hand over his, feeling this week's blisters.

"See what, that I get upset?" he asked, incredulous.

"Yes. The whole time I've known you, you've been so composed, so distant, not even caring about stuff that would make other people get excited ... except when you were fighting with me about fireplaces and furniture, that is." She paused and peeked up at him with a smirk. His answering smile caused her heart to leap.

"And you weren't at all prickly when we met." Michael tugged her into the covering of the bridge, leaning against it and pulling her into a loose embrace.

She smiled at his gentle sarcasm. "Well, OK, maybe a little." Her voice sounded breathless just from his nearness.

"We have different ways of protecting ourselves, right?" As she nodded, losing the ability to form sentences, his caress smoothed the fuzzy corduroy on her back. "You're softer now," he teased. "I like it better."

"Me, too." Responding to the light pressure on her waist, Jennifer inched closer until her cheek rested against the faint stubble on Michael's. Aftershave or cologne tickled her nose. Like before when he'd held her, she kept her hands folded between them. Did she dare embrace him? Reaching out for anyone in her past had always brought pain. Her fingers flexed, longing to touch the dark hair at the nape of his neck.

"You scared?" he whispered.

She decided pretending could present too much risk. "Yes."

"Don't be."

Jennifer reached. Her fingers laced at the collar of his cotton shirt, and she leaned into him, expecting the solidity of his masculine frame to repel or alarm. Instead, she felt the way she did when he placed his hand on the small of her back or opened her door for her, protected. She'd be lying if she denied a tingle of awareness, but for now it remained pleasant, not threatening. His heart beat against hers, and she closed her eyes and let out a sigh of relief and contentment. This was exactly what she craved despite herself.

Michael's fingers now stroked her hair the way one calmed a skittish mare. When she felt his lips graze her ear and cheek, she turned her face toward the affection like a flower sought the sun. "What scares me," he said in a quiet voice, "is how helping you get past your blocks from the past makes me lower my guard, too. I can't do it without connecting with you, without being tender. I didn't seek those moments, but it seems like God's put them in my path. And now there's the possibility that just when I stop protecting myself, the blow could come."

Jennifer pulled back to look into his blue eyes. "You do know the only reason I'd go to Savannah would be if I prayed about it and felt that was where God wanted me."

She saw him swallow, and he suddenly looked sick. "That's just what I expect of Him."

"Why? Why would you expect that?" Jennifer's brow creased.

"It's nothing," he said, straightening and releasing her except for a light tug on her hand. "Let's go. It's almost three."

She allowed him to lead, but, sensing she'd hit on something important, not to end the conversation. "What did you mean, Michael? Do you think God doesn't want us together?"

He sighed, not looking at her. "He just has a way of taking away the women I'm close to."

Jennifer pressed her lips together, then said, "Sickness entered the world with sin, when Adam and Eve chose against God's will. I don't think it's God's will for people to suffer a death like that."

Michael slanted a glance back at her. "So He didn't take them, but He allowed them to be taken. No need to split hairs. Did you know that Ashley got leiomyoscarcoma, same as my mom? What are the chances of that? I believe it's the dirtiest cancer known to man. There's no way they could have suffered more." His face twisted. "Sometimes the spinal block worked for the pain, sometimes it didn't. I kept thinking I must be missing the formula for the right prayer of faith. I tried everything, I would have given anything. I'm still not sure what I did to deserve to go through that with both my mother and my wife."

Jennifer stopped beside him as the anguish radiating from Michael almost took her breath away. She had suffered inner agonies of worthlessness, shame and fear, but here was a pain that, while different from hers, raged no less intense. Worst of all, she didn't have a snap answer. Maybe Stella would have, but Jennifer was new to this faith thing. All she knew to do was to place a tentative hand on Michael's shoulder while drawing close to his side, communicating her empathy as best as she could through her gesture.

He glanced down at her and pressed his lips together in a grim smile. "See why I don't talk about this? I told you it would ruin the day."

"But you're really here," she whispered. "Right now, you're really here with me. And you never will be unless you take an honest look at what's inside, then begin to let go of the past."

Michael gave an unexpected laugh. "Didn't I tell you my turn would come?"

She smiled. "Yes, you did. I'm sorry. I know it's not fun."

By the time they joined the Harmony Grove group, sitting with the Jamses in soft camping chairs on the periphery, the people finished singing, and Pastor Simms stood up at the end of the picnic shelter, holding his Bible. Keenly aware of the exposed pain she still felt from Michael, Jennifer wanted to scoot closer, but the splayed arm rests prevented that. The reverend introduced his text, Exodus 15:22-27, and read of the time shortly after Moses led the Israelites out of slavery in Egypt. After three days in the wilderness, they found nothing to drink, finally coming to Marah, where the water tasted bitter. When the people complained, God showed Moses a tree to cast into the pool that would make it sweet.

"Today, in this beautiful place, I want to talk about healing waters," Pastor Simms said, then paused as if heeding a voice in his spirit. "Mmm, Jesus, I hear you," he added, pointing a finger up to the blue, cloud-studded sky. "I believe He's sayin' to me that some of you here today been wanderin' in the wilderness. Some of you been standin' by the bitter pool complainin'. 'He tested them,' it says. Some of you are failin' that test. Some of you haven't cried out to God to make your waters sweet, because you too busy feelin' sorry for yourself and complainin'!"

Murmurs rippled under the pavilion as Jennifer cut her eyes toward Michael, who sat unmoving as a stone, looking like a man who realized he'd been led into an ambush.

"But God's got a tree for you! Say it with me, folks. 'God's got a tree for you.'" Most everyone repeated the phrase with the tall, middle-aged minister, who wore dress slacks and a white polo shirt that glowed against his dark skin. He read from his Bible, "'If you diligently heed the voice of the Lord your God and do what is right in His sight, give ear to His commandments and keep all His statutes, I will put none of the diseases on you which I have brought on the Egyptians. For I am the Lord who heals you.'" Pastor Simms pointed a finger at the passage. "'The Lord who heals you' in this verse is where God chose to reveal Himself as Jehovah Rapha, Hebrew for 'to heal' or 'to restore.' Now why wouldn't God choose to use that term, that name for Himself, when Jesus healed the sick? Or when He raised Lazarus from the dead? Because I think there's something harder than any disease to heal, and that's the cancer of bitterness."

"Mmm-hmm!" several people cried out.

Jennifer cringed, feeling the heat for Michael. Pastor Simms possessed a gift of spotlighting people with his insightful and impeccably-timed messages. As she glanced at Michael's set features, she prayed the words penetrated.

Pastor Simms again pointed upward. "God always goes for the biggest work. *He always goes for the biggest work.* In your situation, you may want this or that, you may say, 'God, why don't you do this to fix it and get some glory?' But He's gonna get the biggest glory, and that biggest glory comes from healing you of your bitterness!"

People applauded and called, "Amen!" Jennifer put her hands together in a quiet clap. She found it truthful that, even though free choice had allowed others to harm her as a child, God had set her free from her past controlling her, the biggest miracle. Would Michael hear that his freedom from bitterness could trump a physical healing for his mother or wife?

"Mmm, yes, Jesus. And people, I've got good news for you. You call out to Him for that sweet tree—and let me just say there is no sweeter tree than Calvary, where He accomplished it all, took on Himself all the pain and suffering anyone ever felt—and not only is He gonna throw that tree in your waters, He's gonna lead you away from that place of disappointment to Elim, a place of refreshing. See the next place they went? Elim. It says there were twelve wells of water and seventy palm trees. Now that sounds like a dessert oasis, doesn't it?"

"Yes, it does," the congregation affirmed.

"Now why do you think the Bible tells us how many wells and how many palm trees? It could have said 'a lot,' and we would have gotten the picture. Well, we have a God who's in the details. He doesn't throw 'em in there for no reason. I'm gonna give you a little quiz. How many disciples were there?"

Waving her arms, an adolescent girl waited until Pastor Simms placed a hand on her head. "Twelve!" she exclaimed with pride.

"Yes, ma'am, your Sunday school teacher's done good. In Luke it tells us Jesus gave those disciples power and authority over demons and to cure diseases, the power of the Holy Spirit. The power of the Holy Spirit in us is the only way we can get the victory over our bitter places! Now let me ask you a harder one. How many people did Jesus send out two by two, after that?"

Dorace nodded her head, catching the pastor's eye.

"Do you know, Mrs. Watson?"

"Yes, Sir."

"Well, tell us, sister."

She raised her eyebrows. "Seventy."

"Amen. He sent seventy 'before His face into every city and place where He Himself was about to go.' Do you hear that, people? Where He was about to go! Mmm, I want Him to lead me out in power, and I want to go where He's going. Don't you?" When the response fell short of Pastor Simms' expectations, he asked again, "Don't you?"

"Yes!" and "Amen!" the people called. Jennifer nodded, encouraged by the example and promise of a brighter future. Maybe Michael would also realize God had something better for them both if they accepted emotional healing.

The preacher lowered his voice for emphasis in closing. "He has a plan for you. He has a place of abundance and blessing for you. But first you have to be willing to cry out to Him to turn your bitter waters sweet. Will you do that?"

After Pastor Simms had them bow in prayer, Michael folded his chair, shook hands with Earl and hugged Stella.

"You OK, honey?" Stella asked him, pulling back to study his face.

"Yep, fine. We enjoyed the day," he told her. "Thank you for inviting us."

Stella didn't look convinced. As Jennifer hugged her and Michael took the opportunity to step away, Stella murmured, "I don't get a good feelin' about that boy."

"Me, either, Stella. Pray for us. I think some things got stirred up today."

Stella nodded and held her hands. "Well, you know now from experience, God can't heal what's covered. The road may get bumpy for a while, but it's a necessary part of gettin' where you need to go."

When Michael short-fused her attempts at conversation in the truck, Jennifer rode in silence almost to Lexington. Finally she could endure no more. She took a breath and said, "I take it you didn't like Pastor Simms' sermon."

"No, it was great," came the short reply.

"Right. What happened to being open?"

"I'm just a little tired of talking about deep stuff. We're almost to Lexington. Wanna stop for some ice cream?"

"No, I want you to talk to me!"

"I am talking to you."

Jennifer angled her body toward him. "Did you not see where that message was for you? About how God wants you to let go of your bitterness over what happened and allow Him to heal you?"

"Yes. I saw it."

"But ...?"

When he looked over, his glare sliced to her heart. "But I also heard other things. Like what God said about not putting diseases on the people if they obeyed Him. Well, Mom and Ashley obeyed God. They didn't have unhealthy habits, either. So why the cancer?"

Not yet grounded in theology, Jennifer resorted to logic. "Well, if God doesn't always shield us from the bad choices of others, if there's cause and effect in the world, maybe He doesn't always shield us from other unhealthy things that are also here because of choices, like chemicals, pesticides, pollution, free radicals."

"OK, Miss Science Expert, what about what he said about God leading us from Marah to Elim? Where is Mom's Elim? Where is Ashley's?"

Michael's sarcasm alarmed and seared her. She didn't like this side of him. She drew her arms close to her body and leaned toward the window. "Heaven," she whispered.

The one word diffused Michael's tension. He glanced at her, and his voice gentled as he said, "You got me again. But what about a big plan for their lives? Neither one of them got to accomplish anything big for God. Do you really believe their best purpose was to die early and go to heaven? They didn't have anything else on earth to do?"

"I don't think we can judge that. I think God can. Besides, they both made you who you are, didn't they? And I think that's pretty great."

Michael's look melted her heart. "Thanks," he said, genuine now.

If she could have left it at that, maybe they could have moved back into harmony. But that now-familiar urging in Jennifer's spirit to speak what she perceived gripped her and wouldn't let go, so she took a breath and tried to steady her voice. "I think you're really mad at God, not because He took Ashley and your mom early, but because you think He was not faithful to you."

Silence descended in the cab of the truck. Maybe two miles passed with Michael just looking out the windshield. Jennifer cringed. Who was she to tell Michael how he fell short? To offer high-sounding spiritual insight? She batted back tears, certain she'd alienated him with her brutal honesty only hours after he'd opened his heart to her.

Finally, in a level tone spoken still looking straight ahead, he asked, "So how is it again that you don't feel God abandoned *you*?"

She shrugged. "I don't think I was worthy of much notice. I'm sure He had bigger matters on His hands."

"Well, that's just not true."

Jennifer realized she'd repeated what she'd believed for so long, not what God's Word told her. It took time to change old ways of thinking. She tried again. "I didn't belong to Him like you did. You see him as a Father who failed to protect you." As she spoke, a vision of her own father's semi cab disappearing down the road for the last time flooded Jennifer's mind, and along with it, the piercing anguish, panic and rejection. Recognizing the source of the memory, she sucked in a sudden breath.

He looked at her, stirred to mild alarm. "What?"

"I get it. Oh, I get it." She'd been so sure she'd successfully forgiven her mother and stepfather that she hadn't really thought today's sermon applied to her. She'd even been proud she didn't blame

God for not rescuing her from her past. But she'd not thought far enough back to the unhealed wound of her real father's leaving. Now she had something else to reckon with. True, she had hope of comfort, healing and provision from God, but she realized Michael was incapable of moving forward until he no longer felt about God the way she felt about her earthly father.

CHAPTER SEVEN

Saturday's influence extended into the next week, initiating a domino effect Jennifer felt powerless to stop. Although he worked like a machine, each day Michael grew more distant, his focus more inward. Her attempts to arrange private time to talk about what went on in that mind of his all failed. Meanwhile, Jennifer's fears grew that Michael's withdrawal proved he had decided a relationship with her wasn't worth the risk.

Distraught, Jennifer held out for Wednesday night. She envisioned herself getting in her Civic and driving away, using the time to think and pray … and investigate what might not now be a dead end, but made her feel dead inside nonetheless. Pretending to be happy, she told her friends of her plans to drive out to Jekyll Beach Wednesday evening. She'd get a good night of sleep, meet Tandy Sullivan for lunch, tour the company, then take some time to walk through the historic district before driving home. Yet when the third man on Fig's crew fell sick with the flu just as a predicted end-of-week freeze threatened the successful completion of the cabin chinking, Jennifer realized she needed to stay and help the men through twilight on Wednesday. By the time they finished, driving to Savannah proved pointless.

Instead, after bringing the cat in for the night and opening a can of Fancy Feast, Jennifer opted for a long soak in the tub. Lavender Epsom salts helped ease her sore upper body from mixing and daubing and her lower body from squatting and bending. By the time she emerged in her robe and PJs she felt too tired to contemplate watching TV and decided to head to bed despite the early hour. Maybe if she slept well she'd leave early the next morning and do some sightseeing before her interview. Still in her fluffy robe, Jennifer curled up under her quilt and began to drift off to the comforting cadence of Yoda's purring.

When Jennifer jerked awake she got the sense not much time had passed. Yoda sat on the end of the bed meowing. "No!" she moaned. Yoda knew how to use the litter box. "It is not time to go hunting!"

Yoda meowed again, and Jennifer threw a toss pillow close enough to scare her off the bed. Maybe she'd give up. But now Yoda sat on her floor and meowed.

About that moment someone banged on the front door.

Jennifer raised her head. What in the world? Was she having a dream?

"Jennifer! Open up!" Calvin's voice yelled.

Michael. James. Something might have happened to them. Mental fog clearing, Jennifer stuffed her feet into slippers and stumbled toward the living room. She froze when she came out of the hallway. An eerie orange flicker from her back deck illuminated the fact that a smoky haze hovered in her kitchen.

"Oh, my stars!" She ran to the front door and threw the bolt, pushing open the storm door. When her neighbor's wrinkled face and bathrobe-encased, sausage-like form appeared, she gasped, "Calvin, something's on fire!"

"I know, I saw it while lettin' Otis out. You've got to get out of there, Jennifer. I'm afraid your hose was coiled out back and is burnt up. I don't think mine will reach this far. We have to call the fire department."

Jennifer whirled and ran back down the hallway despite Calvin's protests. She hadn't noticed smoke until she entered the main living area. She knew she had enough time to grab her purse and scoop Yoda under her arm before scampering out the front door. As soon as her feet hit the damp grass, Jennifer scrambled for her cell phone with shaking hands.

"I'll call 911," she told Calvin. She prayed the spotty Hermon reception wouldn't fail her now.

"OK, I'm goin' to run for my house and see if the hose will reach with the extension on." Calvin loped away in the darkness, leaving Jennifer to stand shaking in the cold night, trying to hold the squirming feline besides clutching the phone to her ear.

Minutes later, the call placed and the reassurance of a crew on the way offered, Jennifer stumbled around the side of the double-wide to find Calvin shooting water at the blaze crackling below the back deck. The trajectory reached only the edge of the flames, allowing the recently kindled fire to encroach on the kitchen wall.

"I've got a bucket outside my shed," he called to her. "If you can find it you could help douse the side of the trailer."

Jennifer hesitated to put the cat down, afraid she'd run off in alarm and not return for days, but she had little choice. She lifted Yoda into the tree Otis had chased her up, hoping she'd feel safe there, then, with a longing glance toward Michael's dark house, switched on her flashlight ap. She found the bucket where Calvin said. They filled it twice and tossed the water against the blackening wall before red and white lights and blaring sirens announced the arrival of the firefighters. The men pulled the red truck right up to the double-wide, and within minutes of yelled directions and the extension of the thick, black hose, put the blaze out. Before they finished, Michael ran up wearing a coat over T-shirt and lounge pants and grabbed her, wrapping his arms around her.

"Oh, thank God! I was so scared when I heard the sirens. What happened?" he demanded.

"I don't know," Jennifer said, aware that James, too, now placed an arm around her. She looked around to see Stan approaching in his policeman's uniform. "I was sleeping, then Yoda started meowing, then Calvin was banging on my door."

"We're so glad you're all right, Jennifer," James said as Jennifer unpeeled from all but Michael's arm.

"Yes, we are," Stan agreed. "Please tell me we can easily explain this. Do you think you left a burner or oven on in the kitchen?"

Calvin stood nearby with his arms crossed above his protruding stomach. "No, that fire started under the deck," he declared. "When I let Otis out, he started barkin', and I came out and saw the smoke. The deck was burnt up long before the flames reached the house."

"A grill on the back porch?" Stan suggested.

Jennifer shook her head and said in a small voice, "I don't have a grill. So that means … someone wanted … to kill me?"

As Michael squeezed her hand, Stan tried to calm her. "Now let's not jump to conclusions until I have a chance to investigate in the morning. If Mr. Woods' claim is true, we'll find evidence of it."

"Why would I be lyin'?" Calvin demanded, his gruff tone communicating offense.

"Calvin came to my rescue," Jennifer defended him, stepping away from Michael to place her arms around the older man in a loose hug. "And I have yet to thank him for it."

Calvin unfolded his arms and stumbled back, taken by surprise. As he did, Michael reached for Jennifer and pulled her to his side again, glancing at their neighbor with mistrust evident in his frown. "There's serious evidence of a crime. You aren't safe," he told Jennifer. "For now, I think you should come home with us."

James agreed, but he said, "Something's occurred to me, Stan. Jennifer wasn't supposed to be here tonight."

"That's true," the sheriff said, looking back at Jennifer. "Even my sister told me about you leaving for your interview in Savannah. Everybody knows, Jennifer, because they don't want you to go."

Jennifer blinked and looked at Michael. "Whether to scare me or to kill me, someone wants me to go. For good."

An hour later, Jennifer tossed and turned on the leather sofa in Michael's and James' darkened sunroom. The firemen had cleared the double-wide for her to return to her bathroom for sundry personal goods while James and Michael searched for Yoda, missing, of course, from the perch in the tree. Catless, they'd trekked across the yard to their historic doctor's house. Michael offered to give up his bed for Jennifer, but she knew she wouldn't sleep a wink enveloped in sheets that bore his scent. Neither was she having much luck here. The more she told herself she must sleep before tomorrow, the more awake she became. The excitement of the evening left her stirred up, her mind running to a hundred different possibilities.

Stan said her trip to Savannah would give him time to investigate the fire, the house to be cleared of smoke and any damage assessed. But she couldn't stop thinking of who might want her to leave enough to burn all her possessions to a crisp, and possibly her, too. The looming threat made her stomach churn.

Throwing off her blanket, she made a trip to the bathroom in the other hallway, one of the two resulting from the different additions onto the house. When she came out, she paused outside the door. The entrance to the office beckoned, empty, dark. What pictures or degrees had James hung on the wall? Had Michael's protest overruled? If so, what if that box sat in the closet where Michael suggested?

Jennifer tip-toed in and shut the door, then felt for the lamp she knew sat on the computer desk. Switching it on, she looked around at walls in the same state they'd been in when she'd last seen them. James must have joined Fig working on the cabin that day. She opened the door of the closet to find the box of towel-wrapped prints. Holding her breath, she tugged until the box slid over the closet threshold into the light. Reaching for the first frame, she flipped the towel off and stared with disbelieving eyes at ... Michael's M.D. degree from Emory.

Like a balloon deflating, all her breath left in a rush. With her heart thumping a heavy rhythm, Jennifer covered the degree up, put it back in the box and left the room as she found it.

No sleep for the weary and disillusioned. She paced in the glow of a nightlight in the kitchen, running her hand through her hair, flapping the edges of her suddenly hot robe. The cultured speech so unlike most construction workers, the concern about even a high-performing swimming career sidetracking his studies, and even the lingering intensity of loss over Ashley, all made sense. Why had he not told her?

Jennifer turned on the kitchen sink light and started opening cabinets in search of James' stash of hot tea. When she located a box of chamomile, she filled the tea kettle and clicked on the gas burner. Setting the honey beside the tea bag, she bent over the counter, breathing in long drags that soon turned to tears. She wanted out of here. She didn't want to stay another minute in a house with a man who claimed to care for her yet concealed who he really was.

Deciding she'd rather lie awake in her smoky double-wide, she clicked off the burner and whirled around ... straight into Michael's T-shirt clad chest. He took hold of her upper arms to steady her and asked in a rusty, confused voice, "What are you doing?"

Jennifer pulled away. "Nothing. I couldn't sleep, so I thought I'd make some chamomile tea." She took a quick brush at her watery eyes and added, "I think I'll just go home."

All sleepiness fled from Michael's expression as his dark eyebrows shot up. "What? You most certainly will not! Whoever set that fire could still be out there!"

She hadn't thought of that. Jennifer bit her lip and edged back and forth, weighing the risk and possible escape routes around Michael's tall, muscular frame.

"You aren't actually thinking of leaving still?" Michael demanded. "You look like you've been crying. What's got you so riled up? I mean, I know you're upset about the fire, but that's not it, is it? Something's got you wanting to leave. Are you uncomfortable staying here with us?" He lowered his voice. "You know my dad's here."

"That's not it." Embarrassed, she turned her back on him and, for lack of anything better to do, dropped the tea bag into a mug and poured hot water in.

"Then what is it?"

As Jennifer felt Michael's hand rub her shoulder, she shrugged it off and reached for the honey.

"Jennifer." His tone became stern, demanding a response.

She turned around and met his blue eyes with a withering glare. "I don't know, why don't you give me a diagnosis, *Dr.* Johnson?"

His face went blank, then understanding and dismay molded his handsome features. "Dad told you."

"No, the framed degree in your office told me."

His eyes opened wide. "You went snooping?"

Years of reinforced messages of worthlessness stirred at his question, and with them, anger at being forced to feel that way again. "You know what, you're right. It's your business, your past, your private life, nothing I need to know. I get it, Michael. I'm your employee, and maybe your friend, but if I were really more, you wouldn't have hidden something that big for months." When his only response was to stare, then blink, Jennifer plunked down the honey and started for the door. "Forget it. I think I'll take my chances with the boogeyman."

Michael grabbed her hand. "Please, Jennifer, don't. This is what I planned to tell you when I said we needed to talk."

She turned to look at him, miserable. "Michael, that was almost a week ago. And don't you think it might have come up long before now? Like maybe when we went to DePalma's and you told me about Ashley?"

"Yes. It should have. Will you please come, sit in the living room with me and let me try to explain?"

She sighed and stared straight ahead, considering. "I wouldn't have told you about Roy if I hadn't been pretty much forced to at the lake, so I get that there are some things you'd rather not discuss. But this is different, Michael. The fact that you were a doctor is something to be proud of, not to hide."

"But that's the thing. I'm not proud of it." He tipped his head toward the living room. "Please?"

Jennifer pulled her hand free and marched ahead of him, her tea forgotten. Michael switched on a small lamp and sat next to her on the sofa. She pulled a leg up under her and waited.

"So you know my grandmother, Gloria, filled my head with stories of my doctor ancestors growing up. I also thought it pretty cool that her mother had been a WWII combat nurse. When my grades proved strong enough for scholarship money from Emory, and my swim times made me a good fit on their team, it made sense to attend there. Not only is it a respected school for doctors with an associated hospital, their swim team is competitive in the NCAA. And it isn't D1, so I thought I could study without excessive pressure to train." He waited until Jennifer nodded, then continued. "Mom's death to a particularly aggressive and rare form of cancer focused my determination to become a doctor, and then, an oncologist."

Jennifer's eyes widened. "You're an oncologist?" James had mentioned something about that, but she'd never thought Michael had followed through on becoming one.

"Not quite. I met Ashley after I'd quit swimming and was in graduate school. I told you she became a nurse. We married, and I completed my three-year internal medicine residency. I'd gotten one year into the three-year oncology fellowship when she miscarried our first child and her cancer was found."

"Oh, Michael." Jennifer's face fell. Despite her hurt that he'd not shared this part of his life before, it was impossible to remain stoic at the recounting of such a tragic tale. "Was that when you walked away from medicine?"

He looked away from her. "That was when I should have. Instead I threw myself into my work, staying up 'til all hours researching, insisting she try experimental treatments and listening to her when she told me to not cut back on my surgical assisting to be with her. I told myself that was because we believed the gemcitabine and docetaxel would work. Taken together they showed a fifty-five percent response rate, as opposed to about thirty percent for other drugs. But I knew the real reason, and worse, so did she. It was why she told me to not quit the fellowship."

106

Jennifer lowered her leg to the ground and leaned a little closer. "And what was that?"

Michael shook his head, his mouth twisted with disgust. "I couldn't stand to watch her suffer, to watch a beautiful young woman waste away, lose her hair because I also insisted she add chemo even though it's not very effective with leiomyoscarcoma, and suffer from abdominal pain and bleeding. After the tumor metastasized to several places, when the spinal block failed, she couldn't even speak because of the pain." His voice broke, and Michael sat forward and covered his face with both hands. "We brought in ministers and prayer warriors. The elders of our church anointed her. We were instructed in every way how to have faith for her healing. But God didn't heal her. And her husband deserted her. But she remained gracious to the end. The light of Jesus never faded."

When Michael's uneven breathing dissolved into weeping, Jennifer sat forward, too, and pulled his head against her. She wrapped her arms around his upper body and kissed his hair. The sight of his pain made her heart feel like it might split in two. "I didn't mean to make you recount all that," she whispered. "I just wanted to know why you didn't tell me you were a doctor."

He wiped his face and pulled away. "Because I'm not. When Ashley died the same way Mom died, I shut the door on that chapter of my life. If nothing I knew could help the two women most important to me, why continue? It felt worthless. Laughable. Cancer made a cruel joke of me."

"You also shut the door on God along with medicine, didn't you?" Jennifer questioned gently.

"No. I still know He's God. I just realized I didn't understand Him as well as I thought I did."

"But you didn't want to be close to Him anymore ... or people, either, for that matter."

"Maybe." Michael blinked moisture from his eyes and looked at her without expression. "I should have told you. It just never seemed the right time. But can you see why it's easier if I let people think I've always just been with Dad's construction company?"

"Yes. But I think you're denying like what, a decade of your life, ever happened."

Michael let out a disgusted puff of air and shook his head. "So be it. I'd rather that than have to listen to all the reasons I'm wasting my medical training and should go back to doctoring. They tell me how my compassion could be a gift to others. How God wants to use it."

"He could, if you'd let Him heal you first."

Michael growled in frustration and reached for her, pulling her next to him with their backs against the sofa cushions. "Not you, too," he murmured. "I didn't tell you, because I didn't want to hear it from you. I just want you to understand, and I think you of all people should, that it's simpler this way. I pound a nail, and it goes in. I saw a board, and it cuts. No guess work, no disappointment, no watching people suffer and not being able to fix it."

Jennifer took his hand and rubbed her fingers over it, trying to imagine when it had been smooth and uncalloused, a surgeon's hand. She kissed his palm. "I do, if you're truly happy working on wood rather than people."

"I am." He focused a steady stare on her, as if trying to convince her.

"OK. Then I won't say anything else about it now."

"Now?" He smirked at her implied meaning. "Fine. As long as you forgive me for keeping this to myself for so long."

She fell silent, not meeting his eyes. "I'm still a little hurt you didn't trust me."

"I'm sorry," he said again, brushing her chin with his thumb. "I told you, I don't tell this to anyone. And part of me said, why should I if you might still leave me for Savannah. Where you're going tomorrow, I might add."

"Maybe today." She didn't even want to look around for a clock. Her gaze swung back to his and she blurted out the question that had risen to her mind when she'd tried to add up all his years of medical school. "How old are you, anyway?"

A corner of his mouth turned up. "Thirty-two."

Jennifer feigned alarm and dismay. "Oh, my goodness, you're too old for me."

Instead of laughing, Michael cupped her face with his hands and shook his head in amazement, staring into her eyes. "How can you find something to laugh about after all I've shared? After all you've been through? I can't believe how much of you is untouched, preserved.

Your view of things is so simple and clear. Somehow it's still easy for you to see the light."

"I can see it because you and your dad and the people who live here have shown it to me."

"Then please don't leave."

Her heart softened. "It's not my plan," she whispered. Wanting to comfort him, she slid her hand around his neck and leaned in to kiss his cheek, but Michael turned his head and covered her mouth with his. This kiss went deeper, and he didn't wait to gauge her reaction. At first she was OK. She longed to be close to him. So she responded as his mouth moved over hers with an urgency she hadn't sensed before.

When Michael paused, his lips a fraction from her own, something Jennifer saw and felt from him caused her heart to pound and her stomach to churn. Need. He'd just unburdened his heart to her, and he waited for her response. Yes, need, but something else. Desire. The combination created a war of conflicting response. She wanted him to want her, but now that he did, what did she do with that? She wanted to comfort him, but the way she'd been forced to comfort men in the past was wrong, all wrong.

With a soft moan, Michael pressed his mouth to hers again, tangling his fingers in her hair to better draw her in. Sympathy and admiration battled with fear and resentment. She couldn't breathe, and she felt trapped, but she didn't dare pull away for fear of hurting his feelings or making him mad. Still, panic mounted so fast Jennifer prepared to protest and struggle away when he moved back.

Of course he did. This was Michael. She could trust him, she thought with a sense of relief as he tucked her in on the sofa with the pillow under her head. He sat beside her on the outside edge. "I'll heat up your tea," he whispered. She nodded, grateful, but he didn't get up. And a minute later, he put an arm over her and, on his side, stretched his length beside her.

Jennifer's heart hammered. Surely he could feel it under the quilt and would realize he was scaring her. Her eyes wide open, she watched him like a field mouse watches an owl on an overhead branch. He rested his head next to her and just looked at her, his blue eyes unfathomable. Was he testing her? Testing himself? Why? Or did he need something from her? What?

Confused, Jennifer snaked a hand out from under the cover and intertwined her fingers with Michael's. "You OK?"

"Yeah." He buried his face in her shoulder and kissed her collarbone.

A shiver went up her spine, and when she felt the tempo of his breathing pick up, she panicked. "I think you should go," she whispered, and she couldn't stop her voice from shaking.

"Right." Michael raised his head, and when he looked at her, sadness shuttered his eyes. "Sorry," he said as he hoisted himself off the couch. Walking to the door, he glanced back once. He didn't bring her tea.

CHAPTER EIGHT

She'd messed up. She'd messed up so bad she better convince this friend of Barbara's that she possessed irresistible qualifications for this job, in case facing Michael again proved more painful than she could bear. So Jennifer did just that. She drew on every social skill she possessed and prayed for God's help when, on two hours of sleep, those ran out.

Clad in the autumn wrap dress she'd worn to the coffee bar opening, slid on at dawn in her smoky double-wide, and aired out with an open sun roof on the drive down, she managed to mince confidently in her unfamiliar heels through the halls and offices of the restored Greek Revival town house just off Madison Square that constituted Savannah Heritage Trust. Tandy, a tall, slim, ginger-haired woman slightly older than Barbara, told her their company offered the unique services of two teams, preservation and restoration specialists, and the general contractors accustomed to carrying out their directions with finesse. SHT took pride in adhering to the guidelines put forth by the Department of Interior. Their list of clients included some of the most noteworthy private and public buildings not only in the city but up and down the coast. In her interview, Jennifer thought she came across as confident about working with those clients while supervising a crew of contractors. When Tandy asked why she wanted to move to Savannah and work for SHT, Jennifer related how she'd always dreamed of doing just this sort of work in the state's premier historic city.

And she wasn't lying. What history lover wouldn't want to live in Savannah, with its sea gulls, Spanish moss, plethora of amazing architectural styles tracing back to Colonial days, and intricate grid of beautiful public squares, each its own mini-park, laid out originally as military training grounds?

A monument of Revolutionary War Siege of Savannah hero, William Jasper, commanded the center. It was surrounded by St. John's Episcopal Church, the 1841 Sorrel-Weed House, E. Shafer Books, and a Masonic temple housing the Victorian pharmacy-themed Gryphon Tea Room. The Green-Meldrum House, adds historic merit with the story of its Civil War-era owner, who rode out to offer General Sherman use of his home when the Union occupation of the city proved inevitable. Savannah offered Jennifer's ultimate shop of flavorful historic delights.

But she did notice the balmy weather held little hint of fall, while the hardwood leaves turned and the breezes hinted of chill and wood smoke in the Piedmont. And as they navigated to the 1753 Pirate's House, clearly Tandy's condescending nod to Jennifer's tourist status, Jennifer marveled at the traffic and all the people she didn't know walking the sidewalks. Oh, not Atlanta, to be sure, but such a far cry from Hermon. She reminded herself she'd make friends and associates quickly through work. And church. She asked Tandy about good churches. Tandy told her which ones boasted the most historical features.

In the restaurant, Jennifer admired the view down into brick-lined tunnels leading out to the river once used by pirates and smugglers but ordered the buffet rather than off the menu to save time. Her worry over what Michael might be thinking about her today, not to mention wondering what Stan and the firefighters determined about last night's blaze during their investigation made it difficult to focus on Tandy's review of her latest big project.

"So what else are you plannin' to do here?" the older woman asked.

"I thought I would drive down to the beach."

"Oh, are you spendin' the night? If you want real ocean rather than river and marshes, you do know it's a good half hour out to Tybee."

Jennifer blinked. "No, I didn't remember that."

"It's lovely, though. On your way out, check out Fort Pulaski at the mouth of the Savannah River. It's worth gettin' a hotel room and putzin' around the area. What do you have to hurry back to?"

What indeed? Hmm, back to a smoky double-wide with an unknown arsonist-slash-probable-prior-assailant still on the prowl? And a man she loved who'd deceived her? Let's face it, she'd had to corner him to get him to open up to her. Then she'd acted like a fool, showing him a scared and scarred little girl the one time he'd looked for a woman. Like Kelly always said, she didn't know how to deal with what she asked for where men were concerned. She and

Michael, they were both dysfunctional. Both of them would do better with someone who already had their life in order.

"In fact …" Tandy was pulling out her cell phone and tapping the screen. "Let me just contact my friend at the East Bay Inn and reserve a room for you. Off-season, week day, should be no problem."

"Oh, no, it's OK," Jennifer protested, hurrying to touch Tandy's wrist before she could dial.

Tandy looked up, her taupe-highlighted hazel eyes blank with surprise. "Honey, it's on me. Consider it part of my hostessin'. I want you to get the full Savannah experience. I'm only ashamed I didn't think of it sooner. I've just been so distracted with my husband's travel plans."

"You don't need to do that. I … really do need to get back." Her voice attempted to convey decisiveness, but Jennifer's protest sounded lame even in her own ears.

"Are you sure?" Her companion looked disappointed. "I hope you have enough of a feel of our city to make an informed decision. I can let you in on a little secret. I'm goin' to Italy. I've already spoken with the firm owner about Barbara replacing me, so it's almost a sure thing she will be comin' here. So it's just a matter of who comes with her, and we both know she wants you."

The fine hairs on Jennifer's arms raised. "Wow," she murmured. "I appreciate you telling me that. I wonder if Barb has considered what she'll do after the year she fills in for you."

Tandy sipped from her water goblet, then patted her mouth with her napkin. "Well, first off, my husband still has family in Italy, and I expect to love it there. I mean, what's not to love, right? Chances are good we won't return. I'm preparin' my boss for that fact. Even if Barb doesn't stay on with SHT, I can guarantee by the end of the year our rival firm and the local preservation schools will be competin' to gobble her up. She's already got lots of connections here from the field studies she's coordinated for UGA."

"Oh." Jennifer stared at the exposed beams above her hostess' head, then pulled her attention back to the matter at hand. "You've given me a great snapshot of the job and the area." She pressed her lips together in a smile. "There's no doubt Savannah and SHT offer far more than Hermon."

Tandy rolled her lipstick up from its tube. "And that dinky little job in that other town, too, right?" She winked, then painted.

Smiling, Jennifer felt sad as she pictured her two options, the quaint, green, concrete block ex-gas station with a Philips 66 sign still out front, or the crown-molded office the window of which framed the palms and live oaks planted in the wrought-iron enclosed, courtyard garden. "Right." Then she pictured two faces, Michael's and Barbara's, and almost warned Tandy relationships could be game changers. But she bit her tongue. No need to burn a bridge until she knew how Michael would act when she got home. Home ...

She pulled out her cell phone and saw that no messages had arrived, no calls had been missed.

After Tandy dropped her off at the parking garage where she'd left her Civic, Jennifer decided the drive to the beach would be worth it. She put Tybee into her phone's map program and followed the bridges out of town. She sped past the left-hand turn-off to the Civil War fort, feeling only a twinge of regret at not stopping. Exploring empty barracks and mess halls from another century sounded lonely by herself.

Jennifer's thoughts screeched to a halt. Since when had her appetite to tour any historic structure depended on companionship? Another evidence of how Hermon had changed her.

Pulling her hair back into a pony tail, Jennifer locked her car and fed the meter just off the wind-swept stretch of shore. Walking over a bridge of wooden planking, she climbed past sea oats and over sand dunes to get to the water's edge, her spirit opening up at the expanse of sea and sky. She walked, looking away from the line of condos and hotels at the waves. Way out there, the mast of a tall ship appeared. She could relate, alone on a big sea, not sure where to anchor.

God, she prayed, *I need you to show me. Everything logical says Savannah. Everything in my heart says Hermon. But I still don't know if I can be around Michael if he's not mine, and I don't know how to make him mine.*

So what if he'd taken her off guard or required too much last night. He wouldn't have hurt her. But no matter how patient he was, there would come a time when she'd need to trust him with everything, and that made all her old fears and memories foment like those waves. He'd probably realized by her pop-eyed, heart-pounding reaction that marrying such a soiled dove meant a very demanding and sensitive road ahead for a long time to come. What kind of guy would sign up for that? Especially one with money, looks, intelligence, personality and an M.D., for heaven's sake?

Could you make him willing to try, God? And, could you maybe work on him before I see him tomorrow, so I don't die of embarrassment?

Jennifer looked down as a wave swirled too close to the toe of the Mary Janes she'd changed into. To her right, she noticed a flash of white. a sand dollar. Bending down to pick it up, Jennifer wondered that it would be here this time of day. She decided to take it as a sign. She put it in her pocket and searched for butterfly and cornucopia shells.

After an hour she felt relaxed enough to head inland. Still full from her big lunch, she stopped at a Starbuck's for a restroom, latte and muffin, dinner on the road. From there she texted Michael to ask if they'd located Yoda. Her phone rang as she pulled onto the highway. Michael's name came up on the screen, causing her heart to pound.

"Hello?" she answered.

"Hi." His husky, sheepish voice alone made her flush. "Are you on your way back?"

"Yes. What's happening there?"

"We found the cat," he offered as though that was the most important thing.

Maybe to Jennifer's fractured emotions it was. "Oh, good," she breathed.

"A can of Fancy Feast and two bowls of warm milk later, she's sleeping on our sofa."

"OK. And what did Stan say?"

"They believe rags soaked with gasoline started the fire under the deck, like Calvin thought."

It felt like the bottom dropped out of her heart. She closed her eyes for a moment on a pine-lined straight-away. "Oh, my stars."

"So far no other evidence has turned up. They've been questioning all the neighbors, but no one saw anything."

"Of course not."

"It's not safe for you to sleep there alone. Listen, I know you don't want to stay here again, but Stella is very upset and is offering for you to gather some things and stay with her. Stan thinks that would be a good idea."

"I ... don't know, Michael." Right now she just wanted to be home alone. "How bad is the damage?"

"Nothing essential is harmed. I've been in touch with the owners today, and they'll contact the insurance to replace some siding and re-build the back deck. The fire didn't get into the plumbing, flooring or electrical wires in the kitchen. That's a miracle, and thanks to Calvin. Unless of course ..."

Jennifer's fingers tightened on the steering wheel. "You suspect him, don't you?"

Michael released a ragged sigh and admitted, "I don't know. I can't figure what motive anyone would have to harm you, or even to scare you, Calvin included. I feel bad about this."

She grabbed a quick swig of coffee. "It's not your fault, Michael."

"Maybe not, but the quicker we wrap up work on the cabin, the better."

His words pierced her heart as she shoved her cup back into the holder. "Then what?" The words burst out of her mouth, her emotions surging too strong to check. "So I can leave? Or should I go ahead and leave now?"

"No, Jennifer. For your safety," he clarified, sounding exasperated. "Just to another location. To stay with someone, like Stella." But that's not what he'd said. He'd spoken of finishing work on the cabin, which meant her work in Hermon would be done. Jennifer's heart thudded painfully. A moment of silence ensued before he added, "How did it go today?"

"Great." She spit the word out and bit down on her bottom lip.

"I figured." His voice sounded sarcastic. "Listen, about last night ..."

"Please—"

"No, I need to say I'm sorry. You were already shaken by the fire, rightfully mad about finding the degree, and a guest in my home. All reasons I should have respected your space. I acted stupid, and I shouldn't have put you in a position where you felt uncomfortable in any way."

She swallowed. "It's OK. I acted stupid, too."

"I guess we've both got a lot of past junk coming up right now, huh?"

"Yeah. But we can deal with it with God's help, right?"

"Sure. Listen, you've got two choices, Stella's or a police patrol tonight. I'm sure the officer on night duty would rather hang out at the station than in your driveway."

Michael's rush to brush past her spiritual reference rather than reassure her stung. Regardless of his apology for pushing her boundaries, he'd taken her reaction to his advances either as a hurtful rejection or a sign of how hopelessly she was damaged. Either way, a wall had been erected, one she felt too insecure at the moment to try again to scale. She said in a brisk voice, "As soon I get home, I'll call one or the other." Seizing a timely electronic ping that sounded in her ear as an excuse, she added, "I've got to go. Someone's dinging my phone."

It was only Barbara, texting that, as the expected freeze had not occurred and the forecast now predicted a string of milder days, her friend's class would commence the outhouse dig at eight a.m. Monday. When Jennifer got home, she'd have to remember to text Amy, Grace and several other community archeological enthusiasts about the new date and time.

Jennifer lifted her Starbuck's cup, frowning as she sipped tepid liquid. She remembered what Stella said about praise music and turned on the radio. But the tenor of Michael's call had shaken the inner calm briefly found at the beach, and fretful thoughts butted into her prayers the rest of the way home.

Dark had fallen by the time Jennifer punctured the southerly speed zone of Hermon. Her heart lurched as she drove past Michael's house, noticing a light in the parlor window. For a second she allowed herself to envision being there, sitting in front of the fire with a book, or watching a movie with Michael in the sunroom den—using his office computer for her research, waking up in the four-poster bed in the master. Nope. Couldn't go there. If she couldn't even imagine it, how could she think for a second it could ever become reality?

With a sense of weary relief, she pulled into her own driveway, but her homecoming contentment fled the next minute. An Altima with a dent in the door sat where she normally parked … and her mother sat with her head in her hands on her front porch steps.

"Mama? What in the world are you doing here?"

Kelly stood up as Jennifer approached. "I'm sorry, honey, to surprise you like this, an' you got every right to send me on my way." Anxiety made Kelly's twangy voice more nasal than usual. She wrung her hands in front of the tight-fitting black pants and button-busting, tailored white blouse that constituted her uniform for the steakhouse where she waited tables. "But before you do, do you reckon you could hear me out? Just for a minute?"

Jennifer closed her gaping mouth, swallowed and said, "Sure. Let me unlock the door. How long have you been sitting there? Why didn't you go over to Michael's? He would have let you wait there." She fumbled on her key ring as she opened the storm door, struggling to portray calm rather than the dismay and alarm that filled her. If she'd thought the socializing at the gala brought her to the verge of a meltdown, her fragile senses threatened cataclysm of nuclear proportions now.

As she slid the key in the lock, Kelly came up behind her. "About an hour, but that's OK. I could use the extra time to think. Besides, I didn't want your boss to see me like this."

"Like what?" Jennifer turned around, then gasped. In the porch light, she saw that her mother's smeared mascara oozed onto a purpling bruise on her one cheekbone. She grabbed Kelly's chin. "For heaven's sake, Mom, did Roy do that?"

Kelly pulled away. "Don't matter. He won't never do it again. I always told 'im the first time he put a hand to me, I'd leave."

Jennifer froze as the implications of this statement came clear. Her mother had left her stepfather. Finally. And not over Jennifer's abuse, but over a slap to the face. "Come in and tell me what happened."

In the dark house, Jennifer turned on lights.

Kelly sniffed. "Did you burn somethin' in the oven?"

Apparently Kelly's own drama had rendered her incapable of noticing the police tape in Jennifer's back yard. "No, Mom, I had a fire last night. As in, someone set fire to my back deck."

The raccoon eyes widened to half-moons. "Whaaat? Who would do such a thing? And did they get caught?"

"I don't know, and not yet." Jennifer sighed, deciding she was too weary to update her mother on the string of unusual incidents. If Kelly didn't ask, that story could wait until tomorrow. "I've got to go to the bathroom, and I imagine you might, too. There's one right here in the hall."

"Well, yes, but are we safe here?"

It was good question. Jennifer dug out her cell phone and assured her mother, "Stella's brother is the sheriff. I'll call him right now and verify that we'll be staying here tonight and would like his officer to patrol the area, unless, that is, you'd rather us go over to Stella's." In fact, her screen showed that Stella had tried to call while she talked to Kelly on the porch.

Tears swam in Kelly's eyes. "To be honest, I don't think I can handle one more thing at the moment."

Jennifer touched her mother's arm. "It's OK. I'll make the call, then we'll sit down and talk." The Oglethorpe policeman and God would just have to keep them safe. After dialing Stan, receiving his assurance his officer would camp out in the driveway until dawn, and texting Stella of her plans and her mother's arrival, Jennifer dumped her purse and heels and made a quick change into sweats. Returning to the living room, she found Kelly sitting on the sofa, staring straight ahead and looking shell shocked.

"Can I get you a drink?" Jennifer asked.

"Well, I would say yes, but I bet you don't have anything stronger than coffee. So I guess I'll take some coffee."

"I think I have something better."

In the kitchen, she put her tea kettle on and found Allison's "Comfort and Calm" tea bag. On second thought, Jennifer pulled out another one. Not only did she live in a mysterious crime zone, but her difficult mother had just stolen her solitude. And who knew what kind of woeful tale Jennifer was about to hear? She needed "Comfort and Calm" more than her mother.

Kelly looked up from sniffling into a tissue as Jennifer returned to the living room and handed her a mug. "What's this?"

"Chamomile and valerian tea, with honey."

Her mother accepted the offering and took a tentative sip. "Not bad. Thanks." Kelly paused to eye her through the steam coming off her cup. "I know I got no cause to expect you to take me in, but I didn't know where else to go. And I needed to tell you how sorry I was."

"For what?"

Kelly started crying again. "For everything," she mumbled as she reached to set the mug on the coffee table.

Jennifer slid a coaster under the tea, frowning. She was afraid to trust Kelly's contrition. Best to hear the story first. "Why don't you start at the beginning?"

Dabbing with her tissue, her mother nodded. "Well, we got your letter. At first, I have to admit it made me mad. I felt like you were bein' holier than thou and still accusin' Roy of things I couldn't bear to think were true. He wouldn't read it. Finally he did. I knew because I found the burnt pieces in the trash can."

"Oh, wow." Jennifer's stomach sank.

"I've suspected for a while he's been carryin' on with someone. I just didn't know who. Today I came home unexpectedly between lunch and dinner shift. I found 'em in our bed." Kelly's dark-rimmed eyes fired with anger. "It was the eighteen-year-old, skinny as a stick, scraggly little girl they'd hired to answer the phone at the garage. Not even outta high school."

"Oh, my stars, Mama. I'm so sorry." Jennifer's heart went out to her mother. All the years she'd been with Roy, Kelly had thought she'd made a good choice because he'd brought home decent money, schmoozed friends with his redneck charm, and he'd never hit her or cheated on her that she could prove. Jennifer had long believed he'd just been sly about it. Until now. Maybe her letter made him reckless. "What did you do?"

"I drug her by her skanky hair to the door and kicked her out. Then I got my suitcase."

"Good for you. Did Roy try to stop you?"

"He told me she didn't mean anything to him. He started tryin' to tell me he felt neglected by me, that if I'd been there for 'im more he wouldn'ta needed to look elsewhere. You know how he turns things on you."

Jennifer sighed. "Yes, I do."

"That was when I told him that judgin' from his choice of bed partner maybe what you said in your letter was true, and he hit me.

Then he told me if I believed that I should get out and take my lies with me. He stormed out and left. So I packed my stuff and got the boxes of your childhood things. They're all in the car. Everything I need is in the car. I don't care about anything I left. He can have it all. I used my debit card to clean my money out of the account at the ATM in town. I'm done."

Jennifer gaped at Kelly, never having seen her mother so resolute. But then, she'd never found another female in bed with her husband, either. "What about Rab?"

"He's a waste. Roy's ruined 'im." Kelly shook her bleached blonde hair. "Went and got his girlfriend pregnant. Found out about that last week. I ain't raisin' no baby in my old age. The way I see it, this was God's clear call for me to get outta Sodom."

Jennifer's eyebrows flew up at her mother's biblical reference. "Do you have any sort of long-term plan?" she asked.

Kelly's face fell. "Not really. I can go to Alabama where my sister is. She'll help me find a place, and I can always wait tables. But first, I was hopin' to make things right with you." Kelly looked at her, unblinking. "Once I got over bein' mad, the words of your letter kept comin' back to me, about how you found Jesus and He helped you let go of the past. And forgive us." Kelly paused, buried her face in her tissue. "I don't deserve forgivin'.".

"Oh, Mama." Jennifer moved to sit next to Kelly and placed a hand on her shoulder. "None of us do."

Kelly shook her head. "But you didn't do nothin' to warrant what you got. I'm guilty. I turned a blind eye. I denied the signs, all to preserve my own selfish skin. I deserve to be shot as a mother."

Jennifer's heart beat heavy. For most of her life she'd waited to hear Kelly say those words. She felt a warm presence there with them, hovering, guiding the conversation. Could it be that just when everything appeared to be falling apart, God prepared to do something miraculous? "Are you saying you believe me?" she asked, breathless.

Kelly nodded. "I do. I was too afraid of bein' without a man to acknowledge it before, but lookin' back now, I do. And I'm so sorry. I can't even bear my mind to think about what that monster did to you." Kelly glanced at her, reaching for her hand. "Can it really be true what you said, that you've really already forgiven me?" The older woman blinked, and another tear slid out of her blue eye.

Jennifer squeezed her hand. "It is. When we come to accept Christ as Lord of our lives, He gives us strength through His Spirit who comes to live inside us to do things we couldn't do on our own. I've been in counseling, and I also see how your own childhood made you vulnerable."

"Then I think I need to learn more about this Jesus, 'cause He doesn't sound like who I thought He was."

A smile spread over Jennifer's face. "You've come to the right place."

CHAPTER NINE

Jennifer put Kelly to bed in the spare room. The next morning, Jennifer slept past her alarm but dressed quickly, remembering Fig was supposed to apply his second coat of wood preservative to the cabin today. She needed to be active, to keep her mind off the uncertainty of her future decisions and relationships. Mindful that her mother still slept, she got coffee and breakfast quietly, then let herself out the front door into the chilly morning. She waved at the officer in the patrol car parked in her yard. He waved back and, as she headed across the grass toward Michael's, pulled out onto the main road.

Since Fig planned to work alone, he had not brought a second pressure tank and sprayer. "Thought you didn't approve of my chemicals," he said in surprise at her offer to help.

Jennifer gave him a faint smile. "The important thing is to finish the job the way Michael wants. He has the equipment in his shed. I'll just go ask."

Easier said than done. Maybe if she got lucky, James would answer the back door rather than Michael. Of course, that didn't happen. Wearing a flannel shirt with jeans and work boots, Michael pushed open the storm door. However, to her joy and relief, he held Yoda in his arms. Blessed, furry ice breaker.

"Morning," he said. "I'm glad to see you're OK."

"I'm glad to see Yoda's OK!" Jennifer leaned in to pet the cat and press her face against the fuzzy nose. The feline rewarded her with a purr, but the spicy and now-familiar scent of Michael's aftershave made her pull back. "Yes. The officer just left. What are you up to today?"

"Dad and I were just getting ready to meet the guys over at the old store … or I guess we should call it the art gallery now." He grinned, bending down and releasing the cat's lanky length to the freedom of the great outdoors. "Stella's on her way, too, for a walk-through. We want her to see the rooms we marked out before we start framing today."

"Oh, that's great!"

"Do you wanna come in?"

Jennifer declined and explained her need for a pressure tank. "Could you let me in your shed?"

"Sure, just a minute. I'll grab the keys."

A minute later Michael returned and stepped onto the porch with her, offering her a polite smile. Jennifer smiled back, wrapping her arms around herself. Despite his pleasantries, she sensed a difference between them, like they'd taken about ten steps back from the day at the park. Maybe it had to do with the fact that he in no way tried to touch her, and in fact kept some physical distance between them. But the man who'd cried in front of her and kissed her with such need had retreated behind the composed employer-friend from back in the summer. It made her stomach ache with loss.

The crunch of gravel under tires relieved the tension of the moment, and they both turned to see Stella's car pulling in. She waved. They waited while she parked in front of the back porch and got out, wrapping a long, multi-colored, loose-weave cardigan around her cotton shirt and jeans.

"Honey, just you come'ere," Stella called, reaching for Jennifer before the younger woman got down the steps. Her embrace felt like hot chocolate after being out in the snow, making Jennifer realize how much she needed balm for emotions scraped raw over the job situation, Michael, the fire and her mother. "I couldn't sleep last night for worryin' about you! Are you OK?"

Jennifer nodded and started to reply when Michael's attention fixed on the Altima he noticed in front of the double-wide. In a voice roughened by suspicion, he asked, "Who's at your house?"

Kelly herself provided the answer, choosing that moment to step onto the front porch, setting a travel mug of coffee and a pack of cigarettes on the rail. As she lit one and took a draw, she looked around, still somehow managing to appear small and vulnerable. Spotting them, Kelly waved. "My mother," Jennifer supplied in a dry tone.

"What?"

"Well, I knew, I don't know why you didn't," Stella said, frowning at him. "You supposed to be keepin' an eye on this girl. Jennifer, I'm afraid I must insist you and her both come stay with me for a couple of days. I didn't want to be too pushy last night, because I knew your mother had just arrived, and you said she was upset. I knew you'd both want to sleep well and you'd need to get some things together, but please, come on over tonight."

"Why is she upset?" Michael wanted to know, posture stiff after his cousin's mild rebuke.

Jennifer decided she'd better fill both of them in, and fast. Having taken another drag before hastening to extinguish her cigarette, Kelly now walked their way. Her shiner would really glow in the morning sun. "She found my stepfather with an eighteen-year-old girl. And he hit her," she said. "She believes me now about the past. She's left him. Her car is full of her things."

"Oh, no," Stella moaned, putting a well-manicured hand to her mouth. "Dear Lord, please bless her heart, and yours, as if you didn't have enough to deal with. What a mess. How can I help?"

Jennifer reached for Stella's hand and spoke fast. "I do need your help. She asked for my forgiveness last night and said she wants to know more about Jesus."

"Oh, honey, that's great. That's just what we've been prayin' for, isn't it, Michael?" Stella asked, glancing at the silent man beside her, who assessed Kelly's advance with a skeptical stare.

"It is, if she's truly looking for a change and not just a place to stay."

Stella blinked at him before addressing Jennifer, "I tell you what, I'll invite her to come on over to my place. I'll pick her up as soon as we do this walk-through. That will give us some nice, quiet time before the boys get home. Sunday, we can all go to church together."

"Perfect. Thank you so much, Stella," Jennifer said.

"There y'all are," Kelly said as she walked up, hunching over her coffee cup in a self-effacing posture cocooned by the opposing scents of shampoo and nicotine smoke. "I got a little spooked when I woke up in the house all alone."

"Nice to see you again, Kelly," Michael said, and shook her hand.

"You, too, Mr. Johnson."

"Michael, please."

Stella gave her a hug. "I don't blame you a bit for bein' uneasy," she said, "with all the accidents Jennifer's had recently. It makes perfect sense you'd feel the need to come check on her. I'm tryin' to convince her to stay at my house while my brother investigates this fire, but she's a little stubborn. As her mama, maybe you can help me convince her."

Kelly looked blankly from Stella to Jennifer. "Accidents?"

Now Stella had done it. Jennifer sighed. To her relief, Michael spared her by relating the string of incidents occurring on the property in a matter-of-fact and concise manner, stating how bad he felt about them since Jennifer fell under his employ, and how confused they all were about who would want to harm or scare them away from completing the restoration project. He concluded with, "I agree with Stella, Kelly. I think you and Jennifer would be safer staying with her for a few days. We can't keep a county officer out here at all hours."

"My guest room has twin beds," Stella offered. "It would be perfect. Just let Stan do his work. I don't know if I'm supposed to tell you, but he did find some tire prints over on the vacant lot next to Michael's. He's trying to match those to a vehicle make now."

"This is crazy," Kelly said. "And that isn't even why I was spooked."

"Why were you spooked?" Jennifer asked.

Kelly looked embarrassed, shifting her weight. "Just a dream I had, is all."

"What was the dream?"

"When I woke up I thought I saw a man standing at the foot of my bed. A big man. I felt this ... unease." Kelly rubbed her arms.

"Well, I guess you did!" Stella cried.

"Was someone really there?" Michael demanded, glancing at Jennifer.

"I don't think so. I think it was a dream, or I was seein' things. I just got this bad feelin'. I thought I'd sleep like a baby, gettin' away from Roy at last, but I hate to say it ... and no disrespect ..." Kelly glanced at Michael. "But this property gives me the creeps."

"Well, OK," Stella announced in a tone of such assurance you'd think they'd just passed a senate resolution. "That settles it. You two will come stay with me. I'll pick you up in about an hour if that's all right, Kelly. Jennifer can come later. And right now, let's just join hands and pray."

"What ... are we praying for?" Kelly wanted to know in a dubious voice, reluctantly placing her mug on the gravel at her feet.

"For the release of this property from whatever evil is holding it and whatever mischief anyone is up to," Stella said, holding her hands out. "Something we should have done months ago. I'm right ashamed of myself for taking this long to get around to it."

Michael laughed and gave her his hand. "You'll get used to my cousin," he teased Kelly.

She gave him an uncertain smile and took the hands of Stella and Jennifer. When Jennifer's hand slipped into Michael's, a warm sense of safety filled her.

"Dear Lord," Stella said once their heads bowed and eyes closed, "we come before You in agreement that we need You in this situation. We don't know what is going on to cause dangerous incidents and feelings of unease on this property, whether it be spiritual, or physical, or both. We've prayed for Jennifer's protection before, Lord, and we thank you for being gracious to answer those requests, but right now we just lift this property and this situation before You. We ask that you will be with Stan and his officers as they seek to find answers and bring anyone guilty to justice. Let whatever is hidden be revealed and whatever is covered be made known. If there is evil, we bind it, Lord, we bind it in Jesus' name. And we pray for the release of Your power, authority, peace and safety, that this may become a place of peace and fellowship for all who come here. We take authority over this situation and this ground we stand on, in Jesus' mighty name. Amen."

"Amen," Jennifer echoed. She opened her eyes to find her mother staring at Stella as though she'd thrown back her cardigan to reveal a blue and red "S" on her chest. She couldn't resist a quiet laugh. "Now, um, I really need to get that sprayer, or Fig's going to be done with the whole cabin before I get over there," she said.

"Oh, sure," Michael agreed.

"Before you go," Stella put in before they could walk off, "won't you give us a quick recap of how the interview went yesterday?"

Jennifer nodded and shared some particulars. She finished by relating what Tandy said about her desire and ability to clear the path with her boss for employment for both Jennifer and Barbara.

"Barbara's going?" Michael frowned at her. "You never told me that. Like she'd be your boss?"

"Sort of."

"That pushy professor who hugged you at graduation?" Kelly wanted to know.

Jennifer flushed. Funny, even her mother's rusty radar registered concern over Barb, although Roy had duped her for years. "Yes, that's her. Trust me, I was surprised, too. I didn't know myself until recently, and it was all a bit iffy, so I didn't say anything. But Tandy made it sound like we could both be installed by the first of the year if that's what we decide."

Stella pressed her full lips together and said, "Mmmm."

Michael responded with more directness. "I thought the idea was to get away from Barbara and make your own way in the world."

She glanced at him. "It is."

"Well, you can hardly do that if she follows you to Savannah, now can you?"

Her defenses flared, an ingrained reaction at being told what to do, especially by a man. "It's not ideal, but that's the way it is, and it's a strong job offer, much stronger than Lexington."

"Whatever. It has to be your decision. Listen, I'll just grab the pump." With a hand wave behind him, Michael shook out his keys and strode toward the shed. He also waved at Fig, who erected his ladder near a corner of the cabin.

"Gee, what's eatin' Gilbert Grape?" Kelly said, brushing a wet leaf off the bottom of her cup and taking a long draw from the slit on top.

"He been like this since the sermon at the park?" Stella asked Jennifer, who nodded. "Well, that's just more to pray about. Michael and your daughter, Kelly, well, they like each other, but they got some things to work out."

"Like each other?" Kelly echoed. She play punched Jennifer in the side and said accusingly, "You didn't tell me! That hunk?"

"There's a lot I haven't told you, Mama," Jennifer admitted, rubbing her toe in the dirt.

"Well, I can't blame you. I ain't been much of a mama to her," Kelly said to Stella with brutal honesty. "But I want that to change. I really do. I guess it sounds like I might have to follow her to Savannah and wait tables at some seaside pub. Just us two girls, huh?" Kelly bumped her hip against her daughter's. "Might be nice."

Jennifer mustered a smile, uncomfortable and still untrusting of this new side to her mother.

Stella put her hands on her hips. "Well, I sure hope not. This with the professor goin' puts a new light on things. That's one thing Michael and I agree on. And as for changin', you're in just the right place, Miss Kelly, if you're willin' to let the Lord help you."

"I am, Miss Stella," Kelly teased. "I reckon when you're as low as I am, you can't go much lower. Only way to go is up."

"Well, let's start climbin'. Come get you in an hour?"

"Yes, ma'am."

Golden mums exploded from the beds in front of Stella's Gothic Revival cottage, while various-sized white and orange pumpkins crowded the sides of the steps. The smell of meatloaf and the yapping of Truffle the Pomeranian greeted Jennifer when Jamal let her in the front door. Truffle pranced his way into Stella's special parlor and jumped up onto his towel on the prized, peach silk damask-upholstered Belter sofa, right between Stella and Kelly. An open Bible lay on the coffee table in front of them, along with Old Roses tea cups and plates bearing crumb evidence of Stella's homemade cookies.

In her sweatshirt and jeans, her mother looked out of place among the fine antiques, her bleached blonde hair hanging in a side ponytail. But her face glowed, the evidence of tears still glistening in her eyes.

"Mama?" Jennifer questioned.

Kelly held out a hand to her. "Stella's just led me to Jesus," came her simple explanation.

"Oh!" Jennifer glanced at Stella for confirmation, and the older woman nodded.

"Your mother's got faith like a little child. It makes it easy for her to trust," Stella said.

Jennifer enfolded Kelly in an embrace, patting the delicate, jutting bones of her mother's shoulder blades. "I'm so happy," she said, amazed, yes, but in her heart she wondered what in the world this meant. If Kelly was a dissolute harpy of a woman, best she go to her sister's in Alabama. If she was a Christian mother wanting to form a relationship with her daughter, that meant she should stay. But where? In Hermon or Savannah? Jennifer had no idea where she'd be living herself in another month, much less what she'd do with a homeless mother trying to pull her own life together. She figured she'd just doubled her need for God's direction!

"I trust too easy, that's for sure," Kelly said. "With God it's good, but with some folks, dangerous. We've been talkin' about bein' innocent as a dove but also wise as a serpent. I don't ever want to get taken in by a slick-talkin' man again. But Jennifer, sit down here a minute. I do have eyes where others are concerned, and it seems clear to us where your future lies. It only took me a few minutes around you and Michael Johnson to see you're a gonner over him, and he over you."

Placing her overnight bag at her feet, Jennifer sank into an armchair, her eyes cutting between the two women. "You've been talking about me?"

"Only a little." Kelly grinned and shrugged. "I can see Stella's been like a mother to you, and we both want what's best for you."

"I just filled your mother in on some gaps," Stella explained. "I hope you don't mind."

"No. I trust you, but you don't know everything that's happened, Stella."

"What don't I know, honey?"

Jennifer sighed, and her shoulders sagged. "Well, I know you want me and Michael to get together, but I'm just not sure that can happen."

"Why not?"

"The other night, he told me more about Ashley's death." Glancing at Kelly, Jennifer paused to tell her mother how both Michael's mother Linda and wife Ashley died from the same form of cancer. Only she wove in the further knowledge that Michael had been on the verge of becoming an oncologist when Ashley passed away, giving up his medical training out of anger and frustration.

130

"Well, I'll be," Stella murmured, sitting back and stroking her chin. "We always did say he was way too fancy to have just pounded boards his whole life. Mmm, this is a sad turn of events."

"Now, don't you go to work on him about it, Stella. That's why he didn't tell me. He can't stand it when people harp about how he should return to the medical field."

"Oh, I don't think he belongs in the medical field," Stella hastened to clarify. "Not until he gets heart healing himself first."

Jennifer nodded. "He thinks God takes away the women he gets close to."

"And that's why you think it won't work out? He's scared to get close?" Kelly asked.

"Well, that's only part of it. I'm the other messed up half of the problem. Michael knows about my past, and well ... let's just say it's dawning on him that anyone dating me has a hard row to hoe. It doesn't surprise me." Jennifer lifted a shoulder in what she hoped provided a show of strength. "I can handle it. I'm used to men not sticking around. That's why I've thought maybe it *is* best to go to Savannah. Give both of us a clean break."

Stella sat up straight and folded her hands in her lap. "From what I see, Michael's a patient man. I hear what you're sayin' about him needin' to work through his own problems, but what makes you think he won't come around?"

"I'm kind of running out of time for him to do that, aren't I?"

"Not if you stay in the county," Stella said, tossing both hands up.

"But you have to admit that's a big gamble that could lead to a very painful outcome. I just don't see that I should put myself through that again," Jennifer said, trying to think of an excuse to end the conversation. "So anyway ... is that meatloaf I smell?"

Stella wagged a finger at her. "Now don't you try to sidetrack me, Miss Jennifer. And don't you take this out to Savannah just because you're scared. You've got to be brave enough to stay and try if that's what God wants."

Jennifer sighed. "Maybe you should consider that I might just be too damaged for a relationship right now. Maybe we both are."

"You know what that is? Pride. You sayin' you're too messed up for God to fix, and Michael's sayin' God shoulda stopped everything bad from happenin' to him because he was too special. Both just different forms of the same thing, pride. You both got to let go of the past and let God work in the present, let Him bring beauty from ashes like He promises us He'll do. Let Him get you past that pool of bitterness the preacher talked about to the future He has for you."

Jennifer blinked at her, unable to move past the first part of what she'd said to the second. She'd never considered thinking too little of oneself a form of pride. But she could see how it was. All the focus on "me," even her shyness, her awkwardness … thinking too much about herself and not about others and the bigger situation at hand.

Watching Jennifer with concern, Kelly mistook her stunned silence for offense. Now she, too, sat forward, mashing Truffle's paw and causing the Pomeranian to glance at her in irritation. "OK, I gotta say something here. And it's something I've been needin' to get off my chest for a long time. I'm hopin' me sayin' it will help Jennifer where I failed to do so in so many other ways." Placing her hands over her heart, she heaved a deep sigh, then continued. "Jennifer, I know all your problems with men don't come from Roy, though heaven knows enough do. I think what you're sayin' and feelin' is from your daddy abandoning you."

Jennifer nodded, uncertain where she was going with this. "I realized Michael needs to stop feeling about God like I felt about my earthly father. I've been working on forgiving him like I did you and Roy, but for some reason that doesn't make sense, it's harder."

Kelly nodded. "Well, OK, baby, maybe I can help with that. See, I think you believe your daddy didn't love you. I don't know what memories you have of him, but he did love you. Very much. You were the apple of his eye. This is where I need to take responsibility and tell you, it was my fault he left, not yours."

Jennifer didn't know why silly tears filled her eyes. "It's nice of you to say that, Mom."

"No, honey, it's not just nice of me, it's true. What you don't know is your daddy sent you birthday presents and cards for years. And letters, inviting you to come see him in his new home. He and I couldn't get along, but he knew you were his, and it broke his heart to leave you."

"But—but what …?"

"Roy burned them, and I let him."

"You let him? And you never told me?" As the room spun around her, Jennifer struggled to fit this new information into the picture she'd always believed to be accurate. Truffle huffed at her, tongue hanging out in an absurd sort of indifference. "You let me believe he left me and never looked back?"

"I told you there was a lot I needed you to forgive me for." Kelly's face pleaded with her for understanding. "I was stupid. I thought I was helping you bond to Roy, that he was this great man who just wanted that bad to be your real daddy. And I ... I guess it felt good to me at the time to let him act mad at your father like I was. I'm so sorry. So sorry, Jennifer."

Jennifer put her hands over her face. Stella rose and came to stand beside her, putting a hand on her shoulder. Jennifer mumbled, "So you're saying ... I may still have a father out there who wants a relationship with me?"

Kelly bit her unpainted lip. "The letters finally stopped coming when you were a teenager. But yeah, maybe. I remember the town in Alabama they came from. It wasn't far from my sister's. I could look him up, explain ..."

Her voice trailed away as Jennifer doubled over and gave in to the sobs that erupted from her middle. Stella bent over her, putting her arms around her. She motioned to Kelly, calling her over, too. Jennifer felt her come, hesitating. Her mother knelt beside her, placing a thin hand on her knee.

"Baby, I'm so sorry. Can you forgive me for this, too? I understand if you can't. I know I've ruined your life."

"Shh, shh," Stella shushed her gently. "Remember, the here and now. This moment forward. That's the beauty of forgiveness."

Jennifer could only picture the presents in the trash, the cards burned, all the evidence she'd longed for all those years that her father cared about her. And she realized that was how God had been, desperate to reach her, his efforts overlooked ... only He'd never left. In the picture of her own father's attempts to reach her, she understood and felt the love of her Heavenly Father in a new way. A missing piece of herself clicked into place as she looked up at Kelly with tears streaming down her face and said, "I have a father who loves me. He wanted me."

And while Stella and Truffle went to check on the meatloaf, giving time for another moment of forgiveness in Hermon, her mother wrapped her arms around Jennifer and cried, too, assuring her it was true.

CHAPTER TEN

Jennifer tossed and turned until 3 a.m. Monday, when she finally concluded no hope remained for further sleep. She sighed at the red letters of the alarm clock on the walnut Eastlake table and at the soft snores emitting from the form recumbent on the twin bed on the other side of the room. As much as Stella stressed "this moment forward," it was hard to not feel hurt by her mother. Kelly's apologizing and mournful glances, which continued even after Jennifer said she forgave her, did not help. She just needed time to process. She needed to give her hurt to the Lord, and ask Him to help her fit this new piece of her identity into place. And she needed some space from Kelly to do that.

Jennifer craved her own kitchen, Keurig and Bible, away from watching eyes and well-intentioned comments. Right now that solitary time felt worth the risk of intruders or arsonists. But she didn't want to wake anyone in the household, either. She peeked out the window to note a setting half-moon. Good enough for the short walk across town. Flipping back the covers and padding to the bathroom, Jennifer washed her face and brushed her teeth over the Renaissance-style Victorian wash table. She wrote her mother a quick note. Then she dressed in the darkness and crept downstairs.

A little thump sounded as Truffle jumped from sofa to floor, then a huffing and clicking as the wagging Pomeranian chased her to the front door.

"Sorry, I can't let you out," Jennifer whispered to the hopeful canine before she set the lower lock and slipped onto the porch. She pulled her coat around her but immediately felt invigorated by the autumn chill. Hands in her pockets, Jennifer walked with a brisk step toward Main Street, thankful for the street lights that illuminated the sidewalk and the yet-dark houses.

Something else bothered her, knowing Michael was mad at her for still considering the Savannah job with Barbara involved. He felt she was selling herself short, doing another's bidding rather than following her heart. They had to talk. But how could she put into words that her fear of her brokenness exceeding his patience required self-protection? Could she really be that vulnerable and honest with him? Say those things aloud?

Jennifer searched inward and realized something that had been broken now felt firm inside her. Kelly's revelation about Jennifer's father had somehow solidified her perspective of herself, of life. Something had changed just knowing her dad had cared for her, whether they connected again in the future or not. She laughed like she'd just rolled doubles in Monopoly. And with this new clarity, any remaining bitterness toward Kelly fell away.

Isn't that just like you, God? Jennifer asked the pre-dawn sky as she ducked past a low-hanging branch. *Giving me that* aha *moment before I ever asked you?*

She knew lots of people never got to fit that missing piece. Their path would prove harder, but not impossible as they learned to allow God to fill their emotional needs and bring healing.

She took a deep breath. Yes, after a little coffee and prayer time, Jennifer thought she *could* talk to Michael. Maybe if she initiated the conversation her maturity would help override her romantic backwardness in his eyes.

No lights illuminated Dunham Place as Jennifer crossed an empty Highway 77. Not empty for long. Today was the excavation. By eight, the university students would arrive. They'd work from the privy walls inward to reveal artifact layering, tossing shovelfuls of dirt into waist-high sifters. If they were lucky, the vault's country location would mean it wasn't "dipped," or cleaned, too many times over the years. Perhaps the Dunhams had merely thrown in ashes now and again to cut down on the smell and disease.

Jennifer looked forward to seeing what the slice of the past served up: just dishes, buttons, clay pipes, and old bottles, most likely. But a single pontil marked medicine bottle, handmade by a glass blower prior to the Civil War, could fetch thousands of dollars.

What she didn't look forward to was Michael encountering Barb today. No telling what he might say. Yes, Jennifer needed to pay him a little visit *before* the dig.

As she headed toward the trees shielding her house, a strange sound made her steps falter. Jennifer stopped and listened. It came again, a faint scrape like a shovel on a hard surface. The sound issued from Michael's back yard, yet Jennifer saw no light. Deciding to investigate, her heart started pounding when she spied a figure in a hooded sweatshirt digging in the area roped off for the main dig … the very spot where the old outhouse had stood!

Jennifer stood frozen, one hand on her cell phone, debating whether to flee and dial "911." But what if it was just Michael or James, figuring the moon provided enough light to dig … for what? At that moment, the figure turned toward her.

"Hey!" she yelled when she realized the man wore a black ski mask!

He threw the shovel and ran.

"Michael! Michael! James!" Jennifer screamed at the top of her voice, running a few steps towards the house. Then she realized something. The stocky figure that now fled toward the empty Stevenson lot did so with a gimpy knee. "Horace?"

The intruder glanced behind. Jennifer obeyed instinct and ran after him. "Horace, stop!"

A back flood light stained the dark yard just as Jennifer grabbed at the man's jacket. She jerked him backwards, and he stumbled as she waist-tackled a pudgy figure. As they both landed on the ground, she reached for the ski mask.

They wrestled, the intruder trying to pin her arms. "Let go!" The man's voice proved almost unrecognizable with wheezing, but he did sound all too familiar.

Jennifer lunged again. "Horace, what are you doing?" Her fingers just touched the soft material at his neck when a meaty fist shot out and struck her in the jaw, snapping her head backwards. As she cried out and fell, she heard a shot ring out, Michael and James shouting. But the man who'd hit her took one knee, huffed and fled into the woods. Through the stars and a halo of pain, she turned her face toward the sound of a truck engine roaring to life. A vehicle raced onto the main road and sped away, sans headlights.

"Call 911!" she heard Michael shout to his father. "Did you see it? Did you see the truck?"

"As good as the light allowed. Looked like a Ram," James said in a grim tone, then paused to speak into his cell.

Jennifer raised herself to her elbows just as Michael knelt beside her, cradling her head. "Are you OK?" he whispered. "Where did he hit you?"

"Jaw." She rubbed the tender area and moved the joint back and forth.

Michael's tone changed to exasperated tenderness. "You little idiot. Why did you try to tackle him? What in the world happened? And why are you over here?"

James drew close to hear her answer and relay parts of it to Stan, whom he now had on the line. Jennifer sat up. "I don't even know what just happened. I woke up early and wanted to be in my own house, so I was walking over when I heard the sound of digging. I went around to see, and there was this hooded figure. I thought it could be one of you. But when he saw me, he ran. And he ran with a limp. I called out Horace's name, and he looked back."

"When you jumped him, did he say anything?"

"Yeah. He said 'let go.'" Noticing that Michael wore PJ pants and a T-shirt, Jennifer allowed him to help her stand, then jerked back and brushed off her pants. She didn't like being called an idiot.

"Was it really Horace?" James wanted to know.

"He was wheezing so hard I could hardly tell. But I think so." Jennifer frowned at Michael, then insisted, "That's why I tackled him. I figured I could take Horace. And I wanted to know what he was up to."

His face softened, and he tucked her hair back in place. "I know, but that was foolish. He may be older now, but he must have a hundred pounds on you."

"But what was he doing? Did he really think something that valuable was in this privy vault?" Jennifer hurried over to the site, stepping around the small flags. Michael and James trailed her, Michael lowering his .22, James his cell phone.

"Stan's put an APB out for Horace and his truck and is sending a deputy over here," he told them. "Looks like he hadn't gotten far digging under this concrete slab, so whatever he was looking for, he didn't find. I'll get a spot light, and Michael, why don't you grab some ice for Jennifer?"

"Sure."

"I can get it. You go help your dad. You'll probably need your jackhammer, too."

Michael hesitated, then nodded. He stepped closer to her, touched a finger to her chin, and placed a soft kiss on her jaw. Already throbbing like a cantaloupe sprouted there, the area now exploded into sudden heat.

Jennifer gave a faint smile, trying not to let sudden hope sweep her away. "Thanks."

"We're going to get to the bottom of this, and you won't be in danger anymore," he promised.

When Jennifer returned with an ice bag pressed to the side of her face, two county officers joined the Johnson men in the glare of a spot light. One whom James introduced as Officer Lew turned to Jennifer and pinned her with green eyes in his lantern-shaped face. He shook her hand. "You're a little too brave, young lady."

She grimaced. "I realize that now."

Taking out a notepad, he smiled and added, "I'd like to ask you a few questions before they start making noise."

Jennifer again related her encounter, then wondered aloud, "But why would Horace want to beat the excavators to the privy? I mean, I know he's a history enthusiast, but that's ridiculous. Oh, hey... do you think he has some crazy idea about buried treasure? When we first started working on the property, he did warn us about people looking for Silas' missing gold. Maybe *he* was looking for Silas' gold."

"That's an interesting idea," James mused.

"Let's find out," stated the second officer, presumably Lew's partner, as Michael took up his jackhammer and lowered plastic safety goggles over his eyes. Ear-splitting noise woke the neighborhood just as dawn touched the horizon. Next door, Otis began to bark and bay. Jennifer knew without looking that irritated and curious neighbors would be coming out onto their porches. Minutes later, they cleared away the debris and started shoveling.

"Gently, a little at a time," Lew directed.

Jennifer's eye fell on something white gleaming in the spot light. She lowered her ice bag and called out, "Stop! What's that?" When everyone looked at her, she pointed.

The men knelt around the area indicated, James dragging the light closer. Jennifer hovered over them as Officer Lew removed his hat, bent his white head in concentration, and brushed the dirt away from the hard white thing that was not a stone. He met his partner's eyes. "Call it in."

The officer spoke into his lapel mic. "Yes, we're going to need a CSI unit at 160 Main Street, Hermon …"

At the same time, her stomach fisting, Jennifer stepped away and dialed Barb on her cell. "Hey, Barb, I'm afraid we're going to need to cancel the dig today. Yes, I'm serious. Why? Well, I think we just uncovered a human finger bone."

They sat around the dining room table, frozen in shock with untouched cups of coffee before them. The back yard buzzed with policemen and GBI detectives rolling out crime scene tape, taking photos and talking into their lapel mics and cell phones. Michael had overheard one of them say Amy Greene had verified to Stan that the noise of her husband's truck—the Dodge truck the tire prints of which did match those found the day of the fire, and again today— had awakened her in the wee morning hours. Horace then took off on the motorcycle he kept parked in his shop, without a word to her. She suspected he might head for a remote hunting cabin he owned in the mountains.

"The forensic expert uncovering the skeleton said it belonged to an adult male, and quite a large one. We'll have to wait on an autopsy for further details," Michael told them.

"This is unbelievable," James murmured. "I trusted Horace, let him advise me on the property. And he killed someone?"

"And could be behind all those 'accidents' in the process of trying to cover it up," Jennifer added. "Which means he could have killed *me*."

"Now we shouldn't rush to conclusions," Stella said. She and Kelly had arrived a few minutes ago, alarmed at the sight of police rather than archeology students. "There could be things we don't know here."

James shook his head, cradling his mug between his hands and staring sightlessly at the dark liquid. "But Horace did have access to this property when he acted as property manager. There were months, even years, when it sat vacant before Michael and I arrived. Plenty of opportunity for a crime to take place, and be concealed. I'd say whomever did this must have removed the board on the double-seater outhouse, thrown in the body, then come back soon after to shovel in a layer of dirt and pour that concrete slab down in there, just hoping future owners would assume the outhouse pit had been sealed for safety purposes."

"Who knows, Horace could even have told potential renters that," Jennifer said. Then she added, "Calvin talked about seeing lights and people coming and going during that time."

"But what about motive? Who would he want to kill?" Stella asked.

Jennifer looked at her, lowering her ice bag. "Chad Fullerton, Amy's high school boyfriend and quarterback of the high school football team." She sat forward. "Amy told me about how Chad intended to return to the Athens area after he blew out his ACL playing for the University of Florida. He'd resumed contact with her even though she was already in a relationship with Horace. When she told him Chad was thinking of returning home at the end of the semester, Horace got livid. Chad told some friends at his university he wanted to check out rental options here and left in his car, never to be seen again. Do you think … Horace could have showed him this place?"

"Oh! This gives me the creeps!" Kelly cried, throwing her hands up and shaking them. "What if that—that *presence* I saw at the foot of my bed was this Chad dude? Like his murdered ghost?"

"Jennifer, you've got to tell the investigators what you just told us," Michael said in a level tone, ignoring Kelly.

Nodding, she reminded herself that with all that unfolded right now, she shouldn't be disappointed that he didn't attempt to sit near her or touch her in any way, and that his manner of speech sounded more stern than compassionate. "Well, I can, but surely Amy will."

"They'll want to hear it from more than one source, and there's always a chance she could cover things up for him."

"Like … do you think she lied to Stan when she said Horace was home in his workshop … the night your truck was tampered with?"

He shook his head, his mouth forming a grim line. "I sure hate to think that. It's all so hard to believe. Horace seemed like a good guy at heart."

"Consider what a state Amy must be in," Stella urged. "We don't know what's been goin' on at home, what Horace may have told her or asked of her. I'm thinkin' someone ought to be with her during the police questioning. Maybe I should go over."

"Well," Jennifer said, "from what she told me that day we hung the curtains here, I don't think she had a clue. Chad's disappearance still haunts her. She really loved him back then. She's going to be devastated if her own husband actually killed him."

Unexpectedly, Kelly straightened her spine and pushed back from the table. "Well, I'd like to go, too. Is that OK? If anyone can understand a man not bein' what he pretended to be, it'd be me. I'd like to think maybe I could help a little, let her know it wasn't her fault."

Amazed, Jennifer stared at this strange new woman.

Stella smiled her approval. "I think that would be a great idea, Kelly. We'll be underfoot here, anyway. Let's head on out. See you back at the house, Jennifer?" She stood, pausing to kiss Jennifer's head and hug Michael and James. "I can give you a key if you think you'll be done here before we are."

Jennifer waved a hand. "No, thanks. If I am, I think I'll just go on over to the double-wide, I mean, now that I know it's safe and everything. It is safe, right?" She turned a questioning glance on the men.

"Let's just see what the police say," Michael urged.

"OK." Stella waved at them from the door to the kitchen. "Don't worry, y'all, it just looks like trouble and chaos, but God's got this. We prayed He'd uncover any evil doings, didn't we? Now we just got to let Him do His work and pray these policemen get to the bottom of things."

Michael turned to Jennifer after the two women exited. "Your mother seems to be doing well," he commented, but his quirked brow suggested skepticism.

She let out a little gust of air. "Yeah. I don't know what to make of it. I mean, I told you she prayed to accept the Lord, but the change is so sudden it's really taken me off guard. I guess she's hurt and disappointed me so many times I'm kind of waiting for her to do it again."

"That's a natural reaction," James said. "And she may, but by the grace of God it won't be like it was in the past."

"Actually ..." Jennifer hesitated. She really wanted to share this with Michael alone, but that didn't look possible in the immediate future. So she continued, "She kind of made a big admission this weekend. It seems that after my dad left, he tried to stay in touch, sending cards and gifts and invitations to come visit him. Roy destroyed all the correspondence. She said at the time she thought she was doing what was best by not telling me."

"Oh, wow." Michael uncrossed his arms and moved like he might reach for her hand, but stopped with merely leaning forward.

"That must have been hard to hear," James said. "Have you been able to come to peace with it yet?"

Jennifer sighed. "We talked. I prayed. And yes, I forgave her."

"That's good, Jennifer. If it helps at all, I get a good feeling from her. I think she's genuine."

Jennifer raised her hands, palms up, and shrugged. "I have to admit, I do, too. She loved Harmony Grove yesterday, and as you can see, she's taken to Stella like a chick with a mother hen, spiritually speaking, of course. She's even talking about going up toward Athens this week and putting in applications to wait tables." She paused and glanced at Michael, realizing he could interpret that as a decision to stay when she still didn't know yet. She'd indicated to her mother that Kelly's desire to find employment here might be premature, too, but Kelly had insisted she didn't want to just sit around and be a burden on anyone.

Michael seemed to notice she waited on his response. He stirred and agreed, "That's probably a good sign, too."

Warmed by his small effort at encouragement, Jennifer nodded and admitted, "It's really helped me, knowing my dad tried to stay in touch."

"I bet. We're really glad for you, Jennifer." Michael smiled.

Knowing as she looked into his eyes that he meant it, but still feeling the ache of distance between them, Jennifer gave a faint smile in return.

James tried to make up for Michael's understated response. "Of course he loved you. And I'm sure he felt the loss keenly. Maybe the future will even hold a reunion, God willing." He stood and put his hands on Jennifer's shoulders. She glanced up and offered him a genuine, grateful smile. He squeezed her shoulders. "Well, I was thinking of running up to Chicken Express to order a couple of family packs. Everyone's bound to be hungry soon. Michael, why don't you stay with Jennifer while she gives her statement? I imagine she could use the support."

Jennifer bit her lip and glanced at Michael. She resisted the urge to squirm over the fact that even James noticed his son's renewed reserve toward her, but the strength she'd received from the recent revelation about her father allowed her to admit, "I think I could."

Michael gave a nod. "Then I'll stay. I'm sure they'll want to talk to both of us, anyway."

As James looked satisfied and left the dining room, Michael played with the edge of his place mat. "As much as I hate this, for Horace and Amy and that poor dead guy out there, and as unsettling as it is to realize that body's been in my back yard all this time, it feels like a huge weight off to know that soon this will be resolved. I've felt responsible for things that have happened to you while you were working here."

"Well, that was hardly the case. I just keep thinking how desperate Horace must have been, if that is Chad, to conceal his murder. That's why he kept asking us if we intended on moving or demolishing the outbuildings on the property, and he probably put Amy up to finding out the date for the dig, knowing we'd think nothing of her interest. I mean, he and Amy have built up this big reputation in the area. I can't imagine acting so normal with a secret like that."

Michael stared into the fireplace, reflective. "People get good at hiding the darkness inside."

"Yes, they do," she agreed with emphasis. "Do you think he attacked Barb, too?"

"Probably so, in the hopes that she'd cancel the excavation."

Jennifer snapped her fingers and exclaimed, "That's right! He asked us that day at the plantation site about our plans for the dig, and I told him when Barb was coming to mark off the sites!" As Michael nodded and watched her, she quieted, then added, "But it seems he tried to scare us without killing us. I guess that's something, at least.

He probably thought I was in Savannah the night of the fire. At least, I have to choose to believe that."

Michael's face hardened. "But you weren't. And the loose bleeder screw could have killed you if you hadn't been on a straightaway out in the country when that deer made you hit the brakes hard. He deserves whatever justice he gets."

As much as she wanted to take Michael's anger as proof of his protective feelings towards her, Jennifer knew Stella was right that they shouldn't get ahead of the investigation. She held up a hand. "But maybe it wasn't even him. Maybe he was trying to help someone else conceal the murder."

"I'm afraid not," said a deep voice from the doorway. Officer Lew stood there, hands on his hips, badge glinting in the sun from the nine-over-nine window. "I just got off the phone with the sheriff. Rabun County deputies mobilized in time to help the GBI apprehend Horace Greene outside the hunting cabin his wife described to us earlier this morning. When they cuffed him, he fell down into a blubbering heap and confessed on the spot to the murder of Chad Fullerton."

CHAPTER ELEVEN

After Jennifer gave her statement to Officer Lew, they were still processing the stunning turn of events when Jennifer heard James struggling to open the kitchen door with a huge Chicken Express bag in his arms and a gallon of sweet tea dangling from one thumb. Hurrying over to help, she couldn't hide the surprise on her face when she realized he was not alone. A man and a woman who appeared to be in their late forties, dressed for the breezy late autumn day in trench coats, sweaters and slacks that made them look like models for J. Crew and Loft, stood behind him on the porch. Both dark-haired and smiling at her, the woman clutched her Michael Kors purse and a leather satchel and the man another bag of Chicken Express.

"Uh, I brought company," James announced, sounding sheepish. "I hope it's OK, Officer Lew? I met the Jacksons in the front yard as I was pulling in. Apparently, Michael, they're relatives from Valdosta."

"I see no need to bar a family visit, so long as everyone stays in the house," the policeman responded, eyeing the chicken with far more interest than the newcomers.

Impressively uncowed by the visitors' panache even in his jeans and work shirt, Michael stepped forward to shake the man's hand with confidence, but an expression of befuddlement. "Valdosta? I ... wasn't aware of any relatives from that far south."

"I'm Frank. This is my wife, Linnea. I'm sorry to take you by surprise, and at such a bad time, clearly, but we were just on our way home from a game weekend visiting our daughter in Athens and decided to stop by and introduce ourselves. We would have contacted you beforehand, but we actually just read the article at our B & B yesterday." Frank turned his handsome, squared-jaw face toward his wife and prompted her with a pointed look.

The shiny hair of her straight bob, no gray evident, slid over one eye as Linnea opened her satchel and held up the October copy of *Old Houses*. Framing the magazine like a game show hostess, she offered an apologetic smile. "I'm afraid it's my fault. I got very excited when I stumbled on this story about your property. I convinced Frank if you happened to be home you wouldn't mind us stopping in unannounced when you learned he is a descendant of William and Charlotte Dunham's first child, Walker, born in 1873."

"You're kidding." Jennifer's mouth fell open for the umpteenth time that day. Not to mention, week. She quickly closed it at the pain the movement invited.

Linnea smiled at her. "And you're Jennifer. I recognize you from the picture in the article." Her gaze stuttered over Jennifer's jaw, which Jennifer imagined looked quite a sight by now. However, the polished woman didn't comment. "A real pleasure to meet you. What you've done here is so impressive."

"Well, thank you. As you read, I had a lot of help. I just hate that you happened to come in the midst of ... well, a murder investigation." Jennifer cringed and glanced out into the back yard as a police officer walked past the window. Her fingers flitted up to her face. Sophisticated people always made her self-conscious, more so than ever today with her rumpled appearance. To her surprise, she felt Michael's hand touch her back in a gesture of reassurance. Warmth surged in her chest, and as she gave him a quick smile, she noticed Linnea watching them.

"Jennifer had a little encounter with our intruder this morning," Michael explained as James indicated he'd shared the basics with the couple.

"Oh, my goodness, I'm so sorry," Linnea said to Jennifer. "I'm afraid I would have run in the opposite direction! I prefer my drama on paper. We really won't stay long. We just wanted to meet you, and there's something we wanted you to see."

James said from the island where he unpacked boxes and Styrofoam containers, "You have to stay for lunch at least, if you don't mind humble fixings. And Officer Lew, you can spread the word to your colleagues that we've got eats in the kitchen whenever they can pop in for a break. We've got plenty for everyone."

As the policeman brightened and headed outside, Linnea loosened the belt on her coat. "Well, thank you, we appreciate the offer," she agreed. "If you're sure it's not too much with CSI being here on the same day." She grimaced at her own morbid humor.

"Not at all."

As James placed a stack of paper plates and napkins on the counter and began to arrange the food in a serving line, Michael stepped closer to Frank, studying his features with interest. They were near the same height, although the older man carried a little extra weight in husk, if not paunch. "So you're really some distant cousin of mine?"

Frank grinned, exposing charming brackets to his mouth. "Yep, it would appear so. Linnea's the genealogical enthusiast. She dug everything up going for a DAR proof for our daughter some years ago. She says my great-grandfather Walker spent his later childhood years in Atlanta after his parents moved back there in the 1880s."

"I'd bet that was when Hampton, Charlotte's and Stuart's son and Michael's great-great grandfather, took over the practice in the apothecary here," Jennifer observed, encouraging the couple to place their coats and bags on the loveseat near the 1840s fireplace.

"That's what I imagined, since William went back to practicing in the city," Linnea agreed. "Walker's daughter Agatha moved to Valdosta when she married. That's how we ended up there. Look at them. I think I see a resemblance, don't you? This is so exciting." She peered at the two men and smirked.

Jennifer agreed, but her head felt like it might explode with the overload of the moment, especially considering the much more pressing investigation unfolding a few hundred yards away. She moved behind the island to help James get ice in plastic cups while the Dunham descendants chatted.

"Jennifer, I can handle this. Why don't you and Michael take the Jacksons on a quick walk through of the house while I finish?" James suggested. "Tea, everyone?"

The idea of conducting an impromptu tour in the amount of time it took James to pour drinks and while distracted by painful thoughts of Horace and Amy rattled Jennifer's nerves, but she nodded. Following Michael into the sunroom, she couldn't stop the flush that spread over her face at her last memory in the room. Noticing Jennifer's momentary dysfunction as it translated into hands-folded silence, unfazed himself, Michael explained the enclosed porch served as a perfect place for a manly retreat, then led the group up

148

the hallway toward his bedroom. As he took them inside, she hovered at the door but managed to recount how they'd redesigned the awkward attic access and how she'd located the four-poster bed and American Empire wardrobe clustered on the brown, gold, blue and apricot 1840s Oushak carpet at a nearby auction. In the front parlor, she half hoped Michael would tease her by recounting their feud over the "girly," late Victorian fireplaces, but he merely stated that she'd advised them to leave the more recent fixtures. As Linnea and Frank exclaimed over Stella's mural, Jennifer explained how Amy had selected the paint and window treatments from her Lexington shop. She stopped abruptly, the press of tears constricting her throat.

Jennifer didn't know what was the matter with her. A year ago, she'd have become so absorbed in the historical details of the tour that even the Jacksons would have made excuses about using the restroom to momentarily escape her preservationist ardor. Now, she couldn't get through a simple explanation without squirming over Michael or sorrowing over the Greenes. When had people taken the place of old buildings in her affections? When had this house and its residents come to have such personal meaning that the threat of having to leave soon for good wrenched her stomach with nausea?

Clearing her throat, Jennifer detailed how the grand, main hallway and the men's bedrooms had been part of the 1870s addition, while the office and dining room constituted the earlier, 1840s original, with the kitchen of the same period brought up from the rear. Linnea's eager questions made it easier to focus, but Jennifer felt relieved when they circled back to the kitchen and served their plates. The sensation didn't last long.

Linnea bumped up against her and whispered, "So are you and Michael a thing?"

"W-what?" Not another mouth-open moment.

The middle-aged woman lifted a slender shoulder. "Just seems like there's something there. Some ... electricity." She lifted her tea and winked. "If I'm wrong, please forgive me. Frank says I'm forever overstepping my boundaries."

"No, it's fine. We've ... dated a little."

Linnea smiled. "I thought so. Wouldn't it be romantic to marry him and get to stay in this wonderful place you restored together?"

Jennifer shut her mouth and swallowed. "Right now that seems unlikely," she whispered, following their guests into the dining room and not looking at Michael in a terror that he might have overheard their conversation. Linnea sent her a concerned and questioning frown, indicating that she hoped to learn what that meant at a later time.

"So what type of work do you do in Valdosta? And is your daughter at UGA your only child?" James asked after offering a quick blessing which the Jacksons accepted as routine, stating "amens" and reaching matter-of-factly for their utensils.

As Frank related that he was a financial advisor and Linnea an accountant, and their daughter Dee Ann was indeed their only child studying veterinary medicine at the university, Jennifer tried to see the dining room through their eyes. She felt proud of the American Empire table she'd found to coordinate with the mahogany sideboard from Harmon Stone's barn, and the way the sixteen coats of lacquer, applied two days apart, gleamed in the soft, golden light. So did the 1830 coin silver tea set Mary Ellen called her about a few weeks ago, displayed on a dark red place mat that complemented the red diaper pattern wallpaper. The nine-over-nine window framed the lingering, reddening leaves of the dogwood and the gnarled grape vine arbor. She'd even added some fall leaf swags and arrangements in an attempt to instruct two bachelors on how to embrace the season. The room felt rich and welcoming. One would hardly know detectives unearthed a skeleton in the back yard. Jennifer shoved that from her mind.

When the Jacksons asked about Michael's line of work, Jennifer glanced his way, then averted her eyes. He explained that he and James led a crew in the process of restoring the local general store. Jennifer chimed in with details of Stella's plans for the building. Their guests were delighted to hear the renovation of Hermon proceeded as promised in the magazine article.

"I'm just sorry the apothecary is closed today," Jennifer said. "We have a key, of course, but ..."

Linnea laid a hand out next to her plate. "Oh, please. No worries. You have enough going on today."

"We'd love to have you back to see both the apothecary and the art gallery, as well as all the outbuildings off limits today due to the investigation," James offered. "In fact, what about Thanksgiving? Or did you already have plans with your daughter?"

Frank looked over at his wife and shrugged. "She was just coming home for the week. But my parents are no longer living, and Linnea's have yet another senior cruise they're leaving for right around that time. We were going to have the meal a day early so they could get down to the Florida coast for their departure."

"Aunt Bessie?" Linnea asked.

"She can come the day before, then go to her cousin's."

"Well, I guess that would work," Linnea told them, "if you don't mind that we bring Dee Ann. But are you sure?"

"Of course," James exclaimed. "And definitely bring your daughter!"

Jennifer noticed Michael's effort to add enthusiasm to his polite smile, the idea of a crowd not much more exciting to him than to her. "My aunts Patricia and Mary will be here from Atlanta with their families, so it would give them a chance to meet you."

She stared at him, surprised by this information. Would they not want to meet her, too? And she'd assumed the James and Johnson families would get together at one house or the other. "What about Stella and Earl?" she blurted out.

Michael glanced at her. "Oh, they've got so many close relatives, I'm sure they'll have a house full without us getting involved." Softening at her look of dismay, he added, "But I'll be sure to ask."

"OK." Jennifer poked at a corn nugget, then decided it looked too greasy and left it on her plate. They hadn't discussed Thanksgiving yet, and she had no idea where she and Kelly would go. With a sinking feeling, Jennifer realized no reason for them to join either of the families she'd pictured herself with would sound reasonable to an influx of relatives. Especially not with even her questionable dating relationship with Michael on possible hiatus.

"Stella, the lady who painted the mural and the trim in the house, and who's opening the art gallery?" Frank wanted to know.

"That's right," Michael said.

"Your families became close during the work on the house?"

Michael smiled. "You could say that. The fact is, Jennifer discovered while researching for her National Register report that Stella is also a distant cousin."

Jennifer waited to see if he would detail the relationship between Hampton Dunham and his African American housekeeper that the magazine article omitted, its writer remaining unaware of the mixed-race history and instead focusing on community revival as Jennifer intended, but he did not. Maybe he figured the Jacksons were already running on overload. Or maybe he just wanted to see their faces when they met Stella, who had not been pictured with her artwork in the article.

Linnea grabbed her husband's arm. "Frank, isn't this exciting? An opportunity to meet a whole line of your family we didn't even know existed until recently? And to get to see the apothecary your great-great grandfather built? It sounds like an opportunity we can't pass up!"

Frank turned to Michael and James and smiled, repeating in an obedient voice, "It sounds like an opportunity we can't pass up."

Everyone laughed while Linnea rolled her eyes.

"Well, great. We'll plan on you," James said.

"Just for a day visit. And you must let me bring some food. But I'm so glad we came today," Linnea squeaked, transferring her hand to Jennifer's arm.

Jennifer smiled, not minding the contact even on short acquaintance. Watching Linnea with Frank reminded Jennifer of herself with Michael, trying to rouse him to the appropriate amount of enthusiasm over her areas of interest. Only the couple possessed a level of comfort that evidenced their many years of marriage, something Jennifer could hardly imagine but dreamed of. Fighting a wave of unexpected sadness, she rose and offered to clear the table as the conversation turned to the crime and suspect at hand. Michael gave his new relatives a minimal amount of information, only what the police had confirmed so far, saying they should wait for an official statement rather conjecturing what they believed had happened. He did indicate the murder must have occurred during the house's

rental period. The way he spoke, Jennifer guessed the Jacksons concluded the crime involved random strangers. Just as well.

"You must feel a tremendous sense of relief to know the body
will be removed today," Linnea said. "But does it make you uneasy
going forward, knowing a murder was committed right here on the
property, maybe here inside the house?" She gave a delicate shudder
and pushed her plate back, having eaten only half of her chicken
fingers and a serving of slaw.

Jennifer took the plate with Linnea's thanks and heard James
say as she headed to the kitchen, "It is a disturbing thought and one
I imagine we're going to have to work extra hard to not dwell on for
the next little while. But we've committed the house to the Lord and
want it to be a place of healing and rest for all who come here."

"I get that," Linnea said, "and that segues perfectly into what
I wanted to share with you. Frank has a very precious book in his
possession that the university has been after him to lend, but we
refuse. It shows that his ancestors possessed strong faith themselves.
Jennifer?" she called into the kitchen.

Jennifer came to the doorway. "Yes?"

"While you're in there, could you bring my satchel? And join us?
You're going to want to hear this."

"Sure." She preferred clean-up in the kitchen to more of Michael's emotionally exhausting mixed signals, but curiosity stirred.
Doing as the woman asked, Jennifer laid the leather satchel before
her on the table and resumed her own seat.

Linnea unhooked the top and pulled out a slim laptop. "I only
wish I had the actual book with me so you could see it, but in my
historical file on my computer I kept a copy of its transcription along
with all my documents proving DAR for our daughter and SAR for
Frank. I researched both families at once, his and mine, so you can
imagine all the files! I'm pretty type A and keep everything. I guess
it goes along with my obsession over getting my numbers perfect in
my job. Anyway ..."

As Linnea struggled to untangle her power cord, Jennifer pushed
her chair back to help her and plug it in. Growing impatient with the
details, Jennifer cut to the chase. "So what book is this?"

Linnea met her eyes and said with emphasis, "The diary of Verity Dunham. You know who that is, right?"

Jennifer spluttered, glancing at Michael and noticing that he looked as incredulous as she did. "Well, yes, of course, but are you saying you have an actual Colonial-era account written in her own hand? Do you know how rare private documents, much less whole diaries, from that period are?"

Biting her lip, Linnea gave a slow and emphatic nod, relishing Jennifer's response.

"The journal was passed down from Levi to Silas to William to Walker, and so on," Frank supplied. "We keep it in a small, airtight safe. Verity related in her own writing that Levi and some ministers of her acquaintance, including Francis Asbury, encouraged her to keep a journal for therapeutic reasons. She wrote it between 1788 and 1802, when the Creek Indian boundary was moved west. Really the last portion of middle Georgia's frontier period."

"Francis Asbury?" James echoed in amazement. "The famous Methodist minister?"

"Yep. The one and only."

"Let me just pull up the document, and I can read you some excerpts. You'll be fascinated." Linnea typed in passwords and touched the screen of her computer. "Then I'll get your e-mail address and mail you the entire thing to enjoy at your leisure. When we come for Thanksgiving, I'll bring the original."

Leaning in for a closer look, Michael said, "That's ... amazing."

To Jennifer's surprise, he looked like he really meant it. At last. Something with enough antiquity and rarity to elicit his awe. Or maybe his appreciation of his ancestral history had finally grown to a level matching the stature of his family tree.

"Did we glimpse a log cabin behind the house?" Frank asked.

"You did," Michael said. "Levi's cabin. We moved it from the original plantation site depicted by Stella's mural onto the property here. We're almost ready to furnish it." He glanced at Jennifer with the first twinkle of affection that day, making her heart warm and beat fast with hope. "Jennifer just put a big ding on my credit card with an order from some primitive décor place in the mountains."

She smiled. "Well, he and James want to make it a guest house. We even installed a bath. If people are actually going to stay there, it has to be comfortable, doesn't it?"

"Of course it does. Don't let him make you feel guilty," Linnea said with a conspiratorial frown and a firm nod.

Frank rubbed his hands together. "I have to admit, this is amazing. OK, Linnea, are you happy? I just got a chill. I'm sitting in a house William Dunham lived in, albeit briefly, with his doctor's office a few hundred yards in front of us and his grandfather's cabin a few hundred yards behind us."

They all burst out laughing, especially when Jennifer chimed in, "Now, I would have given money to hear Michael say that! You can't imagine how many times I've tried to impress him with his own ancestors."

"I can vouch for that," James exclaimed, while Michael shook his head good-naturedly.

"OK, here it is." Linnea pointed to her computer screen, and they all crowded around like pigeons eager for a chunk of dry bread. "The first entry's from March 1788. 'The child will live. My husband plied me with some type of Asian root in a tea with cayenne pepper and cinnamon sticks. He now keeps the key to his medicine chest upon his person. For my low spirits he prescribes St. John's Wort. Methinks it does not help much. He has also instructed me to write within this book when my soul feels conflicted. Like a dutiful wife, I submit.'"

"She almost lost a baby," Jennifer mused aloud.

James cocked his head. "Or tried to lose a baby."

Linnea held up a finger. "Listen to the next entry. 'After much searching, I found where Levi buried the gorget. A dreadful argument ensued, but he did finally ascent to my keeping the object, as it is all I will have of Tenetke for the child. He made me put it away and promise to never take it out to hold. I promised, but with the spring thaw, the call west stirs in my heart when I am quiet. He found me weeping by the tree along the road and has said he will fetch a Negro woman to help me in the house as the baby comes, but methinks it is to watch me.'"

As Linnea stopped reading, a heavy silence fell. Finally Jennifer whispered, "Tenetke?"

"I looked it up, of course. It's Muscogee Creek and means 'thunder.'"

Michael's eyes popped open wide. "Just a minute," he said, and, pushing away from the table, left the room.

Linnea told them, "I believe we have proof here that Verity's first child, Selah, was the daughter of a Creek Indian, not Levi."

When Michael returned, he held the leather pouch Jennifer expected him to. "We found this behind a stone in the cabin's fireplace," he said. He pulled the silver crescent out and laid it on the table in front of his cousin and cousin's wife. Linnea's mouth formed an 'O' as she placed an index finger on the thunderbolt engraved on the front.

CHAPTER TWELVE

Stella and Kelly took Amy home from the police station after she gave her statement. Kelly later described the poor woman's shock and grief. In tears, she confessed that the evening before Jennifer set out for Augusta in Michael's truck with a loose bleeder screw, she accepted Horace's word that he'd been in his workshop. She had not checked on him and admitted he could have left and returned without her knowledge. Later in the day, word came that Horace gave police a full confession, describing the events surrounding the murder of one-time Oglethorpe County star football player Chad Fullerton.

Kelly, who returned shortly before bed time, confided to Jennifer as they sat in the kitchen, "When Chad wanted to move back to Athens, he made the mistake of contactin' Horace, knowin' his father owned that property company. Horace agreed to show 'im some places." She stifled a yawn, but her eyes gleamed with excitement.

Jennifer realized that her mother had taken to Hermon's tragedy like a long-time resident and clearly enjoyed being "in the know." She added, "And Horace showed Chad historic rentals since Amy loved those."

"You got it. But he really hoped Chad'd be put off by those, bein' ultra modern. Horace just knew Amy and Chad was a bad match. But to his surprise, Chad showed interest in this here place. Guess he was willin' to do whatever to get the girl, the career in football bein' gone." Kelly rose and went to the refrigerator.

"So he killed him rather than let him have Amy?" Jennifer questioned, agog.

Kelly shook her head, turning from the counter where she poured herself some milk to look at her daughter, seated at the table. "Only once Chad started talkin' about how special his and Amy's connection was, that no time, distance or person could break it."

"Hm. Sounds familiar," said Jennifer, thinking of Tenetke and Verity. "Amy said she'd told Chad that she and Horace were dating."

"Apparently Chad didn't think much of that. He was all confident of his ability to get Amy back. Cocky. Horace hated cocky guys, Amy said, always having been heckled by them in school. And when Chad poohed what Horace and Amy had next to how *intimate* he and Amy had been—" Kelly paused to give her eyebrows a suggestive waggle— "well, I guess that must've been the final straw. A crime of passion, as they say."

"Did he reveal where the murder weapon was? And what he did with Chad's car?"

"Well, there was some details the police spared Amy from takin' in right now, bein' as fragile as she is, but Stella did tell me he used a shovel on site, dragged the body to the outhouse to dump it, then sunk the car, shovel and all, in Lake Oconee. I reckon they'll be checkin' the lakebed about where he tells 'em to. He's giving everything up, but on the condition police know Amy had nothin' to do with any of it. He knew he was done in the second he saw police lights."

"I'd say, before. That's why he tried to dig up the body before the UGA students could," Jennifer told her. "He'd covered it up so long. He must have come back with dirt and cement another night shortly after the murder, making sure no one or any animal smelled the decay." Jennifer grimaced and stood, looping the belt of her robe tighter.

Her mother nodded. After taking a sip of her milk, she added, "He's got a lawyer. Stella says she expects they'll go for manslaughter and try to prove it wasn't pre-determined, pre ...?"

"Pre-meditated?"

"Right."

Jennifer shook her head. "What will poor Amy do?"

"I don't know."

"Were you able to help her some?"

"I hope so. I only gave her a snippet of my story, just to let her know someone understands what livin' with a secret monster's like. I intend to go back over tomorrow, after I go up toward town to see about applyin' at several East Athens restaurants." Before Jennifer could open her mouth to protest, Kelly placed her empty glass in the sink, turned and ran a hand over her frazzled hair. "Well, I'm tuckered out. I'm goin' on to bed, sweet girl."

Jennifer stood there mute while Kelly disappeared down the hallway, both her guarded admiration of her mother's good deed and her words of warning about her own future here left unspoken. Exhausted from the rapid unfolding of recent events, Jennifer wanted to go to bed too, but she knew the thoughts of Michael she'd shoved into the back of her head would explode into her consciousness the minute she became horizontal, so she settled for an episode of "This Old House" instead.

The next day when Kelly departed for Athens, Jennifer roosted with a cup of hot chocolate in front of her computer. She opened the document Linnea e-mailed that morning, the Wifi at Michael's having proven too weak to transmit large files the previous afternoon.

To Jennifer's dismay, the gorget had initiated discussion leading them away from further reading of Verity's journal, although Linnea said the document suggested Levi speculated the item magnified, or at the least, symbolized, some sort of spiritual or psychological connection between his wife and the brave who had captured her. Jennifer got that now, how thoughts of a person could constantly dance around the periphery of your consciousness, an unseen cord pulling you to them, making you miserable when you were apart. Afraid to examine the evidence that Michael was distancing himself from her just as she finally understood him and admitted her feelings, Jennifer allowed thoughts of the diary and the murder investigation to take center stage in her mind.

Now, she scanned over the two entries their guest had read. Given the obvious longing relayed in them, Jennifer hoped for more about Tenetke, but the next two sections contained accounts of Levi showing his wife how to search the creek bed for yellow root to create a "spring tonic," and then chickweed, poke greens and waist-high plantain, to be boiled or made into a "salat." Perhaps Verity confined her written expression to the mundane out of fear that her husband read her journal. The entry after that cut to the chase: "The child is born."

August 1788. The child is born, a girl whom Levi delivered himself and named Selah, as in a pause for praise in the Psalms. He says good things always come from bad if we let the Lord God to bring it to pass. I allow I was afeared he would not react well once the baby came, especially if her color be off. And she is a bit dark, but he says we should accredit it to some Spanish ancestry on my side. This would be wise as the Natives have continued their aggression, thieving and scalping among Capt. Fielder and Capt. Autry as near as Scull Shoals. My husband has a plan to take us to Barnett's fort should we need protection, but I am not afeared, although Levi says it is foolish to think my former association with the Creek would spare me future violence.

Levi holds the infant and sings to her and is not vexed when I have to rise during the night to feed her. He says he will take her as his own. He is a good man. But when I hold her I am sad.

Autumn 1788. Oftimes dreams plague me. I feel Tenetke's spirit searching for me, and sometimes about my chores a drowning sensation of aloneness and longing near suffocates me. I feel the winter closing in, and I dread the knowledge of its bitter attack making my separation from him complete. If he knew I was with child last winter, he would never have left me, of that I am certain. And if I returned with Selah, I have no doubt of my welcome. Why can I not cease thinking of this?

Randa, the colored woman Levi brought here to help who sleeps in our loft, knows. Somehow she knows and reports to him. I heard her tell him a dark cord joins my soul to Tenetke's, because he took what was not his and laid down bad magic upon me. Perhaps she is right. I cannot control my emotions where he is concerned. Levi made me pray with him about Tenetke. I said what he wanted me to, but it feels like what happened to me changed me forever, and I will never get beyond it.

Jennifer took a deep breath, saddened for Levi rather than satisfied at the "more" about Tenetke she had desired. During a time when understanding of the psychological and chemical aspects of depression and PTSD remained two hundred years in the future, and "hysteria" was condemned as witchcraft, what hope did Verity have of explaining her inner landscape to her husband? Yet Levi kept on, all through 1789, applying prayers and teas and tonics, waiting for his wife to be "normal" again. Verity's descriptions of historical events and daily chores, while almost absent of mention of her child, led Jennifer to believe she made little progress. Had Jennifer not been so keen on finding evidence to the contrary, she would have found the history lesson fascinating.

July 1789. We have word President Washington prepared to treat with the Upper Creek under their supreme chief, mixed blood Alexander McGillivray, but negotiations failed. McGillivray fears to recognize the United States as protector because that would legitimize the lands Georgia stole from his people and annul his other treaties. It is said he maintains relations with Spain. So it seems the assaults will not cease at this time.

Autumn 1789. Today and the day prior were taken up with the dyeing of my wool yarn, a messy business layering walnut leaves with the yarn, pouring water over all, and boiling all day, then repeating the process from scratch with the morning sun. As we have fair and mild weather, I have hung the skeins to dry several days, but it already appears I have achieved a consistent black color Mother would be proud of.

Autumn 1789. Levi speaks not to me. He says I need to get out, but I find his attempts to pretend the past never happened naïve. I refused to attend the corn shucking at Cherokee Corner, because the last event I went to with him, a spring barn raising for a newlywed couple, folks seemed to not know what to say to me. I saw the looks they gave Selah when her bonnet revealed her face. I am that woman soiled by the savages, with her unholy offspring in tow. Isolation near drives me insane at times but is preferable to disdain or pity.

Jennifer pulled out her phone, realizing the diary gave her an excuse to text Michael. "Are you reading this journal?" she typed.

The waiting reply made her heart leap when she returned from a bathroom break. "Yes."

"I feel so sorry for them," she texted. "He keeps trying to get to her and can't. The pull of the past is so strong." Staring at the words she'd just sent, Jennifer froze, realizing the parallel. Like Verity, she was broken, wounded, unable to freely give the sort of love a man required, especially a man with his own wounds. God had begun a work in her, but too late, too slow, for Michael? Could he be as patient as Levi?

His next answer made her heart thud heavy with dismay. "Maybe too strong for him to break through."

"Maybe Levi couldn't do it alone, but he had God on His side. God can do it," she texted Michael. Surely he saw changes in her and recognized her commitment to reaching wholeness, if he would just be willing to walk the long road ahead with her a step at a time.

"The person still has to reach out to God."

She responded without thinking. "I did. And He was there. He was just as available to Verity. Stella says either thinking we're too damaged for God to fix or so special He should have kept us from ever being hurt are just two different forms of pride."

The phone remained silent for a minute or two, then Michael replied, "OK. Going to keep reading now."

Jennifer bit her lip, staring at his words. She'd done it again, turning around a conversation that started out about Verity and herself and saying more than she should have that applied to Michael. But maybe not. Somehow she knew Michael needed to hear Stella's words, whether he compared himself to Levi, the long-suffering spouse saddled with undeserved heartache, or Verity, stuck in a past that bound his future. As if her current prayers could have effect on the 1700s, Jennifer sent a request upward that this tale of Verity and Levi ended happily, and that something in it would change Michael's heart.

She skipped the rest of Verity's uneventful reports about butchering their hog, chinquapin tree fruit boiled in milk for Selah's teething, successful trapping and winter snow, to where something shifted in March of 1790.

The first of March 1790. Levi's Methodist friends have given report that Rev. Francis Asbury seeks land for a school in Middle Georgia, near Washington. He stays with merchant Daniel Grant and son Thomas on the Little River and will preach at Grant's Meeting House. Levi believes my spirit would take comfort from hearing his address, so we are to set out tomorrow. The heavy rains this season mean travel will prove arduous. I admit, though, the prospect of a trip and the company of Christian souls not informed of my past sounds appealing.

Late March 1790. I return lightened of soul. Unto a packed house, Rev. Asbury preached on Ezekiel 2:7, "And thou shalt speak my words unto them, whether they will hear, or whether they will forbear: for they are most rebellious." Many came unto God, and He smote my heart with conviction that I have resisted Him by clinging like a victim to the darkness of my ordeal. The ordeal does not give identity, God Himself does. Brother Whatcoat and Rev. Asbury proved most gracious, praising Selah without the blink of an eye, confessing they, too, suffer lowness of spirit at times, even, in fact, in that moment, and praying with me to release the past into God's hands. I swear I did feel a chain fall off during that prayer.

Then the strangest thing happened. Brother Whatcoat laid hands on me and said with calm assurance, "Sister Dunham, the Lord has given unto me to know that before this year is expired, you shall bear Brother Levi's daughter, and she shall be great comfort to you."

That amazing prediction bore us home over muddy roads. It was all we could speak of. I could see in Levi's face the gift a child of his own would be to him, for all his goodness to Selah, who quite exhausted us with her restless energy this trip. My husband has the patience of Job, and I have much to repay him for.

April 1790. The effect of our journey to the Little River has proved miraculous. No longer does my soul pine for Tenetke, and Bro. Whatcoat must indeed have heard from the Lord, for I am with child. I expect a Christmas baby. We already know her name, "Comfort." Just as importantly, the Lord warms my heart toward Levi. Finally I can see him again.

May 1790. The world greens, as do I. Levi says never was I more beautiful. I spend much time planting and tending our corn, beans, pole beans, squash, snap peas and sweet potatoes, while trying to keep Selah about my feet. We pen the cattle, hogs and our new sheep at night against wolves but allow them to forage in the river cane and bamboo on fair days. If Levi hesitates to leave us, 'tis now not out of fear that I will flee but out of the fear that all white male settlers share, over the protection of their wives and children. Incidents with the natives still occur, but I trust now in God.

September 1790. Last month, Supreme Chief McGillivray and lesser chiefs in dress regalia traveled to New York and there signed away the lands east of the Oconee River. Levi says Alexander feared war with the United States. The United States feared Spain might sponsor an independent country on its border. People are not pleased with the treaty because it bypassed state leaders and ignored Head Right Grants on the west bank of the Oconee. Citizens of Greene County now must show a pass to cross to that side. Neither did the Creek people receive what they wanted, return of the land between the forks of the Apalachee and Oconee. Some settlers discuss the merits of killing any Indian on sight.

Knowing firsthand how they love the land, I am sad for the Creek people. I believe Tenetke would want peace if he could have it. He must be so

tired of war and has undoubtedly married again, mayhap more than once, and fathered children. But then, there existed a dark and extreme violence in some of the braves that went beyond the natural, giving cause to fear and animosity among their enemies, and feeding many a nightmare, some of them my own.

October 1790. Our new neighbor, George Paschal, who farms six hundred acres south of Scull Shoals, has his eye on Burrell Brewer's daughter Agnes. Hopefully we shall have a wedding soon. And Vines Collier on his four hundred has built a fine new house, with the walls plastered above a chair rail, mantels almost six feet high, board and batten doors, a log walkway out to the kitchen, and a dry well to store milk and butter. Levi says he himself must acquire more land to support such grandeur, but I do not mind our snug little cabin, especially since he did agree to plaster my walls before Comfort is born.

At that point, spacing in the transcription indicated a break in the journal. Linnea had typed a paragraph in brackets, followed by another entry in 1798. Wait, eight years passed without Verity recording anything? Jennifer pursed her lips in frustration, scrolling around and hoping to find the missing time period somewhere else in the document. Finally, disappointed, she returned to the modern note.

"On the next page, Verity recorded two Scriptures, Isaiah 61:1 and Exodus 15:26b. Apparently she left off writing in her journal until 1798. The verses she wrote were: 'The Spirit of the Lord God is upon me; because the Lord hath anointed me to preach good tidings unto the meek; he hath sent me to bind up the brokenhearted, to proclaim liberty to the captives, and the opening of the prison to them that are bound.' And 'I am the Lord that healeth thee.'"

Jehovah Rapha. A person could keep God from working by covering their wounds from the past just as Jennifer had in her memory of shielding the bicycle accident cut from the ineffective ministration of her mother, or they could raise that protective hand and allow the Master Physician to do what He promised He would, heal. Jennifer sat back as a moment of awareness passed over her, raising the hair on her arms. In that instant, she knew God was answering her prayer. He had heard Verity when she cried out for healing, and He heard her, too. He would also hear Michael. She felt a sudden assurance of it so strong that she knew it didn't come from herself, and with it, a sense of peace that scattered all her anxious thoughts. She could see the threads of all the stories coming together, resting in God's hands as He prepared to tie them up.

She also knew what she had to do next. The path illuminated in front of her as clearly as if a floodlight shone. Before she could second guess herself, she picked up the phone to make a call.

Looking out the kitchen window onto a gray November day a few minutes later, Jennifer realized she'd skipped lunch but still wasn't hungry. Her mind swirled with images from the 1700s, and her spirit floated with the buoyancy of joy and confirmation. How strange this bubble of protective peace felt, even when she didn't know what Michael would do. It was different from not caring, for she cared intensely. She'd never wanted anything more than she wanted that man to love her. But somehow she knew in the bigger scheme of things, she would be OK. Her Father held her in His hand.

"God's got this," she said aloud, then chuckled when she realized she sounded just like Stella. That was a good thing.

Kelly probably would not have eaten, either, and would be hungry when she got home. Opting for an early dinner, Jennifer pulled a small shoulder roast out of the refrigerator. As she placed it in a baking dish with cream of mushroom soup, minced onion flakes and pepper, and peeled potatoes and carrots to surround the meat, she marveled at the way God involved Himself in the lives of mere mortals and hummed the chorus of a praise song she heard often on the radio.

But thoughts of Michael intruded on her new-found peace. Something so strong drew her toward the house next door. Shouldn't she give God time to work in Michael's heart? Wasn't this out of her hands? What would she possibly say? "Um, hi, I missed you, and I wanted to be around you. Do you mind if I just stand here in the same room with you for a while?"

Tell him the truth, a voice in her head urged.

Oh, no. Not that voice. The one that could not be disobeyed if one wanted to maintain any personal peace. She argued, *what truth*?

He needs to know you love him.

Jennifer burst out loud: "Oh, good heavens, I can't! I would never! He has to say that first!"

She waited, but no answer entered her brain. Just silence. She cut the vegetables into chunks, covered the pan with foil, and slid it into the pre-heated oven, slamming the door. She leaned on the kitchen counter, hands on her hips in a stance of rebellion, but only a feeling of slight sadness surfaced. Now, why sadness?

Jennifer went back to her computer desk and tried to resume her reading.

May 1798. I fear I have neglected my journal. As life became increasingly full and blessed, despite two infants I miscarried, I no longer needed to write out my despair. My husband and I experienced great happiness in the Lord's provision with our two daughters. But now I find I must write for joy, for I am again with child. I waited long enough to ascertain the pregnancy progresses without cause for concern to make this announcement. Things will be different this time. Randa says the way I am carrying suggests this will be a boy.

Jennifer looked up. That would be Silas. The news ought to capture her interest, but she found her attention wandering, a sense of unease lingering. She couldn't settle into the story like before, and her heart still tugged her toward Dunham House. It ached so badly with unexpressed love for the man who lived there that she could hardly breathe.

"Fine," she said aloud, throwing her hands up. *But you've got to give me the words, God.*

But James was bound to be there, if not GBI detectives, wrapping up their investigation. Not giving herself time to agonize over what to say, she reached for her phone and sent Michael a message. "Can you come over for a minute? It's important."

She hoped he didn't have his phone with him, but a minute later, a text bubble appeared. "Sure, is everything OK?"

"Yes, I just need to speak with you alone."

"On my way."

Jennifer jumped up, the image of Michael striding her way putting her in a frenzy of anxiety. What in the world was she doing? She ran to the bathroom and looked at herself, brushing her hair and drumming her fingers on the counter. Praise music. Stella said praise music helped when one felt worried or afraid. It would also help fill any awkward silences. She ran to the kitchen and turned on the radio to a popular Christian station just as a knock sounded on her front door.

When she opened it, Michael stood there, unbearably handsome in jeans and a navy sweater that highlighted his eyes. Jennifer wrung her hands. She absolutely couldn't do this.

"You read the rest of the journal?" he asked. She jumped back as he stepped inside. He frowned in confusion, taking in her nervous gestures and wide eyes. "Is that what this is about?"

"Through 1798."

"Me, too."

"But I got stuck on something important."

"The Scripture?" Michael stood in the middle of her living room floor, filling the double-wide as he hunched his broad shoulders and hooked his thumbs on his belt loops. His quick movements and short statements bespoke impatience, defensiveness.

She nodded, still wringing her hands and feeling small.

"'I am the Lord that healeth thee,'" he quoted. "Let me guess, you want to know if I caught the significance of that being repeated after the sermon at the park, but you're afraid you'll make me mad if you ask. Yes. I did. I promise not to be too proud to pray about it."

Jennifer's face twisted in dismay. "I didn't mean you were proud like that—"

"Well, maybe I am, but now you've made me aware of it. I'll pray about it. So are we good?"

"No, we're not good, because there's something else I have to tell you," Jennifer admitted, "if you'll stop looking at me like that."

He unhooked his fingers from his waistband. "Like what?"

"Like the big bad wolf."

Michael took a deep breath, then let it out. "I'm sorry. I don't mean to. I guess I don't like feeling I'm being called over here to account." Distracted, Michael's attention wandered to the kitchen. "What is that loud music, anyway?"

"But that's not why I called you at all," Jennifer protested in a faint voice. She forced herself to let her arms hang by her sides. "There's something I think you need to know."

Realizing her distress did not stem from a plan to confront him over some spiritual matter, Michael stepped forward, reaching for one of her hands. His brows lowered in the expression of concern Jennifer loved, because it opened the door of honesty. "OK. What is it?" When she still hesitated, his face shifted into lines of alarm. "Wait, are you going to tell me you're leaving?"

She tightened her grip on his warm fingers, holding on as if they were a lifeline. Did he feel her shaking? "No, I'm staying. I'm actually staying. I just called Marian Dukes to accept the position in Lexington." Michael's mouth dropped open, but before he could speak, Jennifer held up her other hand. "I need to speak plainly for once, because I think it's what God wants me to do right now, so that you can make your own decisions. I know that, like Verity, things in my past messed me up, but like her, I've been given a new life by Jesus. I know that you know that, but you also know that the road to wholeness can be a long one. I think maybe you've ... backed off ... as you realized just how long."

"Jennifer, I—" he began, but she cut him off, releasing his hand and clasping hers under her chin to still their trembling.

"Let me finish, please, or I may not have the courage to."

"OK."

Jennifer gasped in a breath and, even though it seemed to evaporate before making it to her lungs, continued in a voice that sounded high and rushed. "I'm staying not only because of the people here, all my new friends, but because I want to offer you the option to walk beside me on that road. Maybe that's too much to ask, but in reading the story of Levi and Verity, I realize more than ever that's what I want. For you to be as patient with me as he was with her. Michael, not only do I love the people here, I — I love *you*."

The words were out. She stood there completely vulnerable as Michael's face froze in an expression of shock. Time seemed to stop along with Jennifer's heart. But she did not get a chance to witness his reaction, for a sound on the deck, previously muted by the rapturous praise music, caused her to whirl around.

Kelly burst in, threw up a hand like a bull rider, and gyrated her bottom in an embarrassing dance as she twirled in a circle. "Guess who just got hired at Fatz in time for the holiday rush? Me, me, yeah, me! Oh .... Hello, Michael. What are you doing here?"

CHAPTER THIRTEEN

What followed rated among Jennifer's most awkward and embarrassing lifetime moments. They explained Michael's presence on the basis of the Dunham journal, but Jennifer knew her mother realized something else had occurred by the deep red of her daughter's face, and the stunned look of Michael's.

Just before he blinked and focused on Kelly, did Jennifer imagine the sheen of tears in his eyes as he took in her cringing form? Oh, God help her, had her admission caused him to pity her that much?

"Congratulations on the job, Kelly," Michael said in a modulated voice that Jennifer imagined he would have used when giving cancer patients difficult news, showing thoughtfulness but no real personal emotion. "When do you start?"

"Thursday. Thanks, I'm so happy. And so grateful I can pull my own weight and stay close to my baby girl." Smirking, Kelly reached out to squeeze Jennifer's forearm.

Jennifer offered a distracted smile, stepping farther away from Michael but not too close to Kelly's abounding enthusiasm. "I'm glad, too, Mom."

"Well, listen, I'll go and let you ladies get on with your day," Michael said.

"Oh, don't hurry off on my account," Kelly protested. "I'm just going to grab a bite to eat, then I'm off to Stella's to spend the evening with Amy."

Jennifer turned toward Michael but could not quite meet his eyes as she said, "I have a roast in the oven. Should be done within half an hour. You're welcome to eat with us."

"Thanks, but that's OK. But I do want to thank you for what you shared. It … meant a lot to me. Can we talk in the morning?"

"Sure," Jennifer mumbled. As Michael stepped close, touching her arm and brushing a quick, soft kiss against her forehead, moisture sprang to her eyes. She'd been right. He pitied her. He didn't want to hurt her feelings, but he didn't feel the same way about her that she felt about him, or nothing would have stopped him from staying long enough to express his love. Kelly's departure to Stella's would have provided that perfect opportunity. She felt herself sink into an emotional puddle as the door started to close, then jerked herself upright when Michael stuck his head back inside.

"Oh, I should tell you ladies that the coroner completed his report on the body in the outhouse today," he said.

"Yes?" Jennifer prompted, raising her chin as she wrapped her arms around herself.

"It was indeed Chad Fullerton, and he was indeed killed just as Horace described. The family has been notified. I imagine this will give them long overdue closure."

Jennifer nodded. "How sad. Thanks for telling us." Once the door closed behind him, she let out a deep breath and hung her head.

Kelly turned toward her, hands on her hips as she demanded, "Forget the dead body. What was all the rest about?"

Jennifer covered her face with her hands and let out a moan. "I've done the stupidest thing in the world. I told Michael I loved him."

"No way! And he didn't say it back?"

"No, but then again, you came waltzing in the door right after I'd made my big pronouncement."

"Oh, honey, I'm sorry. I'm an idiot," Kelly said, wrapping Jennifer in her arms.

"It's not your fault. You didn't know he was here." Jennifer heaved a sigh and wiped tears from her eyes with both palms. "I've messed everything up. I went against everything I've ever done and told him how I felt, that I was staying in Hermon and actually asked him to be patient enough about my past to work on a relationship."

Kelly drew back to look at her, her dark-rimmed eyes widening. "Wow, that took a lot of courage!"

"Uh, yeah, and made me look like a needy fool," Jennifer said with disgust.

But Kelly shook her head. "No, it didn't. Jennifer, I'm proud of you. You didn't do anything wrong. Michael is a good man. Even if he's not the man for you, it was a huge step for you to reach out toward a guy like that."

"I thought God wanted me to," Jennifer wailed.

"Then He probably did." Kelly patted her back. "But you got to let Him work. Men get scared sometimes. Maybe you took him by surprise. He probably needed a minute to process this. If he has any feelings for you, which I believe he does, he'll come around. In the meantime, don't beat yourself up. You got nothin' to be ashamed of, an' if that man has any sense, he'll be amazed and grateful at what a gift's been offered to him."

Jennifer wiped her face again and managed a tentative smile, saying something she'd had precious few occasions to say in the past, "Thanks, Mom." She couldn't believe Kelly actually proved capable of comforting her.

Kelly made a shooing motion. "What are mamas for? Now, let's check on that delicious-smellin' roast in the oven!"

Kelly's words were easier said than applied. While her mother scarfed down the meat and vegetables with the appetite of one just given a new lease on life, Jennifer picked at her food and stared into space, replaying the exchange with Michael and searching for any hint of responsiveness. In light of her daughter's continued moroseness, Kelly offered to stay home that evening, but Jennifer insisted Amy needed support far more than she did.

She saw Kelly off, deciding to walk around the side of the house for a view of Michael's back yard. Wrapping her sweater around her and peeking through the line of evergreen trees, Jennifer noted that two uniformed men worked around the second privy vault, shoveling in dirt and taking down crime scene tape. Today ended a long nightmare for the Fullerton family and began one for Amy Greene. What did it signal for her and Michael?

Amazingly, Jennifer didn't question her decision to stay in Oglethorpe County. Tomorrow, she'd call Tandy, and she'd have to call Barbara, too. She dreaded that conversation almost more than the next one with Michael, but she knew her decision to break off that connection was right. Sensing the relationship would not go down a good future path, she needed to shed the controlling weight of it. Hadn't Barb herself always said that sometimes one had to break off things from the past that held you back? The professor had just never thought that advice would apply to herself.

Yes, she'd found herself here and made friendships that would last for life. Her mother could thrive here, too. If things didn't work out with Michael, she and Kelly could find a little apartment closer to

Lexington and both of their jobs. She wouldn't have to see him that often, but the thought of any future encounters if Michael didn't love her, and especially if he found someone else he did love, pierced Jennifer with emotional kryptonite.

Jennifer went back inside, praying that if a future between herself and the brooding widower next door constituted part of God's plan for their lives, Michael, too, would be able to release the silver gorget in his past. Wondering whatever became of Verity, Selah and the mysterious crescent, she returned to her computer.

October 1798. The birth of our son, Silas, changes everything. Dear Levi has an heir. With this in mind, he forsees the need to provide for the family of the future. The prosperity and success of our neighbors induce him to purchase more land and draw up plans for a fine plantation home. Joel Early on the eastern bluff of the Oconee built Fontenoy. He had his children dress for dinner at six like they dwelt in Boston rather than the Georgia frontier, and his son Peter returned from Princeton to practice law in the area. An Italian merchant named Ferdinand Phinizy who came to America with French troops during the war has moved from Augusta to Long Creek and also builds a grand house, China Grove of sand brick, with mantels of carved mahogany and three large upstairs bedrooms. Our acquaintance with the Phinizy family grows, for their Sarah is the same age as Selah, and their Jacob that of Comfort. Phinizy opens both a store in the new community forming northeast of here and a hotel on the stage route to Greensborough. He even has a race track on his property! Levi hopes to be of good influence on him, since his cruel overseer causes his slaves to flee, and of course there is the matter of gambling.

Yet I am pleased the forward-mindedness of these men urge Levi to consider the future. So much has changed, we will hardly remain frontier much longer. The Indian attacks in the early part of the decade that led to the governor ordering a dozen log forts to supplement settler compounds along the Oconee and old Indian fighter Elijah Clarke establishing his own militia give way to the government's condemnation of Clarke's "Trans-Oconee Republic" and the 1795 arrival of Benjamin Hawkins as Indian Agent to the Creek Nation. I do not believe the Creek will remain in our state much longer.

January 1799. We passed a joyful yuletide at China Grove, complete with firecrackers, evergreen decorations, brandied peaches and eggnog, and a Twelfth Day Ball. I had not danced since receiving lessons in Augusta. I had forgotten what a joy it is. For so long, I had forgotten joy itself. I made up the burgundy silk muslin Levi gifted me with for a beautiful gown.

Everyone conveyed congratulations on Silas' birth, eclipsing my sorrowful past and the shadow of my older daughter's ancestry. My joy would have been full, but in observing Selah among the other children, I fell prey to concerns that would not lift. Having obtained a greater perception at ten years of age, she seems to find more equal footing among the slave children than the white. She says she is as displaced as they and will not be persuaded otherwise. I can only assume comments were made to her out of our hearing.

Selah also made the acquaintance of a slave woman named Luca at China Grove who calls herself a healer, but the maid assigned me during my stay says she practices the dark arts. She is known to make up "love teas" for those interested in making someone fall in love with them, and far worse, she was caught once putting a bottle with nine new pins crooked three ways under her hearth, a step in cursing someone. The servants fear her. I forbade Selah to go near this woman. Selah thinks what she does is the same as what Levi does. Her fascination alarms me. During the last half of our visit, I made sure the girl remained in the company of other settler children.

On a happy note, Phinizy begins to see the error of his ways. He wishes to employ a new overseer, discontinue flogging as punishment for his bondsmen and institute morning prayers on the estate. He and Levi had many profitable and spiritually enriching discussions over the yuletide.

February 1799. Selah's discontent grows. Comfort hovers over her baby brother like a little mother, but Selah employs herself with chores that take her out of his periphery. She has always been a withdrawn, inner-focused child, but now she seems to feel extraneous even in our own family, as though Silas fills a gap she never could. As though the two of them, boy and girl, fully mine and Levi's together, equal her exclusion. Nothing I say convinces her otherwise. She begins to ask questions about her father, knowing he is not Levi. She no longer wishes to sit near Levi when he reads from the Word, or play nine pens or dominoes with him. She snuck off yesterday and caused us great alarm. She was not found until eventide, coming home on the road that runs to China Grove. She claimed to have spent the day in the woods, but she was not chilled through enough for that and had a closed and sullen look that made me think of Luca.

March 1799. I have told her how I was taken by her father's people and lived among them for a time. A distant light glazes her eye as I catch her looking to the west. In an attempt to make her feel she has a piece of him, I gave her Tenetke's gorget. She wears it about her neck on a black ribbon. When Levi told her to take it off, she protested so violently he relented, not wanting to further alienate her.

April 1799. With the spring, Selah begs us to take her to visit her father's people. We explain this is not possible. She has wept and told me she has never felt she belonged here, and now she knows why. This is exactly what I feared. My heart breaks for her, but I do not know what to do. Levi does. He takes her with him to the fields and forests in search of herbs and tells her what he has learned from the Indians and Africans as well as from his schooling about how to use the earth's bounty to heal people. Thank God, she responds to his tutelage, helping him dry the herbs and roll his pills. I hope this will satisfy the want that caused her to run off several times now to Luca's cabin. She is bright and quick and will make a good healer if she will heed her stepfather's instruction. But will she ever find her place? And someone to love her?

Jennifer raised her head and untucked her foot from beneath her, looking out the window to see the gray twilight fade into an early nightfall. Verity's questions echoed in her head, reflecting on her own life.

Following less personal accounts of colonial existence, an 1802 entry stated, "The Fort Wilkinson Treaty has moved the Creek boundary to Middle Georgia. Settlers can now travel west of the Oconee and Apalachee rivers and congregate in fledgling towns nearby. I pray this settles Selah's restless spirit, her avid curiosity about the native healing arts and beliefs. Would that she yearned after the truths of our Lord in like manner. Regardless, she must now make her life here among her mother's people." The diary ended soon after.

Sighing in an attempt to relieve the heavy pressure on her heart, Jennifer closed the document and turned off the computer. From local hearsay, she knew Selah had not aligned with her mother's wishes. She had continued in her path as a local healer, eventually aiding her younger brother Silas in his work at his sanatorium, but she had died an old maid hiding her valued gorget in Levi's cabin where she dwelt while the rest of the family entertained antebellum gentry in Silas' grand new plantation house. Folks said the one sweetheart who'd looked past her mixed blood died in the War of 1812, causing her to revert to the introverted state Verity described in her journal. And evidence hinted Selah continued to remain open to the dark side of her profession in a time when common receipts for curses and magic wormed their way even into medical books.

One thing Jennifer knew, she did not want to end up like Selah, like Barbara, alone in her twilight years, using her work to compensate for her bitterness toward men and God. Now, Jennifer wondered if Selah ever found peace and the healing and belonging only God could provide. Well, she had God, so even if Michael rejected her, she would never be alone like Selah and Barbara. Taking some comfort in that, Jennifer ran a hot bubble bath. But she prayed. Oh, how she prayed, all evening and through the night she spent tossing and turning and dreaming of the tenderness she longed to see on Michael's face when he looked at her.

Her mother woke her far too early the next morning, leaning over Jennifer's bed and shaking her shoulder. "Hey, let's go into town to buy Christmas decorations."

"Mom, it's hardly worth it. It's not like this is our permanent home," Jennifer mumbled.

"So? It's our home right now, and I want to have Christmas! Don't worry, it's on me."

Jennifer rolled over to face the wall, pulling the pillow over her exposed ear. "You haven't even started work."

"I have all that ATM cash burnin' a hole in my pocket. Better Santas than cigarettes, right?"

Jennifer groaned. "Please no Santas!"

"OK, we'll get whatever you want. Snowmen? Manger scenes?"

"Can't we go later?"

Kelly pulled on the pillow and leaned down until Jennifer rolled an eye back toward her. Her mother gave her a mischievous wink. "I was thinkin' breakfast at Huddle House. It'll be fun, and get your mind off Michael Phelps, Olympian."

"*Mom.*"

"OK, just humor me. I need some good shoes for waitin' tables anyway."

Jennifer let out a breath. "Fine. But I need coffee now."

"I turned on your magic machine in the kitchen. I'm hittin' the shower."

As Kelly danced off to the guest bathroom, Jennifer washed her face, brushed her hair and pulled on a fluffy robe. Since they were heading out for breakfast, she also brushed her teeth. Then she made her way to the kitchen, where she selected a hazelnut K-cup and set the Keurig to brew. She noticed out the kitchen window that an especially brilliant horizon with shades of orange and pink burned off the foggy gray of dawn in a haze of splendor. Maybe some fresh air along with the caffeine would get her up near her mother's speed. Besides, Kelly was singing a really annoying Christmas jingle over the hiss of the shower. With her full mug in her hands, Jennifer padded across the living room floor.

Stepping out onto the front deck, Jennifer froze before the door closed behind her. Michael sat on the step, bundled in a thick brown coat, dark head down, a Bible in his hands.

"Michael?" she gasped. "What are you doing here?"

He looked up, and the sight of tears standing in his eyes made her blink in surprise. "I feel like I've wrestled all night with the Lord like Jacob did," he said. "I think He's telling me to go back to medicine. And more important, I had to come tell you what I should have yesterday when you told me you loved me."

Her trembling hand sloshed her coffee so violently in her cup that Jennifer placed the mug on the rail. Leaving his Bible on the top step, Michael stood up as she turned to look at him. "And what was that?" she whispered. Her heart slammed against her rib cage.

To Jennifer's astonishment, he was looking at her in the way she'd pictured in her dreams, like a prospector who finally struck gold. She blinked to make sure she was awake.

"That I've been a fool, and I love you, too."

He clasped her to him and covered her mouth with his, the toes of her fluffy slippers perched atop his work boots. In that moment, what had been long caged inside her broke free and took flight.

CHAPTER FOURTEEN

Jennifer put her hand on the dashboard of Michael's truck as the vehicle turned off 77 south of Union Point and bounced over a rutted dirt lane beneath low-hanging branches flagged with sparse brown leaves.

"What are you doing?" she squeaked. "We have to get Donald. He'll be waiting for us in front of the VA home, freezing to death!"

Michael cut a glance over at her and smiled. "We have time for a little detour. I told him we'd be there in time for lunch at Long John Silver's. If he freezes sitting outside too long, it's his own fault."

It was the day before Thanksgiving. Linnea decided at the last minute to ensconce herself, Frank and Dee Ann at a B & B in Lexington. Michael's aunts and their families arrived from Atlanta tomorrow. And to Jennifer's surprise, Stella had agreed to bring Earl and the boys to Dunham House for Thanksgiving dinner. At this very moment, in fact, Kelly chopped, boiled and sliced in Stella's kitchen, preparing several casseroles and desserts alongside her new friend. Jennifer hoped her mother learned something. Tonight, Michael planned to give up his bed for his grandfather in favor of the sunroom sofa.

Jennifer had been touched when Michael had asked her to accompany him to Milledgeville to pick up Donald, his maternal grandmother's husband who had shed so much light on the story of Georgia Pearl back in the spring. Now, in consideration of all that was going on, she could hardly believe Michael chose to tack on an extra stop.

But when she saw where they were going, Jennifer let out a squeal of delight. Michael parked the truck at the side of the abandoned, white, Federal-style mansion she'd admired—and he'd teased her about—on their first trip to the VA home. She turned to look at him with widened eyes. "Are we going to trespass?"

He laughed, cutting the engine and opening his door. "We most certainly are."

"Oh, good gracious." She sat there biting her lip, studying the dried ivy twining the whitewashed, brick chimney in front of her as she absorbed that bit of rebellion.

"Well, are you coming?" Michael asked from the open extended cab door.

"I sure am!" As she jumped out, Michael lifted a basket she hadn't noticed yet from the back seat. "What's that?"

"A surprise."

She blinked. "What surprise?"

"An excuse for us to sit and talk a minute without your mother or my father interrupting us for a change. Now go."

"Front or back door?"

"Well, if I know you, you'll want the grand entrance."

"If possible."

"It's possible."

Standing in the limb-littered front yard, Jennifer admired the nine-over-nine windows, five across the top and most missing shutters with faded and peeling black paint, and the tooth-like dentil molding at the cornice. "How do you know it's possible?" she asked Michael, who stood patiently behind her holding the basket.

"If I can't get in the front door without creating too much damage, which I know you'd protest, I'll go around back and do what I have to while you wait here."

She turned to look at him and broke out laughing. "You wouldn't."

"To see your face when you get inside, I would. I looked this place up on the Internet and couldn't find a thing. Like it didn't even exist. Which tells me you were probably right, it's probably caught up in some decades-long family squabble. I'm betting one of the doors have been accessed by vagrants many times over."

"OK, let's see." Jennifer tip-toed her way onto the single-story entrance porch, testing for rotten boards and finding most sound. She approached the door under an impressive fan light and turned the knob. To her surprise and delight, it opened just as Michael predicted. "I can't believe it. Oh!" She pushed the door open and stared inside, clasping her hands beneath her chin.

At her customary statement of architectural awe, Michael chuckled. As expected in Southern country houses of the early 1800s, the stairway and entrance hall were both pretty plain, the six-panel doors providing the most visual interest. Despite the home's simple trim, the peeling plaster, black and white late autumn lighting and empty stretches of dusty yellow pine flooring spoke to Jennifer of whispering petticoats, roasting nuts on crackling fireplaces and the laughter of children long since buried in forgotten graves. Her heart thudded with joy. Michael came up behind her, setting the basket down inside the door and wrapping his arms around her from behind. He kissed her cheek.

"See? I knew it would be worth it."

She turned her face toward the slight scratchiness of his jaw, and butterflies exploded in her stomach as she inhaled his spicy scent. "You're amazing."

She felt his fingers curl around hers. "Let's explore."

They went through all the rooms, finding evidence in the form of tattered blankets and tin cans that drifters indeed had camped out inside the farmhouse in recent decades, although no furniture remained. Jennifer admired the Adamesque trim on the fireplaces and the view of wintry branches and what once was a bustling road through wavy glass, but her favorite discovery was that of the main parlor's oval-shaped plaster walls.

"This is incredible to find out here in the middle of nowhere," she stated. "Reminds me of some of the surprises in Dunham House. I'm just glad your place is no longer falling down and full of spider webs like this one."

"Maybe now that you'll be working in Lexington you can comb the countryside for abandoned beauties and bring them the proper attention in your spare time," Michael teased, winking at her. "This seems like the perfect room for our picnic. Be right back."

He whisked into the entry hall before she could question further, returning with the basket. He opened it and spread a flannel blanket in the middle of the floor, then pulled out a thermos and a plate of what appeared to be Montana's goodies. Jennifer covered her mouth with her hands. "You did this all for me?"

"Why not?" Michael gestured to the expanse of plaid material beside him. "Sit down. I have the last of Mary Ellen's pumpkin spice coffee for the season, and Montana had a lot of fun making this assortment when I told her what I was up to."

"Oh, I bet she did, the little stinker." Jennifer laughed as she knelt beside Michael, remembering the first time Montana had predicted Jennifer would marry Michael. She didn't know about that one yet, but things were certainly moving in a more promising direction now.

"She told me she was going to pray I stayed in Hermon rather than going to Savannah. I guess God heard her. I haven't even told her the news yet." Jennifer gave a brief grimace of guilt.

Michael smirked. "Don't worry, I did." He uncovered the plate of muffins and cookies and set out matching coffee mugs.

"What did she say?"

"It was more like a squeal. She threw herself at me and I thought for a minute she was going to kiss me. It was a little awkward."

Jennifer laughed. As Michael poured the coffee, she shook her head in amazement, her heart too full for words. Framed in the magical setting he'd gone to such lengths to create just to please her, the man before her could not have looked more rugged or appealing. "What happened to you?" she asked softly.

Michael handed her a mug. "How do you mean?"

"I'm sorry, but you're like ... a different person. The one I always thought was under there. I wanted to talk to you so much that morning on my porch, but my mother ..." She squeezed her eyes shut and covered her face with her free hand. "My mother! Oh, my stars, I know she adores you and she's so happy about all this, but I can't believe one day she burst in on us, and the next day she came out in that crazy Christmas sweater and invited you to go shopping with us. And you went! And then she made you help us decorate the whole house. For two days. And then your dad was there, and it was time to go to church, and it was always something. I mean, we talked on the phone some, but I feel like you never got the chance to tell me what changed so much that night before you came over."

"Which is why I wanted to take this moment where we were sure to not be interrupted."

Jennifer nodded, settling onto her bottom and reaching for half a muffin.

"What you said really got to me, you know."

"What part?"

"About pride."

She swallowed and placed her remaining bite of muffin on the plate. "Oh, yeah. That. I could tell I'd ruffled your feathers, but after Stella said it, I just couldn't get it out of my mind."

"So that night when you made your big admission and your mom came in, I know I should have stayed. I just ... couldn't." Michael hung his head. "I certainly was not expecting what you said. And I think I was under conviction. What you said about pride hit the nail on the head. I'd been telling God for years I didn't deserve what happened. But if it's true that sickness and death entered the world when evil did, and was not part of God's plan, but part of the consequences of human choices and the work of evil in the world, why was I any less deserving of suffering than the next man? Especially when I'm as much a mess inside as anyone. How arrogant to believe I deserved to go through life in a perfect bubble. And then, what I read in the Scriptures just transformed my view of death and eternity."

"What verse was that?"

Michael dug in his back pocket for his phone. "It was 1 Corinthians 15," he said, turning on his Bible ap. "I mean, I've read all this about how when believers die they get a new body, a better body, that the last enemy Christ destroyed was death. But this time, it was like I saw it from this whole different perspective. 'The spiritual is not first, but the natural, and afterward the spiritual.' I realized we look at life with tunnel vision. We think what's here on earth is where it's at, but it's not. For Christians, it's just the beginning. A step. Listen to this part: 'what you sow is not made alive unless it dies.'"

"Like the seeds from last year's crop," Jennifer said.

"Right. Last year's crop has to die for a new crop to grow. A whole eternal life awaits us when we die, in a perfected body. And I read somewhere God has things for us to do in His kingdom. We won't just be sitting around on clouds. So if Ashley and Mom left this life to go sooner to that one, who am I to sit around down here complaining and feeling cheated? That's just thinking of myself, because *they* weren't cheated. They got a head start on the rest of us."

"That sounds reasonable to me," Jennifer agreed. "But you also struggled with the fact that they suffered. Are you still trying to get your mind around that part?"

Michael's face clouded with memories. "Somewhat, but something we talked about helped me there, too."

Jennifer's eyes widened as she struggled to believe any wisdom from her short supply could have proved worthwhile. "What?"

"You asked me about Ashley's last days, and if you remember, I told you she never lost the light of Jesus."

A pregnant silence descended for a moment. Jennifer whispered, "Yes."

"It was me who did. As I looked back, Jennifer, I believe Ash was closer than ever to God in her last days. Scripture reveals He never gives us more than we can bear without God's help. So I have to believe that to be true. And in her dying, what grace she reflected and what a testimony she had of something stronger than the grave."

Jennifer blinked tears from her eyes and reached for Michael's hand. "That's beautiful. I wish I could have met her."

He pressed his lips together to still their trembling. "She would have liked you." Putting down his phone, Michael brushed her hair back with a thumb.

"Thank you for that." Somehow it meant more the way he said it than if he'd said "you would have liked her." And somehow Jennifer knew Michael knew that, which made her love him more.

Michael squeezed her hand and continued. "So I was wasting my life in bitterness and regret, not so unlike Verity. I was being nothing like Levi, who pressed forward in faith and never gave up. I had to change that. Levi's example convicted me. So that night I asked God to take all that from me and forgive me for thinking I knew better than He did. And when all that was taken away, that dark ... wall ... I'd erected in bitterness, I could see what was in front of me."

"What?" Jennifer breathed.

Michael touched the pert tip of her nose. "You."

She ventured an uncertain smile, still insecure that she had spoken her feelings first. "Did you really not know how I felt about you?"

He cocked his head. "You have to admit you gave me some mixed signals."

Jennifer hung her head. "Mostly I think that was fear from my past. I figured I was too messed up for you to want me."

"I'm sorry I made you think that. It's true I did use that as an excuse to justify stepping back, but the main problem was within myself. It was me holding onto the past more than you."

"So you don't think I'm hopeless?" She couldn't help herself. She had to hear it again. And probably again.

Michael scooted over close to her and wrapped her in his arms. "I don't, and I promise to be patient. I just want you to tell me what you need and be very clear with me about how fast to take things, OK?"

Jennifer nodded, eyes wide as she stared into his.

He stared back pointedly. "Like right now. You're going to have to say things that you might rather I read your mind about."

She nibbled her lip. "And you might have to ask things you'd rather I read your mind about."

He burst out laughing. "So can I kiss you?"

"You don't ever have to ask that particular question again, because the answer is always going to be yes."

Smiling, Michael sealed her lips with his. In the silvery silence of late morning, the parlor warmed and glowed like a magical place. Funny, Jennifer thought, to have such a moment in such a place, when she'd spent so many moments alone and afraid at another abandoned place, the Lockwood Plantation, as she grew up. Now, she was finally grown, and she was no longer alone or afraid, in or out of a man's arms. The right man, that was.

"So what's in our future, Miss Jennifer Rushmore?" Michael whispered as he drew back and smoothed her hair. Jennifer was surprised that she didn't want him to stop kissing her, but thankful for his sensitivity. Who knew when she'd come up against another wall they'd have to scale together, but it was probably best not to ruin today with that experience.

She couldn't get past part of the question to the answer that fast. "There's an 'our' future?" she asked, amazed at hearing such a concept put to words.

"Well, I sure hope so. You told me you wanted me to walk that road with you, didn't you?"

"More than anything." She just had trouble believing he wanted to.

"So what's the next step, then?"

"Well, Mom and I can look for an apartment or another rental next month," she offered, straightening her back.

Michael's expression looked veiled, speculative, as he sat back on the heels of his hands. She wasn't sure what to make of it. "I can probably convince the family who owns your double-wide to extend the lease if you'd like, maybe another six months. You could pay them directly instead of me."

Jennifer brightened at the idea of not having to move, and remaining so close to James and Michael. "Really? Will you?"

He nodded. "I'll call this weekend. I don't want you going anywhere, not even to Lexington."

She flushed with pleasure at the possession evidenced by his statement. "And what of your future? Here you and your dad are starting a local construction crew, yet you told me you thought God wanted you to return to medicine. You never explained that, either."

Michael flipped over his phone and pressed a few buttons, then read, "1 Corinthians 15:58: 'Therefore, my beloved brethren, be steadfast, immovable, always abounding in the work of the Lord, knowing that your labor is not in vain in the Lord.' I wasn't a preacher or evangelist, but I believed when I went into medicine God called me into the field of healing. I let go of that when I let go of God. For me, the two go together. That reminder at the end of the passage on death and new life really stood out to me. To fully live, I have to embrace that calling even as I let go of the hurts of the past. Dad can always manage a crew until he gets ready to retire, then hand it over to a good foreman."

"Have you already spoken to him about this?"

"Yes. He was very happy."

"I imagine so! That's wonderful, Michael. So what will you do? Can you finish your oncology residency?"

He shook his head. "I don't think I need to do that now. I need to release that whole part of my life and never wrestle with cancer again. That battle's done. I'll make some calls and see what's available for an internal medicine physician in the Athens area."

"That sounds perfect."

"Then why are you looking at me like that?"

"Like what? And wasn't I asking you that same question a couple days ago?"

Michael grinned and took a sip of the pumpkin coffee, making a face that caused Jennifer to give his arm a play shove. He spluttered and lowered the mug. "Like you don't believe me or something."

"I don't know. I guess I'm just trying to get used to the nice Michael rather than the guarded, brooding one."

He pretended to gasp in offense, set the drink off the blanket, and lunged at her, then suddenly drew back. The playful look left his face.

"What's wrong?"

"Nothing." He shook his head.

"No. What?"

"I don't want to scare you. You've seen the guarded, brooding Michael so much you probably don't even realize I have a very mischievous side." A smirk played around the corners of his mouth.

"Were you going to play a trick on me?" Jennifer asked with suspicion, grinning but drawing up on her knees in readiness to flee.

"I was going to do this." Michael tackled her, wiggling his fingers up her ribs and under her armpits until she fell squirming and gasping with laughter on the floor, twisting up the blanket in her attempt to escape. He hovered above her, the teasing leaving his face as his one hand curled behind her ear, brushing her hair back and stroking the tender skin he exposed. "Sorry. I was dying to know if you were ticklish. I don't know why, but you seem to bring out the feistiness in me, and other things I've never felt before."

An image of the petite and lovely Ashley flashed into Jennifer's mind. "Never?" she asked with a reasonable amount of disbelief.

"No, never. Things are … different … with you. You stand up to me and challenge me, and sometimes even get my back up, but at the same time, I want to protect you. But I never want to scare you. Not ever."

"You're afraid I'm going to start screaming like I did when I had my sprained ankle and you picked me up."

"And maybe a couple other times I touched you unexpectedly," he admitted wryly.

Jennifer shook her head and stared into his dark-lashed blue eyes. "You don't scare me like that anymore. I know you now. You can tickle me, and pick on me … and kiss me. I won't fall apart." He seemed to require further urging, so she raised her chin a fraction until her lips met his. Like the artsy nerd fantasizing about the quarterback, she still couldn't believe she got to be close to this man. But as they breathed as one, their parted lips moved in a natural dance that was anything but fantasy.

"See?" Jennifer slid her arms around his neck. "I trust you."

His gaze narrowed and the teasing spark returned, but he asked in all seriousness, "Then why did you look at me like you didn't believe what I was saying about the future?"

"I'm sorry, I guess I'm going to need a lot of reassurance. This all feels too good to be true." She lowered her lashes. "Everything that seemed like it might be good before turned out to be very much … not. I'm used to being used, hurt, left behind. Nothing good."

Michael tipped up her chin, making her look at him. "Well, we'll just have to change that, won't we?" When she pressed her lips together in a wobbly smile and gave a brief nod, he kissed her again, lightly, then pulled her up into a sitting position. "And that makes me think of something else I need to say before we leave."

Jennifer eyed him as he started covering Montana's baked goods with plastic wrap. She took a sip of her cooling but still flavorful coffee. She didn't want to go, to end this time of truthfulness alone together. "What?"

"I don't ever want you to feel used or controlled, either. That means if any part of you needs to take that Savannah job, I don't want you to turn it down on account of me."

Jennifer shook her head. "I didn't. I turned it down because Hermon is where I belong. I feel peace about that."

"Are you sure? Because if we decide to pursue this, and your future lies in Savannah, I'd follow you to Savannah." Michael placed the plate back in the basket and capped the thermos, glancing up at her with a look that entreated honesty. "I could keep the Dunham house for vacations and let Dad stay in it."

"I'm sure. I can't imagine life without Stella, Earl, Montana, Rita, Mary Ellen, and so many others. I think this is best for my mom, too. And your dad. He'd be lonely without you nearby, and he's clearly settled into Hermon. But it means the world to me that you'd say that. It's very … freeing. Thank you."

"I meant it."

"And what about your swimming?"

Moving the basket off to one side, Michael made a face. "What about it?"

"Well, you love it, and I know you gave it up in medical school, but that doesn't mean you should forever. Didn't you say there was some sort of club you could swim for as an old person?"

"What?" He started poking at her side again, causing her to twist away and stand up.

She reached for a corner of the blanket. "Well, isn't there? I really want to see you swim for real, not in a lake. I have to admit, you looked pretty good." Blushing, Jennifer held the flannel against her and waited for Michael to bring his side up against hers.

As he did, he placed a kiss on her nose. "Well, since you who rarely give compliments admit that, I might consider it, *if* you'll come cheer for me. Every meet."

"I would love to cheer for you every meet."

Michael smiled as they finished packing up and made their way back out onto the porch. Jennifer couldn't conceal a look of regret as he closed the door. "Poor old Grandfather Donald … freezing," he teased.

"OK, ok. But thank you for bringing me here. I'll never forget it."

As they got into the truck and turned on the heater, Michael asked, "Speaking of Savannah, are you feeling any better about your conversation with Barbara?"

Jennifer grimaced, holding her chilled hands out in front of the flow of warm air. "Not really, but I don't think it matters. Nothing's going to change."

"You're not going to call her back out of guilt or pity?"

"That's exactly what she expects, but I don't think I should do that."

"And you'd be right. I wish I had told you before you broke the news to her, but I want to give the gorget to the university on an indefinite loan."

She turned to him with surprise. "You do?"

"Yeah. I just think it's best. To me it represents the type of ties to the past we're both letting go of. It symbolized a lot of pain for my ancestors. I thought it could be put in some collection on display somewhere, or used as a teaching tool. I just don't want it in my house. But I don't want you to have to speak with Barbara about it now, either."

"Oh, it's OK. I got the name of the professor who dated and cleaned it for us. I could contact him directly, if that's what you want."

Michael nodded. "It is."

As they drove south on 77 toward I-20, Jennifer's mind went back to the afternoon when she'd called Tandy, then Barbara, giving them both the news that she'd decided to stay and work in Lexington. Astonished would be an understatement in describing Tandy's reaction. As for Barbara, she'd immediately said, "This has to do with Michael Johnson, doesn't it? I knew it, Jennifer, I knew it." Nothing Jennifer could say could convince her Jennifer wasn't "compromising her future" out of some insecurity-based need for a man.

"I made this decision before I knew if there would be a chance for a future relationship with Michael," Jennifer explained. "I looked at how I felt about the work environment and how I fit into the community. I'm sorry, but I think the position in Lexington would be better for me. It's not about Michael, and it's not about the money."

"Nor for me, either. It was about the job, and working together. You would have had a chance to work with *me*." The frustrated longing and hurt seeped through the older woman's wistful statement, stirring Jennifer's sympathy but also her certainty she had made the right decision.

"And I appreciate the offer professionally, but personally ... I'm needed in Lexington."

The voice on the line softened. "You're also needed in Savannah. And by me."

Jennifer paused a moment, surprised by both Barb's tenacity and neediness, especially considering what a strong woman she'd always portrayed herself as, and encouraged Jennifer to be. Finally Jennifer stated, "I told Tandy I hoped my decision wouldn't affect her arrangements with you in any way."

"Well, thank you so much for looking out for me." Drawing back from the sudden sarcasm in Barb's tone, Jennifer remained silent and let the older woman finish venting her emotions. "I'm sorry I misjudged you, Jennifer. I thought we wanted the same things. It's clear I was wrong. You're not ready to embrace all that life could offer you. Good-bye."

Jennifer sat staring at the silent phone for some time. She had expected the professor to be disappointed, but the personal attack hurt, and the reservations Barbara expressed about Jennifer's long-term future with Michael raised doubts. Staying in the trailer sounded snug and reasonable now, but what happened if she signed a lease and things fell apart between them? There she'd be, stuck right next door in the most uncomfortable situation possible. Chewing her lip, Jennifer looked out at the country road continuing south of the interstate and considered whether she should at least see what rentals might be available closer to Lexington. But then she felt Michael studying her with a frown of concern, and he reached over for her hand.

"It will be OK," he told her.

Warmth washed over her. She nodded and put aside her worries. Hadn't God led them this far? What if things really ended as wonderfully as she dreamed? Jennifer found that hard to imagine, but faith, after all, was "the substance of things hoped for, the evidence of things not seen."

In front of the VA home in Milledgeville, Donald waited in a fluffy red warm-up jacket and a WWII veteran ball cap, hands folded over his walker, ready to take off the minute Michael's truck pulled in. With the respect of an earlier generation, the white-haired man stood as Jennifer approached. As much as Donald loved his grandson, he didn't hug him first. He hugged Jennifer, then, with an arm around her, turned to Michael with approval and said, "You brought her back!"

Michael smiled at the sight of the two of them together. "I did."

"You did good, boy. I told you she was a keeper." He turned to Jennifer, his blue eyes gleaming brightly despite macular degeneration. "And that job? The one in Savannah?" he asked her.

Jennifer winked. "What job?"

CHAPTER FIFTEEN

A round eleven the next morning, Jennifer put the finishing touches on her hair and make-up. In anticipation of meeting Michael's aunts Patricia and Mary and their families, she'd taken extra pains with her appearance, making sure the layers of her brownish-red locks gleamed with a fresh washing and a coat of hairspray—"since when do you use hairspray?" her mother had cried—and the browns and peachy pinks of her eyeshadow and lip gloss complimented the embroidery-overlaid, fitted brick red top she wore with a long gold necklace, slim-fit khakis and heeled brown boots.

"Wow," Kelly commented as Jennifer slung on a belted brown trench coat. "Aren't we just going next door?"

Jennifer made a face, knowing her mother teased her.

"They'll love you, sweetie."

"Thanks. You know how I am with big crowds and chaos. I just hope I don't get rattled and make a bad impression."

Kelly handed her a casserole dish and a Tupperware pitcher of sweet tea. "You won't. You always say the right thing these days. You sure didn't get that from me."

Jennifer smiled. "I just really want Michael's relatives to like me." Anxiety churned in her stomach as they stepped out onto the porch and locked the door. So much rode on the way Michael acted today. She wanted him to feel proud of her.

Glancing toward Calvin's house, Jennifer was surprised to see the older man seated on the porch of his bungalow. She frowned. "I wonder why he's at home," she said to her mother. "I think I need to check on him."

Kelly grunted in dismay. "But my green bean casserole! I've got to get it over to Michael's while it's still warm!"

"I'll only be a minute. You go on."

Jennifer turned and strode across the yard, not giving her mother time for further argument. When Calvin noticed her approach, he looked up and smiled.

"Whatcha doin', young lady?"

"Coming to see why you're sitting out here alone on Thanksgiving rather than feasting at your nephews' house," Jennifer answered, stepping up on the porch and resting the glass dish on the wide rail.

"Oh, I don't much like goin' over there for Thanksgiving."

"Why?" Jennifer noticed Calvin wore a plaid flannel shirt and dark gray work pants. The knuckles of the hands resting on his knees looked considerably less knotted and inflamed since he now swore by Allison Winters' arthritis tea and cream.

Calvin gave a dismissive wave. "Oh, they start off at the crack of dawn huntin' with their daddy while my brother's wife spends the whole day slavin' in the kitchen. They come home to devour all the food like a pack of young wolves, then head right back out to the tree stand, leavin' her complainin' and fussin' about cleanin' up. Now that I can't go with them anymore, I'd rather not to be left to keep her company."

"But I thought your arthritis is better. You look like you feel better."

"It is, but I'm gettin' too old to spend the whole day in the tree stand. Besides, they don't really miss me. When you get old, you just become a burden on people."

"I can hardly believe that," Jennifer protested.

"Well, it's true. It's no big deal, just a day like any other."

"No, it's not." Jennifer remembered the photo of the wife who'd left Calvin for a younger and more successful man and as sympathy for the old man's solitary state washed over her, said, "I'm going to Michael's. Mom and I don't really have any family around, either. Why don't you come with us?"

"Oh, no, I couldn't crash their party."

"Lots of people will be there. Stella and Earl and their boys, my mother, Michael's grandfather and his aunts and their families."

"Too crowded. They won't have room for me."

"Yes, it's crowded, and I hate crowds. To be honest I'm really scared about meeting Michael's relatives since we're dating now. It would help me to have another familiar face there." Jennifer held out her hand and flexed her fingers. "Please, will you come?"

Calvin's lips drew up in a bow under his bulbous nose. "So you're datin' now, huh?"

She blushed. "Yes, I guess we are."

"Well, he's a smart boy. Heard about his wife. Sad business. Glad he finally noticed what a cutie was livin' in his own yard. He'd get far too lonely out here without a woman. Trust me, I know."

To Jennifer's surprise, Calvin put his hand in hers and allowed her to help him rise from the sofa. The pungent scent of mothballs accompanied their descent down the leaf-encrusted front steps. Just as Jennifer drew in a breath of cool air and savored the thought that someone thought her cute, Calvin asked, "So what's the story with your mom? She single? She's a real looker."

Jennifer laughed and gave him the abbreviated version of Kelly's restart in Oglethorpe County, then added, "But I think she might be a little young for you, Mr. Woods."

"Well, a man can look, can't he?"

She'd have to make sure to tell her mother to draw the blinds tight.

At the door of the kitchen, where Stella, Kelly and James labored over the stove and sink while unfamiliar children of various sizes whisked in and out and stole samples of turkey, ham and nuts, Jennifer stuck her head in and called, "Have we room for one more? I made Mr. Calvin leave his front porch to join us."

"Oh, good, of course we have room!" James cried, coming forward to shake the mechanic's hand. "Welcome. I have tables set up all over, in the dining room, the sun room and on the back porch."

"The back porch is fine for me," Calvin said as Jennifer delivered the casserole to the island where her mother set out serving utensils.

Dorace wobbled into the room with her cane. "Me, too. I like the warm sun. Put all us old folks on the porch. Maybe we won't mold out there." She winked at Calvin, who laughed and nodded.

"But you all should have a place of honor in the dinin' room," Stella protested, pausing from setting out crystal goblets for adults and plastic cups for the children.

"Nonsense. It's more important you and Earl talk with Michael's relatives."

"Are they all here yet?" Jennifer asked. "I see some kids, but not Linnea and Frank."

"They just texted they're a few minutes out," Michael announced as he filled the doorframe, then suddenly bent over with a grunt as a freckled boy of about eleven tackled him from behind, hanging on his shoulders. Michael grabbed one of the skinny hands twisted in his cotton button-down shirt and pulled the interloper around in front of him. "Jennifer, this is Peyton, my cousin Jeff's oldest boy. Peyton, say hi to Jennifer, my girlfriend. Go shake hands, little man."

Brown eyes widened as Peyton yelled, "Girlfriend? Ew!" and tried to dart back out of the room. Jennifer felt her face flame as Michael seized the boy and gave him a knuckle haircut.

A petite blonde strained to see over Michael's shoulder. "He's scared of girls, especially pretty ones," she said. "But I'm happy to meet you, Jennifer. I'm Rachel, Peyton's mom. We've heard so much about you!"

Bemused and self-conscious, Jennifer offered her hand to first Rachel, then Peyton, whom Michael shoved forward. As she bent to speak to the shy boy, she caught Stella and her mother murmuring and smiling over Michael's introduction. Her heart warmed that she'd gone from the employee who restored his house to the girlfriend everyone wanted to meet.

That began a parade of relatives she felt hopeless to keep named and in order, Patricia, who was plump, short and around sixty, Mary, who shared her dark coloring but loomed over her older sister with willowy height and grace, Pat's sons Jeff and Connor and their wives and children, and Mary's daughter Kate and her husband and children. The kids called Michael "Uncle Mike" even though they were technically cousins, a practice everyone encouraged since Michael was an only child. It didn't take Jennifer long to notice what a natural he was with them.

To her delight, since Jennifer had missed the Atlanta crowd meeting the Jameses, she got to witness Earl's and Stella's introduction to Frank and Linnea. Linnea didn't try to stop her mouth from falling open, but instead of acting awkward after her moment of surprise, Linnea grabbed Stella's arm and insisted she sit beside her at the dinner table and explain each and every connection between the white and African American parts of the Dunham family.

With all the leafs in, she and Kelly, James and Michael, Earl and Stella, Frank and Linnea and Patricia and Mary barely crowded around the American Empire table, leaving the offspring to fend for their own families in the sunroom, kitchen and porches, which they did with no complaint, also serving the "old people's table" on the back porch. Jennifer found herself seated between Michael's aunts. While the others present discussed the family tree, the two women asked her polite questions about herself, the work she'd done at Dunham House and her plans for the future. Sensing their interest was genuine, Jennifer managed to answer while nibbling her turkey and dressing dinner. She felt Michael smiling at her, and the approval she saw in his eyes gave her courage.

"We're just so glad things have worked out this way," Patricia told her. "We all encouraged Michael and his dad to come here, feeling a fresh start after their losses would be wise. We all prayed Michael would find what he needed here, and looking around this table, and especially at you, Jennifer, it's clear he has."

"Yes, what a blessing," Mary agreed. "So much to be thankful for. When we work with Him instead of against Him, God has such a beautiful way of giving back tenfold for our losses."

As Mary patted her hand, Jennifer blushed and glanced at Michael.

"Well said, Aunt Mary," he agreed. "But I heard the little jab in there."

"I can't help it that you're stubborn like your mother was," Mary teased.

"I have to say, even though they were trying to fight it, I saw this connection in the works when we visited earlier," Linnea exclaimed, pointing her fork in the air. "Didn't I tell you, Jennifer?"

"You did."

"They couldn't keep their eyes off each other," she continued, adding to Jennifer's embarrassment. "And it just keeps getting better because this time we got to meet Earl and the fabulous painter Stella we heard and read so much about. We've always been so racially boring, we're excited to learn we're related, aren't we, Frank?"

Frank nodded dutifully. "Very excited."

Linnea elbowed him. "And to see the cabin! We can go in the cabin this time, can't we?"

"You surely may," James said. "We can go right after lunch."

"And I want to see the old department store, too. Stella's been telling me about all the work the crew's done with James and Michael to get her classrooms and gallery space ready. I want to come up for the grand opening this spring."

"Anyone who wants to can join us for a tour," James offered.

Jennifer spoke up. "I do have to warn that the cabin is sparsely decorated. Mary Ellen who owns the antique store next door found a pie safe, rope bed and a primitive table for us, but we're having cane-bottom chairs made. And it's not decorated yet, although I just got some primitive Christmas decorations in."

Kelly perked up. "Christmas decoratin' on Thanksgiving Day is a great tradition. Maybe we could help."

Stella intercepted Jennifer's panicked glance as she imagined the extra snowmen and gaudy garlands her mother would insist on bringing over from the double-wide when she concluded the cabin looked too bare. "Maybe we should let Jennifer and Linnea do that, since Frank has a special connection to the cabin. Besides, after our walk to the store, I really need your help gettin' the desserts ready, Kelly."

"Oh. Right." Basking in her new-found usefulness in the kitchen, Kelly glowed, rubbing her hands together as she looked around the table. "Pumpkin bread pudding, everyone!"

Groans of delight and repletion rippled through the gathered company. As Stella and Kelly cleared the table and put away food, Jennifer made herself useful loading the dishwasher while the aunts insisted on hand washing bowls and platters. Glancing through the wavy glass window following their clean-up, Jennifer spied Dorace, Donald and Calvin talking up a storm on the back porch, while Dee Ann, Gabe and Jamal organized a game of badminton for the younger children in the yard.

"It's a beautiful sight, isn't it? What the Lord can do?" Stella murmured to her, rubbing her shoulder.

"Yes, it is." Jennifer's heart felt full at the picture of family uniting across racial and generational divides, so different from the fragmented dysfunction she'd grown up with. Noticing Kelly chatting happily with Linnea as they set out dessert dishes, she added, "I'm glad to be part of this. And it will take longer, but I think we should see if the older folks would like to go along to see the gallery."

Stella smiled. "I agree. I'll go get 'em movin'."

Minutes later, the odd procession set out, walking on the grass parallel to the main road, led by Stella, Earl and James with the key.

Rather than strolling with his aunts, Michael came back to join Jennifer as she trailed the rear, making sure the older folks found sound footing. In a gentlemanly gesture, Calvin held Dorace's free arm while she wielded her cane with the other.

When Michael tried to hold Jennifer's hand, Donald shoved his walker toward his grandson, saying, "Get away, you young varmint, she's with me," and causing everyone to laugh.

The bright sunshine from the many, long windows, can lighting and open floor plan made it easier for Donald to see the improvements in the old Gillen store. Stella showed them the meeting room, classrooms, and office space surrounding the gallery, the portion encircling the wrought iron double stairway and the balcony space above, where special lighting would highlight framed art on the brick walls. As the group murmured about how the white interior walls freshened the place up and the newly restored and polished heart pine floors glowed, Jennifer noticed Calvin seemed especially attentive, but quiet, hanging back behind the group.

She went up to him and, touching his arm, asked, "What do you think, Mr. Woods? Do you remember this place when it was a store?"

"I sure do. My daddy was the last clerk who worked in here."

"Really? You never told me that."

"You never asked."

Stella and Dorace drew near, along with Michael. "I remember your daddy workin' in here," Dorace commented. "I'd forgotten that."

"I bet you didn't know he saved up and bought the place after it closed."

"What?" Stella gasped.

He nodded, glancing at her. "Sure 'nough. He had plans to reopen it and make it all modern, but he had that heart attack."

"The one when you were just finishin' high school," Dorace recalled.

"That's right. When I had to go to work in the automotive shop to make a quick buck. After I got married, my wife used to talk about turnin' this place into a restaurant. I had it gutted for her, but she gave up on me before I could get enough money together and ran off. Even after she left, I just had a restaurant stuck in my head and kept thinkin' the right buyer would come along wantin' to make that happen. But I can see the right buyer did come along."

As Calvin nodded at Stella, her mouth fell open. "Are you tellin' me you're the one who the city council bought this place from?"

Calvin spread his hand over his rounded plaid belly. "In the flesh."

Jennifer's expression matched Stella's, causing Calvin to break out into a deep chuckle.

"I always thought it was old man Stevenson," Dorace mused, shaking her head in wonder as she stared at Calvin. "I thought that was why the buyer asked so much, to keep anythin' new from happenin' downtown."

"No, it was me. I admit I was stuck in a rut, too, mad at the world and just holdin' out for top dollar."

"But then why did you accept a lower price when the council offered?" Stella wanted to know.

"Well, this little lady made me come to the party for the apothecary store," Calvin said, looking at Jennifer. "She was real nice to me even though I'd been a bear to her, almost shootin' her the first time I saw her. I could see all you folks had done in the doctor's office and at the antique store to make things nice. Folks looked real happy gettin' together as a community. I heard about the plans for the store. I knew you, Miss Dorace, and you, Miss Stella, was good folks, and I decided it was time to let the old place go."

"Well, I never ..." Dorace murmured, shifting her weight on her cane.

Realizing the kindness the Holy Spirit had prompted her to show to Calvin had provided a step toward Stella getting to open her art gallery, Jennifer blinked in astonishment. She and Michael stared at each other, amazed, as Stella said, "Well, let me just hug your neck, Mr. Calvin, and tell you thank you for sellin' this place. You're goin' to be my guest of honor at the grand opening."

Rouged by the first blush Jennifer had seen the old man wear, Calvin turned to Jennifer and asked, "Another thing, since you're stickin' around, do you think you might help me get my house fixed up kind of like you done Michael's?"

"Sure I do!" Jennifer laughed.

Calvin patted her hand. "You come over one day next week and we'll talk shop."

Donald edged in with his walker, head cocked to one side, until Calvin and Jennifer stepped apart. "Hey," he challenged Calvin, "now *you* movin' in on my girl?"

Everyone burst into laughter. Donald grinned at being the butt of his own joke. "I'm just kidding," he said, adjusting his cap over his fluffy white hair. "Even I can see my boy's already gone on her, and she's makin' calves' eyes at him."

Michael agreed by putting his arm around Jennifer. "I'll fight you for this one, Grandpa."

The afternoon held further surprises. Following a delicious serving of bread pudding with coffee, Michael wrangled Jennifer into a game of badminton with his junior cousins. He seemed to find the repeated contact of her racket with air and her tripping over the ground endearing while he covered for her with the speed and agility of a pro-tennis player. Jennifer felt grateful when Linnea came over to steal her away to decorate the cabin. Michael kissed her cheek in dismissal, causing Linnea to smirk.

"You're so cute with him," the older woman said as they entered the dim interior of the little house under the pecan trees.

"Oh, my goodness, I'm so awkward, I don't know what he sees in me," Jennifer groaned, switching on the light which powered the wrought-iron chandelier over the table.

"I do," Linnea said with emphasis. "I mean, look at this. How many women have the gusto and the know-how to make this happen, then also be able to decorate it with antiques and doilies? So what if you can't hit a birdie? You are so incredibly talented. I want to move in."

"Thanks," Jennifer murmured. As Linnea peeked into the tiny bathroom and ran her hand over the smooth-finished, chinked walls, Jennifer set the box that came from Homestay House the previous week on the table. "Christmas trees weren't common in the Colonial period, so I ordered some natural-looking greenery, faux fruits, and homespun table linens in green and red. Oh, and stockings, because some settlers did believe in Father Christmas."

Linnea joined her and peered into the box, noticing several smaller boxes. "What are these?"

"Hospitality candles. Battery powered, but they look real. I thought we could put them in each window and maybe hang one of these crocheted angels on each sash."

"That's perfect. Let's do it!"

In her element now and encouraged by an enthusiastic companion, Jennifer enjoyed the next hour of decorating. The yells of the kids and the scent of wood smoke as James lit a fire on a big house hearth filled the air. Absorbed in arranging pewter plates, clove-studded oranges and a swag of greenery on the mantel, Jennifer jumped when Michael spoke from the doorway.

"Did you show Linnea where we found the gorget?"

"Oh, no, I didn't think of that."

Michael came forward, capturing the attention of his cousin's wife as he said, "We asked the stonemason to recreate the hidey-hole in the chimney." He reached for the loose stone and slid it out in demonstration. "It was right back here."

"That's so cool. Are you gonna put it back there?"

Michael and Jennifer exchanged glances, then shared a smile. "Definitely not."

Nodding in understanding, Linnea asked, "Did you enjoy the journal?"

"Oh, very much. Thank you for sharing it with us," Jennifer said. "As a historical reference, it was fascinating. I must admit, though, personally, I felt really let down when it ended. Verity wrote about her struggles with Selah, about how Selah didn't fit in and kept going to see the slave woman. We've heard Selah never married and became reclusive after her sweetheart died in the War of 1812. She practiced her healing arts, but according to local folklore, the children in the area feared her. Said she was a witch. I don't want to think she died lonely and lost. I can't help hoping she found peace in the end."

Linnea's face brightened, and she pulled her phone out of her pocket. "I think I can answer that for you. Let me text Frank to come out here and bring my things. I actually brought the diary for you to see today in person, and something else, too."

Jennifer could hardly contain her curiosity as they cleared the table of packaging. When Frank arrived, he handed Linnea the same leather satchel she'd carried on her first visit. She pulled out a small strongbox and unlocked the lid. Inside, modern tissue paper swaddled a hand-bound journal the leather covers of which sandwiched yellowed stationery. Linnea laid it on the table and opened it with gentle fingers, turning the pages to show the correlation between the spidery, faded quill script and the words they'd read on a computer screen. It was all there. Jennifer didn't realize she'd been holding her breath until they reached the last page. She let it out when she saw the diary really did end in 1802.

"Now, for the *piece de resistance*," Linnea said and reached into the box again, bringing out a small sheet of parchment paper in a plastic bag. "This letter was passed down with the journal from the time Selah gave it to William. I think you can read this without me taking it out. If not, I have it memorized." She placed the letter before them.

"Why Selah to William? Why did Silas not give it to his son?" Michael wanted to know.

"Because Verity's journal remained in Silas' possession until his death just after the Civil War. At that time, Selah still lived at the Dunham plantation. Look at the date on this letter, 1880. She was ninety-two. This letter states that she summoned William and Charlotte from Atlanta to her bedside with the intention of giving the journal to her last remaining nephew. She wasn't sure if they would arrive before she died. I guess we'll never know, but what we do know is more important. Listen." With a finger on the letter, Linnea began reading aloud.

Dearest William and Charlotte,

As I dictate this letter you are on your way to my bedside, and I do not know if you will arrive before I flee this world. In case you do not, there are things I must say.

I have in my possession the journal of my mother, Verity Miller Dunham, written during the decade after my birth. You will know she suffered much hardship in her life, and I took that hardship as my own. She found relief in Christ her Savior but against Him I turned my back, embracing instead the fickle power I found in the darkness and my herbs and potions. They did not comfort me much in my old age. But you did.

I watched you, Charlotte, bear up under your own load and the cruelty of your first husband, William's brother. From our first meeting I knew you were better suited to my William, whom I loved best of my brother's children. But you remained faithful to Stuart even when he came home half senseless and crippled, and faithful to God, from whom you drew your strength. In the last days of nursing Stuart your gentle spirit left no room for my own bitterness.

I was so pleased when the two of you could wed, and I treasured the years you spent in Hermon and the many times you insisted I visit you there, bringing me from my lonely cabin into your joyful company and that of your babes. I rued the day Hampton took over the practice and you, William, returned to Atlanta, and indeed have fought much misery this last year since you departed. But you left something with me, the witness of your faith, its sweet, lingering scent turning my withered heart to its Maker at last. I wish you to know that, despite my regret for many wasted and bitter years, when I die I go to glory. I wish you to have this journal to keep for your sons and theirs, and while Anne has been good to me and I leave her a faithful sum, the bulk of mine inheritance I bequeath in my last will and testament to you, William, for the love and care of your family.

Your Aunt, Selah Dunham

"Oh," Jennifer sighed, and moved to snuggle into the arm of the soft, fleece pull-over Michael wore. He drew her close and kissed the top of her head, but Jennifer got the impression the gesture attempted to hide tears in his eyes as much as to express affection. She understood. She tingled down to her toes with awe and reverence. "That was beautiful."

Linnea smiled at them with joy and pride.

"So now we know everything," Michael said. "The stories of all the Dunham ancestors back to the first one who built this cabin, their mysteries, their heartaches and joys, who did what, who lived and died when, and the legacy they leave. And you know what I see?"

"What?" Jennifer whispered, looking up at him.

"Over and over, God's healing trumped brokenness. It was a legacy of faith. One I want to help carry on."

Jennifer couldn't tear her eyes away from him. They may have thought they were putting back together the puzzle pieces of Michael's ancestors, but the lives being reconstructed were their own, and those of the community of family and friends surrounding them. For sure, the Master Renovator still had work to do, but Jennifer knew she could rest in the confidence that He finished the task He began, and did all things well.

CHAPTER SIXTEEN

Something was wrong with Kelly. Jennifer knew she was hiding something, she just didn't know what. Marian's invitation to Lexington's old-fashioned downtown celebration the Saturday before Christmas forced her mother's evasion into sharper focus when Kelly said she had other plans but wouldn't give Jennifer any specifics.

"Oh, I might do some shopping," she said, then poked Jennifer in the side. "You know this isn't the time of year to be nosy. Stop askin' questions." But something in her eyes—not to the mention the all-day timeframe Kelly planned to be gone—hinted the outing entailed more than malls and dollar stores.

What could she be up to? Had she caved and reconnected with Roy, allowing his pleading, excuses and promises to lure her back in? Had she met someone new? Or picked up a darker habit? Or maybe she wanted to talk to her sister about the possibility of moving to Alabama. As well as her job at Fatz seemed to be going, if she got a better offer over there, would she up and leave?

As she got ready for Stella to pick her up, Jennifer tried not to let her worries cloud her anticipation of the downtown shopping day complete with Santa's stop at the courthouse, hot chocolate and cookies set up at a table by Montana, and carriage rides through the historic district. Marian had told her she wanted Jennifer to organize a tour of homes next year. The idea of scouting out exciting new opportunities added relish to the holiday spirit.

To her shock, Stella pulled into the driveway with another person already seated in the front of her Cadillac. Amy Greene. Jennifer had not seen her since before the police investigation. Jennifer planned to avoid any involvement with the trial, but the Fullerton family attorney contacted her and pled that she file assault charges and testify. They told her Barbara would. No surprise there. The argument that swayed her was that Horace's repeated tricks and attacks supported intentionality and malice in the murder. Finally, after much prayer and unanimous advice, Jennifer agreed.

Now, even though Kelly assured her Amy bore no ill will, Jennifer felt uncertain how Amy might react to her. But she took a deep breath and opened the older woman's door. "Amy, I'm so happy to see you."

The scent of musky perfume enwreathed her with Amy's frail arm, as Amy's brilliant smile melted away any fears. The woman had lost weight she didn't have to lose, but she embodied the spirit of country Christmas in a red, cable-knit sweater, plaid scarf, boots and designer jeans.

"I hope you don't mind me crashin' your plans," Amy told her. "Stella twisted my arm."

"I told her I knew you wouldn't mind."

"Of course not. I'm so pleased you joined us," Jennifer said, getting into the back seat.

"She insisted I had to quit hidin' in my house."

"She's exactly right. We'll have a better day than we'd even thought." As the car headed north on 77, Jennifer asked, "What are your plans for Christmas, Amy?"

"I'm going to spend it with my family. They've been great. I don't know what I would do if I didn't have them, and Stella and your mom, of course." Amy glanced back over the seat. "She's been wonderful, Jennifer. I can't say how much it's helped to have someone to talk to who's been through somethin' similar. The way she's kept her head up and charged forward really inspires me. She keeps reminding me we can't let the horrors other people do dictate who we are."

Jennifer smiled, pressing her lips together and hoping Amy's words still proved accurate. "I'm glad she's helped. Is there ... any word on Horace?"

"Well, as you probably know already, he pled guilty to a voluntary manslaughter charge, statin' that Chad baited him until he lost reason. The jury will have to decide if words alone were enough provocation, along with the threat of losin' his fiancée. Of course if Horace's lawyer can prove there was a struggle before Horace hit Chad ..." Amy's voice trailed off. "That would go in his favor. And he'll need it. Everyone's bound to see how much evil took hold of him by the lengths he went to, covering up the crime for years, and threatening other lives in the process. It makes me so ashamed."

Jennifer reached up to touch her shoulder. "I'm sorry I brought it up. You don't have to talk about it."

"No, I need to." Amy patted her hand. "This whole thing has torn me right in two. But I want to you to know I think you're doin' the right thing by pressin' charges and testifying for the Fullertons."

Jennifer squeezed the fragile fingers. "Thank you, Amy. And I want you to know I didn't want to."

"I know, honey. But not to would be irresponsible."

"Will you have to testify also?" Stella asked Amy.

"Horace says he's goin' to do all he can to keep me off the stand."

Stella nodded. "Whatever sins Horace committed, you can at least be sure not lovin' you was not one of them."

Amy fell silent, then said, "I know that, but I ... can't bring myself to visit him. I have been able to forgive him, just not face him. I don't know what I'd say, how I'd act. To think how twisted he'd become and I didn't even know it ... well, I just can't be around him anymore."

"Boy, do I get it," Jennifer blurted. She almost covered her mouth, then she realized Amy would know about her past abuse because of Kelly's sharing about Roy. So she added, "Give yourself time, Amy. You'll know when and if you're meant to go."

"And if you want me to go with you, I would. I'm sure Kelly would, too," Stella told her as she veered right to intersect Highway 78.

Amy nodded. "Thank you both." She sighed. "In some ways, it would have been easier if he'd died."

Sensing how much Amy needed their support, Jennifer linked her elbow with the older woman's as they headed toward the downtown after parking off the main street. Amy rewarded her with an appreciative smile. With Amy sandwiched in the middle, the women perused the antique and specialty stores. The kind manner in which the people of the town responded to the victim of the latest local tragedy confirmed yet again that Jennifer had made the right decision to stay among them. Amy was smiling by the time they stopped at Montana's booth for hot chocolate.

Montana hugged Jennifer's neck. "I'm so happy you're staying," she whispered. "I have something for you."

"It's not more makeup, is it?" Jennifer teased.

Montana made a face and put her hands behind her back, leaning back and forth as she murmured speculatively, "Maybe..."

Jennifer rolled her eyes. "Well, I have something for you, too. We'll get together soon to exchange gifts."

"Do you think Michael will propose to you for Christmas?"

The question took Jennifer aback. She wrinkled her nose as Stella and Amy hooted. "It may be a little early for that," she said.

A customer holding out a bill forced the young girl to turn away from her romantic musings, and Jennifer sagged with a sigh. "I admit, though, I was hoping to find a Christmas gift for Michael today," she told the women. "I've already looked in Athens. Nothing seems right. I'm getting a little desperate."

Amy startled her by parting the red lips she'd just screwed up to blow steam off her cup of chocolate. "Oh! I think I can help you there."

"What? How?"

"You won't believe this," Amy said, putting a hand on Jennifer's arm, "but back durin' the time Horace managed the Dunham property, when we were first married, he came across a pocket watch in an antique store in Madison. It was inscribed 'Hamp Dunham.'"

"No way!" Jennifer cried.

Amy nodded. "Yes way. Horace always had a fascination for the Dunhams and that house, so he bought it. I know where it is, and it would be the perfect gift for Michael. He's the rightful recipient."

"Wow," Stella murmured when Jennifer couldn't seem to find words. "I wonder if it might have been a gift from Luella, or maybe even Charlotte? That is so cool, though, to think about Dr. Hamp pullin' out that watch and lookin' at it during the time Georgia Pearl grew up here."

Jennifer shook her head. "I can't imagine a better gift, but if you're sure you're willing to part with it, you must let me pay you for it."

"No," Amy said. "I don't even know what Horace gave for it in the first place."

"That doesn't matter. Just let me pay you what I would have for another nice gift for Michael. Please, Amy?"

"Oh, OK. I admit, it will help this time of year." She smiled. "It will make me feel good to know Michael has it, and that it can be a blessing to a relationship I hope turns out better than mine did. I can give it to you today, if Stella drops me off first."

Unable to contain her excitement, Jennifer executed an in-place quick step. "So, are you guys ready to go?"

The fine condition and handsome appearance of the gold watch with filigree lid, contained in a wooden box, prompted Jennifer to write her check for a hundred dollars more than Amy suggested. She did it without blinking, knowing the money would help Amy and the gift would bless Michael with so much personal meaning.

In her empty double-wide, she took out the watch again and ran her finger over the cursive name on the back. Her phone dinged with a text. Hoping it was her mother, Jennifer put the gift back in the box and went to check.

A message from Michael read, "Lighting the first fire of the season in the cabin to test this chimney. Come hang out?"

Yes. Yes! A million times, yes!

Jennifer texted in the affirmative, ran to brush her teeth and grab her coat, then paused in the living room. Responding to a strong urging, she stuck the watch box in her coat pocket and turned toward the door. At that moment, she heard a car pull into the driveway.

Jennifer met her mother on the porch. Kelly approached with the rumpled look of someone who had been in the car for quite some time, and she held no shopping bags. But as Jennifer frowned in suspicion, her mother's face broke into a tremulous smile, and she held her arms out.

Confused, Jennifer went into them, trying to make sure her sniffs for hints of alcohol, drugs or cheap cologne remained discreet. But all she detected was her mother's now-faded floral perfume and the wispy tang of Michael's fire beckoning her from the log cabin. "Mom? Are you OK?" Jennifer asked. "Are you going to tell me now where you've been all day? I've been worried."

Kelly pulled back but kept hold of her daughter's hands. "Yes, I am, but can we go inside first? It's cold out here, and I'm plumb wore out."

Jennifer twisted her bottom lip. "Uh, sure. I just need to text Michael. I was on my way over."

"I won't keep you but a minute. I'm wantin' nothin' more than a good, hot bath, but this news will be important to you," Kelly told her, leading the way into the house while Jennifer sent her message.

In the living room, Kelly tossed off her coat and plopped down on the couch while Jennifer remained standing over her. "You're gonna want to sit down," Kelly said.

"Fine." Stifling her impatience to join Michael, Jennifer did as her mother directed, taking a seat next to her but not removing her own coat. "So where did you go? And why all the mystery?"

"Because I couldn't tell you until I saw how things would work out. I went to Alabama today."

Jennifer's head lowered, and her eyes popped open wide. "Alabama?"

Kelly nodded.

"To see your sister?"

"No, honey, to see your daddy."

Jennifer couldn't have been more stunned had the subfloor beneath her collapsed from its risers onto the ground. "You found him?"

"Well, it wasn't hard. He was right where I thought he'd be, livin' with that shameless truck stop hussy he left me for ... only she wasn't as shameless as I'd pictured. Maybe she changed, or I admit my comparison of her to me back then coulda been a bit skewed."

Jennifer sat forward and shook her hands. "Mom! My father ... Jake? Jake Rushmore? Tell me about him! What did you do, just show up on his front step?"

"I called him first and talked to him on the phone, explained how things had changed for me and told him about you. Told him about how you'd done so good with your schoolin' and job and found God and all. I even confessed I'd let Roy throw away and burn Jake's presents and cards for you."

"You did that? For me?"

Kelly blinked her mascara-encrusted lashes. "Of course, honey. I'd do anything for you, now that Jesus brought me to my senses."

"How did he react?"

"I must say, he was real shocked. Here he thought all those years I talked trash about 'im and made you take to Roy. I didn't go ... into things ... about that, just told him Roy had been the worst choice I ever made, for both of us. I asked could I come see him in person to discuss things more. He and the wife talked and invited me out."

"That was where you were today."

Kelly nodded. "I wanted to see for myself he was decent and believable. We had a good talk, cleared the air on several matters and made peace ourselves. After that, I told Jake you'd probably be open to gettin' in touch with him."

"You did?" Jennifer swallowed, her mouth suddenly bone dry and a wash of cold leaving her numb. "What did he say?"

Kelly sat up and reached in her pocket, producing a folded envelope. "He wrote you this. I haven't read it. I left that for you. When he handed it to me, though, he had tears in his eyes."

Jennifer couldn't rip the top open fast enough. With shaking hands, she unfolded a plain piece of stationery. Licking her lips, she read aloud, "Dear Jennifer, I learned today from your mother the real reason why I never heard back from you all the years I tried to stay in touch. I'm so sorry I settled for believing the worst rather than driving to your house myself when you were still a kid." She paused to clear the wobble of emotion from her voice. "I never wanted to leave you. At that point in time, I just thought it best for all involved. But I always thought I'd get settled and you'd come to spend summers and lots of visits. Now I know you've suffered because of the many mistakes your mother and I made when we were young and selfish. I know I can never make up for that, but Kelly says you might be willing to talk. I would love to talk on the phone, meet you, come there, or for you to come here, whatever you want to do. I never stopped loving you. Your father, Jake."

Kelly's hand wrapped around her wrist, and Jennifer looked into Kelly's tear-misted eyes. "Aw, honey, it's just as I hoped," her mother said. "See, there's all his contact information at the bottom. So you can choose. The power's all back to you now."

Jennifer covered her mouth with her hand to stifle a little sob. She stared at the plain, masculine printing, the honest words of a blue collar man owning up to his past and asking for a chance at a better future, and knew they could not be worth more to her had they come on gilded letterhead and been expressed with the highest class and education. Kelly held her for a few minutes, patting her head.

"I can't think what to do," Jennifer murmured.

"You don't have to, baby, right now," Kelly told her. "Just take the time you need. He'll wait. He's waited this long."

Finally, sniffling, Jennifer placed the letter on her bedside table and left Kelly to her bath. She wanted nothing more than Michael's arms around her right now. With a full heart and trembling limbs, Jennifer set out across the yard. A haze of wood smoke hung low and gray in the pecan grove, tickling her nose with spicy pleasure and making her heart leap with anticipation. Her feet sped through the crunching leaves of autumn to the door of the snug cabin. Smiling at the fresh evergreen wreath with red ribbon she'd hung there, she knocked.

"Come in!" Michael called.

To Jennifer's surprise, as he stood up from putting a small log on the crackling orange fire, he wore not the expected jeans and flannel, but khakis and a dark green sweater over a collared shirt. His gelled hair slicked back behind his ears in dark waves. He took her breath away.

"Missed you today," he said, coming forward to kiss her and help her off with her coat. Drawing back from her, he frowned with concern and asked, "Have you been crying?"

Jennifer sniffed and smiled. "Only a little, and it's good news. So much has happened today. Let me start at the beginning." Jennifer laid the garment over the arm of the checked loveseat she'd purchased last week in Greensboro and told Michael about her outing with Stella and Amy.

"I think of her a lot, how hard this season must be for her. I'm glad she went with you," Michael told her, sinking down next to her on the cushion and wrapping a long arm about her shoulders.

"I think Amy's going to be OK. Like most Southern women, she's a lot stronger than she looks."

"You're right about that. But that's not what made you cry, was it?" Michael traced an index finger down the side of her face.

Sighing, Jennifer related her mother's recent return, where she had been, and why. She told him about the letter from her father,

Jake Rushmore. Michael's look of disbelief increased in proportion to the amazing tale.

When she stopped, he exclaimed, "Oh, my word, Jennifer, that's wonderful. I'm so happy for you. This could bring you great closure."

"Or a whole new relationship for my future. My kids could know their grandfather." Jennifer stole a shy glance at the man beside her.

"So you're going to contact him?"

"I can't see why not. It's what I've always wanted, only now that it's here, I'm kind of scared."

Michael's arm tightened around her. "I can understand that. I think your mother's right. Pray about it, and you'll know what step to take, and when. And if you want, I'll be there with you."

She smiled up at him. Like Amy, she had support. "That would help so much."

He planted a kiss on her forehead and twined her hand with his, rubbing his thumb across her knuckles. In the moment of silence broken only by the comforting sizzle of the fire, they both focused on their joined hands.

"You know, seeing the words printed on that page, that I was loved and wanted, did something to me," Jennifer murmured. "It was proof of what I hoped for when Mom told me Jake tried to stay in touch."

"Then thank God," Michael agreed. "But if that hadn't been the case, if he really had intentionally abandoned you, would you have been OK? Because it's important to know that wouldn't have affected who you are and how much you're worth in God's sight … or mine."

She kept thinking her heart couldn't swell any more. She squeezed his hand. "Yes. It would have been hard, and I admit I would have needed more support to deal with that rejection I've battled my whole life, but I would have gotten there. Because God really is enough. He really is the God who heals us, and never abandons us. That alone is enough to stake a life on."

Michael gave a murmur of approval, and his hand smoothed up and down her sleeve. "But He likes to give us the desires of our heart, too."

Nodding, Jennifer sank into his side and turned her face up. As she hoped, he took the opportunity to kiss her with more attention to detail. She extended her toes toward the warmth of the fire and shrugged in bliss.

"Fire looks good," she murmured.

"You look good."

When Michael lowered his lips to hers again, deepening the contact, Jennifer slid one arm around his back and raised her other hand to stroke the hair at the back of his neck. She couldn't even remember now how it ever felt to cringe away from him in fear. The tender respect, protectiveness and possession of his touch slowly but surely chased away all her ghosts. At his side, she was a new person, an extension of who she'd become in Christ.

When they broke apart, Jennifer laid her head on Michael's chest and listened to his heartbeat, palm beside her cheek. His hand stroked her back.

Her heart throbbing inside her with that uncontainable emotion, Jennifer whispered, "I love you."

"I love you, too. It's getting more and more annoying to have you over at that double-wide."

"But I thought you wanted me close."

"I want you closer."

Jennifer peeked up at him, pleased but embarrassed that he finally thought of her in those terms. She chewed her lip. "So I know it's not Christmas yet, but I can't contain myself. I bought your Christmas gift today from Amy."

"From Amy?" Michael's eyebrows shot to the top of his forehead. "What, did you get me more layers of curtains I have to hang?"

She slapped at him. "Be respectful. This is a very serious moment." Fishing in her coat pocket, Jennifer went on to explain how Horace had come across a Dunham family heirloom in an antique store years ago. "Amy and I both feel this item needs to be redeemed by a return to its rightful owner. You." She extended the box and opened her hands.

With a look of intrigue, Michael took it from her and sprung open the lid. He sat stunned for a minute. "No way. This belonged to one of my ancestors?"

"Turn it over."

Michael drew out the pocket watch, the chain links sliding over his long fingers, and flipped it to the other side, reading the inscription. He stared at her. "Jennifer. This was Hampton's, Georgia Pearl's father."

"And now it's yours, Dr. Johnson ... Dunham."

Her heart lurched and tears flooded her vision as Michael clasped the watch against his heart and closed his eyes. "'To everything there is a season, a time for every purpose under heaven,'" she quoted aloud.

Michael pulled her down against him, pressing his mouth on hers in a kiss that made her breathless. Leaning against him, laughing, she helped him put the watch away. Then, with her arm across him, she glanced up at his face.

He put a hand up. "Stop looking at me. You're going to make me cry."

"Thank goodness. I couldn't tolerate a man who can't show emotion," Jennifer teased. "I guess that's why I didn't like you at first, that guard you had up, right?"

"What? Like you weren't as bristly as a porcupine."

Jennifer nestled against his sweater. "I was. I'm sorry."

His arm tightened. "Stay. Stay here with me. You belong here, not just in Oglethorpe County, but here on this property that we restored together."

In shock, she looked up again, lips parted, expecting to meet a gaze that matched Michael's words in intensity. But the man's attention had fixed beyond her head, somewhere above them. "Aw, man, something's wrong with that spot in the chimney."

"What spot?" Jennifer glanced around, searching for missing chinking or some other evidence of poor craftsmanship she had missed during her inspection.

"That hidey hole. I just adjusted it before you got here, but the stone won't stay in all the way. I guess I'm going to have to fix it." Michael released her like he was going to get up.

Concerned that he might get away, might actually go fetch tools and ruin the romantic mood right on the heels of his startling request, Jennifer put a hand on his chest and hastened to rise instead.

Approaching the fireplace, she located the stone in question and attempted to push it in. "It won't budge," she said, pulling out the culprit and peering into the opening. She saw something leather inside. "Something's in there! I thought you met that professor in town last week to donate the gorget."

"I did."

Jennifer reached in for the draw-string bag. It looked newer. She frowned in confusion. Then she noticed the item in the bag was decidedly smaller. "What in the world?" Sliding her fingers into the bag, she pulled out a little black box. She looked at Michael, frozen in a moment of blank shock.

He just looked back at her, hands on his knees, calm. "Open it."

She flipped the lid. The firelight glancing off a generous but delicate oval diamond, mounted with antique-looking filigree, set in a ring of white gold and surrounded by smaller stones, dazzled her eyes. Her hand started shaking so bad she almost dropped the box. In fact, her whole body started shaking. "Is this real? Is this what I think it is?" The look she sent Michael communicated pure terror.

Instantly he was on his feet, his hands on her arms. "It is, but you don't look happy."

"I'm happy. I'm happy, I'm … just so scared I'm thinking this means something it doesn't, like maybe this is an heirloom, too, or I'm misunderstanding …" She'd actually babbled that out loud. Years of insecurity and doubt battled with her new identity that she could ever deserve a ring like that, or much more, a man like this.

"Come here." Michael took the ring box from her limp hand and pulled her to him, holding her firm while she shook like a leaf. But his attempt to steady her only produced gut-wrenching sobs. "Gee, I sure didn't think I'd get this reaction. Maybe you've had too much for one day."

Wordless, she nodded in agreement.

"You're not misunderstanding." Michael knelt in front of the stacked stone fireplace, the ring box held up to her. "Jennifer Rushmore, I'm asking you to marry me."

She clapped her hands over her mouth. "N-now?"

"It's OK if you need time. We can have a long engagement if you want. But I thought both of us could use some certainty."

Jennifer tugged on his hands until he stood up again. She threw her arms around him.

"Are you going to make me ask again?" he muttered into her hair.

She looked up at him and blinked the tears out of her eyes. "No. You don't ever have to ask that question again, because the answer is always going to be yes. Yes, yes, for the rest of our lives, yes. Now I think I should put that ring on so we can go show it to all the amazing family and friends God has given us."

DISCUSSION QUESTIONS

Historical Section and Chapters One and Two

1. What is your impression of Tenetke? How does the gorget symbolize a type of slavery to Verity?

2. What different kind of attack does Jennifer face in chapter two? Why is she more vulnerable to this type of attack than another person might be? In what ways does her support group rally around her? How does a new spiritual support structure also help?

3. Why does Bryce Stevenson not want change? What type of overall spirit does James say drives him? Have you encountered people like that, and if so, what type of response did you find effective?

4. Despite her professional success and her personal improvements, why does Jennifer fear she still might not appeal to Michael? How does she find strength and courage to deal with her lingering self-doubt?

5. How do Michael and Jennifer differ in their restoration goals? How do their mindsets reflect where they are in life?

Chapters Three and Four

6. What do you make of Barbara's accident? Do you think it was related to Hermon? What do you think of her revelation that she, too, might accept a job in Savannah?

7. Do you think Calvin Woods is a good person at heart? Is Jennifer right to be cautious of him? How does the Holy Spirit encourage Jennifer to show him kindness, and how does Calvin surprise her in their chapter four conversation? Why do you think Calvin decides to attend the apothecary opening?

8. During the apothecary opening, what does George Stevenson reveal about his father? Was he right to have stood up to Bryce despite Bryce's age and position as George's father? Do you think Bryce got what he deserved?

9. What fear does Barb express about the gorget, and about Jennifer's future in Hermon? Does she really "see" the local people for who they are? Is she concerned for Jennifer, or could there be a more selfish motivation at play?

Historical Section and Chapters Five and Six

10. How does Tenetke's kindness contrast with Verity's captivity to create her emotional confusion? Why does she long for him when he returns her to Levi? What makes Verity attempt to return? What "treatment" does Levi find to be more effective against his wife's turmoil than his medicine?

11. What does Jennifer discover about Michael when James is hanging photos in the office? How does Michael react?

12. Why does Jennifer keep asking Michael how he feels about her staying in Hermon? How does Jennifer being brave enough to demand answers lead to greater intimacy? Even though she yearns for closeness, how does Jennifer still struggle with some aspects of that intimacy?

13. Who does Dorace suspect to be behind the many accidents surrounding Dunham House?

14. What does Michael say at the park that he expects of God where his relationship with Jennifer is concerned? What does he share about his wife's and his mother's cancer that helps explain some of his bitterness over the past? How does the sermon address that very issue?

15. On the way home from the park, what issues with God does Michael reveal he struggles with? Have you ever asked these same questions? How does Jennifer argue that his reasoning may be flawed? Why is it harder for her to challenge Michael spiritually than professionally?

Chapters Seven, Eight and Nine

16. After the fire at her double-wide, what does Jennifer find in the closet of Michael's office? Can you understand Michael's explanation of why he turned his back on that part of his life, and why he hadn't revealed all of his past to Jennifer? What does he need from Jennifer after he makes those revelations that she doesn't feel prepared to give?

17. What pros and cons does Jennifer consider about the jobs in Lexington and Savannah? What is her biggest fear about taking the Lexington job? How does she ask for God's help with the decision? According to Michael's behavior, are her fears founded?

18. What surprise awaits Jennifer when she returns from Savannah? How has the tragedy Kelly faced with Roy forced her to re-examine the past and made her willing to turn to God? Has God ever used a low point in your own life to point you back to Him?

19. What does Stella's prayer in chapter eleven claim authority over? What reaction did her prayer evoke in you? How do you see answers to her requests?

20. What confession does Kelly make to Jennifer at Stella's house? What effect does that have on Jennifer? Has a tiny piece of information ever made a huge difference in your life?

Chapters Ten, Eleven and Twelve

21. What effect on the property and its occupants do you think the murder had over time?

22. What does Jennifer realize about herself as she gives Michael's "new" cousins a tour of Dunham House? How is this evidence of God at work in her?

23. How does the unexpected visit of Frank and Linnea bring another piece of the Dunham family puzzle?

24. How does Kelly find a new sense of belonging and usefulness in Hermon?

25. What kind of connection did Verity describe in her journal to Tenetke, and what helped break it? Have you ever experienced a very strong but unhealthy or destructive connection to someone?

26. How do Michael and Jennifer see themselves in the historical characters? How do the Scriptures in the journal inspire Jennifer to share her true feelings?

Chapters Thirteen, Fourteen, Fifteen and Sixteen

27. What struggles does Selah face as a result of her ancestry? How does she let bitterness color her decisions and impact her life? In what ways does Jennifer decide she doesn't want to be like her, and how does this decision impact her choices?

28. What truth convicted Michael that he, too, needed to release the bitterness of his past? How did Scripture change his view on death and suffering? What does he decide he wants to do with the gorget, and why?

29. How does Calvin surprise the group at Thanksgiving?

30. How does Jennifer receive a beautiful answer to her question about whether Selah ever found peace?

31. How is it fitting that Hampton's watch find its way back to Michael, after all that happened with Horace?

32. What two gifts does Jennifer receive in the last chapter? Have you ever received a gift that God arranged and delivered in a special way?

AFTERWORD

While the restoration process and buildings in The Restoration Trilogy are based on an actual project, and the Dunham doctors are based on an actual line of historic doctors, names and facts have been changed to suit the story line of *White*, *Widow* and *Witch*. You'll find the series cradled by the real county of Oglethorpe in Piedmont Georgia, with larger towns and topographical details unaltered ... but rest assured, no real characters from the series exist. That said, I wrote The Restoration Trilogy with the same goal in mind as The Georgia Gold Series: to weave an entertaining, fictional story among the sturdy framework of history, with its true-to-life people, places and events. I hope you enjoy it! And remember, real history is often the most shocking part of any story!

I would like to thank several local experts consulted by interview for The Restoration Trilogy, including: Richard Thornton, Creek Indians of 1780s-90s; Jim Carter, 1800s architecture and interiors; Debbie Cosgrove, herbs and herbal medicine; Dr. Allen Vegotsky, historic medicine; and Bill Summerour, log cabins. Also, my thanks to the helpful staff of the Oglethorpe County Library. For readers interested in further study on the topics touched on in The Restoration Trilogy, I include a list of sources consulted. These are offered not in MLA format, but merely in the order I consulted them. Many historical threads overlap and interweave in all three books of the series, but in bold are the sources most pertinent to *Witch*.

SOURCES:

The Travels of William Bartram: Naturalist Edition, University of Georgia Press, Athens, GA, 1998

Bartram: Travels and Other Writings, Literary Classics of the United States, Inc., NY, NY, 1996

The History of Oglethorpe County, Georgia, Florrie C. Smith, Wilkes Publishing Company, Inc., Washington, GA, 1970

Woman of Color, Daughter of Privilege: Amanda America Dickson 1849-1893, Kent Anderson Leslie, University of Georgia Press, Athens, GA, 1995

The Story of Oglethorpe County, Lena Smith Wise, 2nd Ed. by Historic Oglethorpe County, Inc., Lexington, GA, 1998

Scull Shoals: The Mill Village That Vanished in Old Georgia, Robert Skarda, Fevertree Press, Athens, GA, 2007

White Flood Red Retreat, Robert Skarda, Old Oconee Books, GA, 2012

Antebellum Athens and Clarke County, Georgia, Ernest Hynds, University of Georgia Press, Athens, GA, 1974/2009

College Life in the Old South, E. Merton Coulter, University of Georgia Press, Athens, GA, 1983

Confederate Athens, Kenneth Coleman, University of Georgia Press, Athens, GA, 1967/2009

Cotton Production and the Boll Weevil in Georgia: History, Cost of Control, and Benefits of Eradication, P.B. Haney, W.J. Lewis, and W.R. Lambert, The Georgia Agricultural Experiment Stations College of Agricultural and Environmental Sciences, The University of Georgia, Research Bulletin Number 428, March 2012

New Georgia Encyclopedia: History & Archaeology: Progressive Era to WWII, 1900-1945, online: World War I in Georgia / Athens / Oglethorpe County / Ku Klux Klan in the Twentieth Century ... and many other online resources

An Hour Before Daylight: Memories of a Rural Boyhood, Jimmy Carter, Simon & Schuster, New York, NY, 2001

Behind the Mask of Chivalry: The Making of the Second Ku Klux Klan, Nancy MacLean, Oxford University Press, New York, NY, 1994

Dr. Durham's Receipts: A 19ᵗʰ Century Physician's Use of Medicinal Herbs, Debbie Cosgrove and Ellen Whitaker, 2008

City of Maxeys Historic Interest Group Interview Report, Bereniece Jackson Wilson & Regina Jackson Wilker by Dennis and Faye Short, April 13, 2014

The Negroes of Athens, Georgia, Thomas Jackson Woofter, Phelps-Stokes Fellowship Studies, No. 1, Bulletin of the University of Georgia, Volume XIV Number 4, December, 1913

Send Us a Lady Physician: Women Doctors in America: 1835-1920, "Co-Laborers in the Work of the Lord: Nineteenth-Century Black Women Physicians," Darlene Clark Hine, W. M. Norton & Company, New York, NY, 1985

A Pioneer Church in the Oconee Territory: A Historical Synopsis of Antioch Christian Church, Billy Boyd Lavender, 2005

A Scythe of Fire: A Civil War Story of the Eighth Georgia Infantry Regiment, Warren Wilkinson and Steven Woodworth, HarperCollins, NY, NY, 2002

Resources of the Southern Fields and Forests, Medical, Economical, and Agricultural, Francis Peyre Porcher, Charleston, SC, 1863

"The Preservation & Repair of Historic Log Buildings," Bruce Bomberger, National Park Service web site

ABOUT THE AUTHOR

DENISE WEIMER

Native Georgia author Denise Weimer holds a journalism degree with a minor in history from Asbury University. Her writing background prior to The Restoration Trilogy includes numerous regional magazine and newspaper articles, romantic novella *Redeeming Grace*, and the four-book Georgia Gold Series (*Sautee Shadows, The Gray Divide, The Crimson Bloom* and *Bright as Gold*, Canterbury House Publishing), sweeping historical romance with a touch of mystery. *Bright as Gold* won the 2015 John Esten Cooke Fiction Award for outstanding Southern literature. Denise is a wife and the swim mom of two teenage daughters.

CPSIA information can be obtained
at www.ICGtesting.com
Printed in the USA
LVOW08s1250190317

527521LV00006B/3/P